DREAMS OF BALI

by

C. J. Harte

2008

DREAMS OF BALI
© 2008 BY C. J. HARTE. ALL RIGHTS RESERVED.

ISBN 13: 978-1-60282-070-8

THIS AEROS EBOOK IS PUBLISHED BY
BOLD STROKES BOOKS, INC.
P.O. BOX 249
VALLEY FALLS, NY 12185

ORIGINAL BOLD STROKES BOOKS EBOOK EDITION: NOVEMBER 2008

CREDITS
PRODUCTION DESIGN: STACIA SEAMAN
COVER DESIGN BY BOLD STROKES BOOKS GRAPHICS

CHAPTER ONE

Madison Barnes ate people for lunch. One of the most sought-after attorneys in South Florida, she'd earned the nickname "Barracuda." Her clients, many with questionable reputations, either feared or adored her. In either case, they paid whatever she asked. She rarely lost a case. She was thorough and competent, but it was her willingness to do just about anything to win that made prosecuting attorneys detest her. They could never prove she did anything illegal to earn her courtroom victories, and she was careful to stay inside the law.

Madison looked down at her watch and sighed. Fuck, she was already fifteen minutes late. The traffic on I-95 was backed up from the Broward County line south into downtown Miami. She would barely make it for the end of the lecture. Reaching for her cell phone, she dialed her sister, Dee. Voice mail answered. She left a message explaining the traffic problems and assuring Dee she would be there. She put the phone on the dashboard and swore beneath her breath as she edged her Lexus SUV to the right. Ignoring the angry gestures and blaring horns, she pulled onto the shoulder and drove the final mile to the next exit.

Her GPS mapped the route, droning directions as she zigzagged her way to Coral Gables. Madison still couldn't believe she was doing this, even for her younger sister. She never volunteered, and if anyone else had asked her to host some straight romance writer for the weekend, she would have bitten off that person's head. And her "guest" wasn't just any romance writer, she was Karlie Henderson, Dee's best friend since their freshman year in college.

Madison had never cared for the woman. Karlie was an upstart New York kid from a working-class family and not in the same league as Dee, the young debutante and high school valedictorian. Karlie had entered the University of Miami on a full-ride scholarship and then began to attack the institutions that enabled her to attend the university. Madison was familiar with the attitude. Some of the poor scholarship kids who enrolled at the university were awed by the money and influence many of their classmates possessed and adapted in negative ways. Some became parasites living off the money and reputations of their well-connected classmates, while others were determined to find fault with all the wealth and power.

Madison put Karlie in the later category. Every time she picked up the campus newspaper, it seemed a certain New Yorker was quoted. *Karlie Henderson, member of Young Democrats, demanded the administration divest its portfolio of war profiteers. Karlie Henderson led a protest rally seeking full domestic partnership benefits. Among those arrested during the recent unrest downtown was campus activist Karlie Henderson.*

Karlie's involvement in social causes and politics often resulted in her dragging the trusting Dee with her, unfortunately for Madison. She'd even had to bail the two of them out of jail during their sophomore year. Everything about Karlie irritated her. She was an obnoxious, troublesome, opinionated opportunist who eventually abandoned her politics enough to marry some Wall Street broker. Madison hadn't seen her in nearly ten years and carefully avoided being available whenever Karlie came to town for a visit with Dee. Now she was going to spend three days with the bitch. Damn it, why the hell did she let Dee talk her into these things?

❖

"Is that *her*?" Madison stared in astonishment at the blonde taking audience questions from the podium. The awkward, loud, sarcastic troublemaker had matured into a beautiful, poised woman. "She's turned out nice looking."

"Sorry, she's on the wrong team."

"Doesn't mean I can't look. I know she's married."

"Mad, please, you promised to behave."

Madison stared into the bright blue eyes that mirrored her own. "I know. I will."

She kissed Dee on the cheek and continued to watch Karlie work the audience. There was a confidence about her, a sensuality Madison could feel even from the back of the room. From the enthusiastic questions tossed at the speaker, Madison was sure she wasn't the only one feeling the heat. Karlie pulled off her glasses, laughing at a question. She then gave an answer Madison couldn't hear. The audience seemed to find the interchange amusing.

"Guess she's still a smart-ass," Madison remarked.

"She's my best friend," Dee said in an injured tone. "And right now she's going through a rough time. Be nice."

The hurt look on her face stopped any further mean-spirited comments. Madison held up both hands. "I'm on my best behavior." She waited for the applause to provide cover. "As long as she is."

"Thanks, I really appreciate this. I mean it." Dee hesitated. Apologetically, she whispered, "I hope I didn't disrupt your plans. Jim didn't know about the conference until three days ago, and I really didn't have anyone else to turn to."

"It's no problem. I had nothing special planned." Madison thought of the redhead she was about to disappoint by canceling their date. "Really, nothing of any consequence. Go have a great time in Atlanta. You and Jim deserve a break. I can manage what's-her-name for a couple of days."

"Mad, you know her name."

"I'm just teasing. Don't sweat it."

Madison checked her unkind thoughts. She liked seeing her sister happy. Dee was five years younger and had been Madison's shadow throughout their childhood. As they grew into teens, Madison protected and cared for her, filling the void left by parents emotionally vacant and more involved in Miami's social life than in raising their two daughters. The Barnes family was one of the wealthier, more political families in South Florida, and Madison and Dee had grown up among a powerful elite. They'd both bucked their parents' expectations in different ways.

Madison cast a quick glance at her sister. They were often mistaken for each other by people who didn't know them well. Both tall and dark-haired, they shared a certain look and sense of style inherited from their mother. But the resemblance ended with their brilliant smiles and lean builds. Dee was much softer and more giving, whereas Madison set her life plan and then followed it. No one would own or control her. Personal relationships were secondary to achieving her goals. With one exception: Dee was allowed within the well-protected walls of her heart. She was much more than just a younger sister, she was Madison's loving and accepting friend, virtually her only friend. The only person she completely trusted. And only Dee could have talked her into spending *days* with a woman she detested.

"Are you coming?" Dee rose to her feet, and Madison realized the presentation was over and the audience was dispersing.

She followed Dee down to the podium and they stood waiting for the stragglers to finish asking questions and shaking Karlie's hand. When they were finally alone, Dee and Karlie hugged and spent a few minutes talking as though Madison wasn't there. She gave them their space, in no hurry to pretend she was thrilled to see Karlie.

"What a wonderful audience," Karlie said. "This guest lecturer opportunity was so well timed. It paid for the trip and I get to spend time with you and the family, as well." She hugged Dee again. "It's just what I needed. Thank you."

A serious expression crossed Dee's face. "Anytime. You know how special you are." She drew back a little. "Speaking of family, I know you remember my sister, Madison."

"I'm sure Karlie will never forget me bailing you two out at three in the morning." Madison kept her tone cordial but cool. She put her hand out, allowing her gaze to wander down Karlie's shapely figure.

"How could I forget?" Karlie shook her hand briefly and

impersonally. Her professorial demeanor seemed distinctly at odds with her physical allure.

Madison finally met her eyes. "It's been a long time. Congratulations on your success."

"Thank you. Nice to see you again, Madison." There was no trace of warmth in her expression.

This was going to be a long weekend.

❖

An hour later the three women were eating lunch in a restaurant at Bayshore.

Madison, making a determined effort to be charming, asked, "Karlie, how did you get to be a romance writer? I thought you were going to be the great social liberal and change the world." She hoped her smile conveyed sincere interest.

"I've never tried to change the world. I just wanted to educate people about issues and find some peace and fairness."

Madison smiled and slipped into her legal persona. "Life isn't fair. I thought you would have learned that by now." She was preparing to offer her best defense of an unfair world when she noticed Dee's hand on Karlie's arm. Karlie seemed nervous suddenly. When she spoke, her voice was calm but her eyes were a cold slate color.

"Life may not be fair, but it doesn't mean I can't live by standards of fairness." She turned her attention to Dee. "So, when do we need to get you to the airport?"

The abrupt question signaled the end of *that* topic. No one ever dismissed Madison as if she was inconsequential. What a bitch. Madison wanted to strangle her. Karlie hadn't changed. She was nothing but a social-climbing snob. Madison frowned as Dee stroked Karlie's arm and murmured something to her in a soothing tone. The tears in her eyes surprised Madison.

"You're the best," Karlie told Dee huskily. "Always have been."

They smiled at each other like conspirators in a secret no one else could be trusted with. Madison had seen that look before. She eyed them suspiciously. What the hell was going on? If Karlie was up to something that involved her sister, she would find out and stop it. She would not allow anyone to hurt Dee or use her. The conversation turned to Karlie's newest book and its backdrop of Bali, and Madison opted for watching the two women talk rather than joining in. When the bill came, she automatically reached to pick it up.

"No, this is on me," Dee said. "My thanks for you taking care of my best friend."

Karlie shook her head and quickly tucked her credit card into the payment folder. "No, please. You've done more than enough, Dee. As for this weekend, I can take care of myself. I'll play with the nanny and the kids."

"I don't know." Dee looked uneasy. "Cindy has a pretty busy schedule for the kids, and I'd rather you weren't alone all the time."

As the other women debated the weekend, Madison covertly replaced Karlie's credit card with her own and handed the folder to the waiter before anyone noticed.

"I like my own company," Karlie continued.

"I know but Madison has already agreed," Dee said.

Karlie heaved a loud sigh. Obviously the prospect of Madison's company didn't appeal.

Enjoying her discomfort, Madison insisted, "It's my pleasure. I planned on taking the boat out tomorrow, so we can spend the day sailing. I hope you like the water."

"I've sailed some," Karlie said stiffly. "If you're too busy, however, I can just read. I'm sure you have enough to worry about. It must be exhausting defending people most attorneys wouldn't want to represent."

Her concern was transparently phony. *Don't give up your day job for acting,* Madison thought. Not that her writing was any more convincing. She could barely suppress her sarcasm as she insisted, "Nope, I promised. Wouldn't hear of you spending the weekend alone."

"Please. For me," Dee added.

Madison couldn't believe her ears. Dee was actually *begging* this woman, like the weekend would be some kind of nightmare. Peeved, she signed the check and pushed Karlie's credit card across the table. Karlie's eyes glittered and she seemed about to say something, when Dee whispered in her ear and they both stood. Madison followed them out of the restaurant, quietly simmering. God, a day on a boat, where there was no escape. What had she gotten myself into?

"By the way," Dee said innocently, when they reached Madison's Lexus, "I made dinner reservations for the two of you at Le Bouchon du Grove for seven this evening."

Appalled, Madison plastered a smile on her face. She refused to make Dee feel bad when she was only trying to do the right thing, but Le Bouchon du Grove was the kind of charming, truly French bistro she would take a date to if she really wanted to woo her over superb food.

Before she could respond Karlie said, "Only if I can pay for dinner."

"I can afford it," Madison snapped back.

"I know, but this way I can at least say thanks." Karlie sounded sincere. "We haven't always gotten along, but I'd like to try."

Hesitating, Madison looked into the gray eyes staring back at her and wondered why she had never noticed their color before. She glanced sideways at Dee, who was waiting expectantly. "Sure. Why not?" she replied, rattled to have been outmaneuvered.

Karlie couldn't stand her any more than she could tolerate Karlie. During their long history of low-level warfare, one thing was accepted: They didn't need to pretend they would ever be friends. So why the olive branch now? What was that manipulative bitch up to?

"I'll have Dee's car," Karlie said. "I'll meet you there."

"It's no problem to pick you up." Madison liked to be in control, and this woman was not playing by her rules.

"It's just as easy for me to meet you there." Karlie made it seem as if she was being gracious and agreeable, but the point was made. She didn't want to have to rely on Madison any more than absolutely necessary.

Want to play one-up in front of my sister? Madison thought angrily. Two could play that game. "I insist," she said. "You're my guest for the weekend, after all."

Dee intervened, as she usually did when she saw an argument coming. "Madison, if Karlie takes my car she can do some shopping beforehand if she wants. And I know how much you hate shopping."

"Fine," Madison retorted. At the stunned look on Dee's face, she took out a business card and softened her voice. She handed the card to Karlie. "If you change your mind, call me on my cell phone."

After a long hug with Dee and a brief glare at Karlie, she got into her car and immediately hit the ignition. She couldn't believe she was going to be stuck with that bitch for dinner. A whole night wasted. Something didn't feel right about this entire situation. Watching her sister link arms with Karlie as they strolled off toward Dee's Subaru, she wished she knew what they were hatching between them. If the past was any indication, they were up to no good.

CHAPTER TWO

Karlie wasn't surprised to see Madison sitting at one of the small round tables with another woman. She almost left the busy little bistro before she was seen, but she didn't want Dee to think she'd stood Madison up. Sighing, she approached the daunting figure. "Hi, I see we're both early."

Looking up, Madison was stunned. Karlie wore an emerald green silk shell that draped softly over her full breasts. She carried a white jacket casually over one arm, the companion to a pair of tailored linen pants that accentuated the curve of her hips and the long, slender thighs Madison had always forced herself not to think about. Struggling to put a hold on her libido, she lifted her gaze to Karlie's face and lost track of the casual greeting the moment called for.

Something had changed. Karlie seemed softer, almost vulnerable. Her gray eyes held a troubled uncertainty Madison had never seen before, and her sensual mouth was slightly open, as though she was about to speak but had reconsidered. She lifted a hand to her gleaming shoulder-length blond hair, casually pushing it back. Madison wondered if it felt the way it looked, silky smooth and as warm as sunlight.

"Is this your date?" the woman next to her asked, dragging her back to reality.

"This is my sister's best friend," Madison responded quickly, getting to her feet. "We're just having dinner. Maybe I'll catch you later."

The woman stood. "You've got my number." She glanced down at the cocktail napkin with a number scrawled across it.

Karlie tried to hide the smile spreading across her face. *Boy, has she got your number,* she thought. A sly taunt wound its way out of her mouth before she could stop it. Lowering her voice so only Madison could hear, she said, "You'd probably have more fun with *her* this evening than with me. I don't mind eating alone if you prefer a different...menu."

The barb irritated Madison. Karlie's humor had always bordered on the caustic, daring the intended victim to duck. Normally Madison enjoyed such sparring, but there always seemed to be a sinister undercurrent with Karlie. She was sneaky in her timing, usually tossing her verbal grenades when others were around and Madison would have to mute her responses.

"I know how to get in touch with her. If I want to." Madison made a show of pocketing the cocktail napkin. "I promised Dee I would take care of you, and I'm not one to shirk my duty."

Karlie sighed and regretted her hastily made remark, fearing retribution was imminent. Madison Barness' temper was legendary and she rarely considered anyone's feelings but her own. She took the chair Madison pulled out with a slight bow. "You're too gallant, Ms. Barnes." *And so full of yourself,* she added as she sat.

"Nothing is too good for my sister's *best* friend."

Fortunately, the menus were brought quickly and Karlie studied the selections, thankful for the excuse to avoid conversation. But Madison wasn't going to be ignored, especially not by her.

"Dee's always trying to get me to read your books."

The inference was clear. Madison Barnes, hot attorney to white-collar crooks, did not read lightweight romance novels. She had more important things to do.

Karlie considered playing along, but decided to be honest. "Look, I know you don't like me, Madison, and you're not my favorite person either. We're only sitting here because we both love Dee. But I'm willing to put aside our differences for the weekend if you are. I don't see much point in both of us being miserable."

Madison hid her astonishment. The district attorney could have said her client was innocent and she wouldn't have been as surprised. She'd expected sarcasm or sullen silence from Karlie, but not the offer of a truce. She stared suspiciously across the table, trying to fathom Karlie's intent. The calm gray eyes gazing back at her showed no sign of wavering, but Madison knew Karlie too well to be fooled. That weasel was angling for Madison to reject the offer so she could be blamed for everything that went wrong over the weekend. No fucking way. She was too smart to be set up by an amateur like Karlie. This bitch would make her life miserable if she backed out now or, if they fought all weekend, because Dee would hear all about it. And she was also going to make Madison's life miserable if she *did* spend the weekend with her. Not a pretty picture.

There was only one possible course of action. Madison had to call her bluff and beat her at her own game. "I'm willing to try," she said with the kind of sincerity that worked on juries.

She extended her hand, and a warm feeling coursed up her arm as Karlie's palm slid against hers. Trying to ignore the heat, she made her grip extra firm, letting Karlie know who was really in charge. Karlie didn't return the pressure, and as her hand slid away, Madison was startled to glimpse a deep sadness in her expression.

Karlie lifted the menu once more, screening her face. "I think I'll try the chicken fricassee," she said after a few seconds.

Madison had already made her choice. They placed their orders and chatted politely as the waiter poured their wine.

"I thought you wanted to be a journalist," Madison said after they'd exchanged a few remarks about the impending hurricane season. "How did you become a romance writer?"

A genuine smile danced across the lovely face opposite her. "I worked as a journalist for a while, but I also began teaching creative writing to adults. I often complained about lack of depth in many romance novels. One night one of my students challenged me to do better. I couldn't very well complain and be one of those people who teaches what they can't *do*, so I spent the next eight months agonizing over my first novel. The rest, as they say, is history."

"This started out as a dare?" Madison felt herself relaxing, a smile forming despite her dislike of her companion.

"Yes. Nothing more noble than that."

"And then you continued writing them?"

Karlie shrugged. "Writing is a great job if you can make it pay."

Madison laughed. "So you ended up buying into the formula you criticized. How ironic."

The smile on Karlie's face faded a little. "Do you read romances?"

"I don't read much fiction at all. When I have spare time, I tend to do something more…physical. Besides, aren't all romances more or less the same seduction scene?"

Karlie paused as their meals were served. "Actually, there's very little seduction in most romance. Very little of the wooing and courting. The tall, studly hero exudes masculinity and causes the sweet virginal lass to swoon. Immediately she is fantasizing about him. He can barely control his own arousal. Soon they are locked in a passionate embrace and then off to bed for incredible sex. At this point the author throws in some obstacle for the next fifty pages before the couple again is off for more incredible sex."

"What's wrong with incredible sex? If some of my divorce clients had mind-blowing sex, I might not see them in my office."

"I agree, but that kind of sexual relationship seems rare."

"Life gets in the way for long-term couples." Madison had heard the same story countless times. Long working hours. Kids. Money worries. Good sex was the first thing to go, once the pressure was on. The stories she heard were enough to put anyone off marriage. Not that they factored into her choice to be single. She simply preferred a life without complication. And yes, sex was important, too. There was no way she could settle for the sterile cohabitation so many people put up with.

"I think seduction is even more rare," Karlie said after sampling her food. Her expression was pensive, as though she'd given this topic great thought. "You know what I mean? The seduction that can allow two people to get to know each other, to learn what pleases or excites the other. Anticipation can set the mood for some incredible sex. I think the reason more people don't have 'mind-blowing' sex is that the emphasis is on the act and not on pleasure and pleasing. And intimacy."

Madison sipped her wine. She couldn't believe she was discussing sex with Karlie, and she didn't intend to go any further down that trail. Steering the conversation to less personal terrain, she asked, "So, for you, what makes for a romantic encounter in one of your novels?"

Karlie didn't answer immediately. Between mouthfuls, she said, "It varies. I try to explore what it is that's arousing for each person. In my latest book, my lead character is a schoolteacher who manages to get through each day by dreaming of romantic encounters in romantic places."

Madison recalled the conversation over lunch. "Like Bali?"

"Exactly. Her life is ordinary and her fiancé is more concerned with financial success than romance. A stranger enters her life, a single father, and he talks about some of the places he's been, including Bali. He's exciting, mysterious, and exotic, and he treats her with respect and adoration. She is flustered but drawn to him. The thought of changing her life is even more frightening than he is."

"But since it's a romance, they overcome their issues and live happily ever after," Madison concluded, unable to resist making the point. Karlie seemed to think she wrote deep and meaningful books, but hers sounded just as predictable as the rest. "Pretty setting, though. Have you actually been to Bali?"

The melancholy briefly returned to Karlie's face before she took cover behind a resolute smile. "No. But I will. And soon."

"It's a beautiful place. I usually go there for Christmas. I can't stand the sudden do-good feeling people have during the holidays. Walking around, smiling, wishing everyone a happy holiday. What a crock. All that good cheer and the same people spending the rest of the year being assholes. I avoid the schmaltz and have a quiet vacation in paradise."

Karlie paused as though editing her comment. In a neutral voice she said, "I'm sure it must be the perfect place to escape to with someone special, especially during the holidays."

"Nope, I always go by myself." Madison realized she sounded more emphatic than she'd intended, and modified her tone. "I enjoy it more that way. I can walk around exploring shops, having leisurely meals, and sitting on the beach. I don't have to worry if someone else is having a good time. It's the only place I can be at peace."

She stopped talking, startled to find herself revealing so much. From the surprised look on Karlie's face, she wasn't the only one puzzled by the lapse. Madison quickly produced a casual shrug. "In other words, I can do what I want when I want and not have to justify my choices to anyone. The rest of the year my life is so regulated, I need a time-out."

Karlie was unsure how to respond. Since when did Madison Barnes talk to her like a human being? "That must be relaxing for you," she said carefully. "Not having a schedule. Getting some space."

"Exactly." Madison looked relieved. They concentrated on finishing their meals. Then, over coffee, she asked, "What happens, by the way? In your novel...how do they end up getting together?"

"You'll have to read it." Karlie threw down the challenge with gentle humor. "Dee has a copy."

"Okay, if I'm ever feeling romantic, it's a deal. But don't hold your breath."

Several appropriate, cutting replies sprang to mind, but Karlie didn't want to begin another verbal battle. Glancing at her watch, she waved for the check and said, "I didn't realize the time. I want to do a little more writing before I get to bed, so I need to be going."

"Me, too," Madison said. "There's some work I should be doing tonight." She glanced toward the counter, obviously planning to grab the bill before Karlie could pay it. "Should I pick you up in the morning?"

"No. Thanks anyway. I'll drive Dee's car. That way we can both do whatever we want afterward." Karlie opened her purse and rifled around, tucking her credit card into one hand before producing her car keys with the other. "Thank you for a pleasant evening." She slid the card into her jacket pocket, then stood. "I must stop and ask them to give my compliments to the chef. That was the best fricassee I've ever had."

"I'll walk you out to the car," Madison offered.

"There's no need. It's not far away." Karlie offered her hand, making her farewell as brief as good manners allowed. "Thanks again. I'll see you in the morning."

Madison stared after her with mixed feelings. As she'd suspected, Karlie wasn't serious about paying for dinner. Or perhaps she'd simply realized she would never win the point-scoring contest. Madison watched her at the counter, talking to their waiter. Although she exuded the confidence of a beautiful, sensual woman, there was something sad about her. Madison wondered what lay beneath her calm poise. The Karlie she remembered had never bothered to hide her opinions, or her passions, but the woman she dined with tonight seemed far more measured. Madison was intrigued. An odd sense of anticipation altered her breathing and she dragged her gaze away from Karlie. Instead of dreading the outing tomorrow, she was suddenly looking forward to it. Disconcerted, she drank the last of her coffee and moved her thoughts along a more comfortable track.

It was only a little after 9:00 p.m. and a certain redhead would be more than happy to see her. The talk about sex had left her aroused. She wasn't in the mood for seduction, just sex. No commitments. No ties. Nothing to interfere with her life. Just some incredible sex.

She turned back toward the counter. Karlie had gone and the wait staff seemed preoccupied. Impatient to move her evening to the next phase, she rose and intercepted their waiter as he passed the table. "I'll pay the check on my way out, if you don't mind."

He smiled politely. "Your friend already took care of it, ma'am. I hope everything was to your satisfaction."

Madison masked her irritation with a polite nod. "Dinner was perfect. Thank you."

She stalked out of the restaurant and fumed all the way to her car. She'd fully expected to be landed with the check and she didn't know what bothered her more: the fact that she'd been outplayed or the possibility that she didn't know Karlie as well as she thought.

CHAPTER THREE

Karlie left the cool sanctuary of the Sanderson home an hour before she was expected at the marina. Needing some quiet, calm time to prepare for the day ahead, she drove to the nearest coffee shop, ordered a latte and bagel, and made a phone call to a close friend and colleague, Sandra Bailey. After a chat about work and politics, she read the *Miami Herald*, then set out. June was not a great time to be in Miami. Already the temperatures were in the upper 70s. The heat and humidity wore down even the heartiest Floridian, much less visiting Northerners. Spending time with Madison was not going to make the day any more palatable.

She thought about the previous evening. In the many years that she and Dee had been friends, she'd never spent as much time around Madison as she had over the past day. She also couldn't remember having a conversation with her when they weren't arguing. Last night had been a surprise. Karlie didn't know what possessed her to talk about seduction and romance to a woman who went through lovers like Kleenex, using them once and then discarding them. Dee despaired of her older sister ever changing her modus operandi, and Karlie could see why. Madison obviously thought hot sex was the only important element in a relationship, and she could get plenty of that without having to make a commitment.

Karlie bought enough coffee to fill the thermos she'd borrowed from Dee's kitchen and drove to the marina with a sense of dread. She doubted last night's truce would last, and it was going to be a long day if she had to listen to any more subtle putdowns about her writing. Madison had always been patronizing. Karlie should have guessed her success as an author would change nothing. Madison had made her feel defensive about her work instead of proud.

She parked near the entrance and approached the gatekeeper. He never looked up as she requested directions. "Henderson?" he repeated the name, chewing on the word as if determining the flavor. Still fixed on the newspaper in his hand, he continued, "Yep, she told me to let you in. It's the next slip, last boat on the leeward side."

He rose slowly from his rickety barrel and opened the gate to the series of boat slips containing both motorized and wind-driven vessels. Karlie followed his directions to a large sailboat docked at the end of the pier.

"Hello!" she called. Not receiving a response, she stepped aboard. "Madison? Are you there?"

From below a voice called, "I'll be right up," and Madison emerged a few moments later looking like she'd just pulled on her shorts and T-shirt. A ball cap failed to tame her unruly dark hair. She slid on a pair of sunglasses, but not before Karlie noticed her tired eyes. *Guess she had a long night.*

Karlie half expected to see another person come up the stairs after her. "Good morning," she said pleasantly.

Madison returned the greeting, bending to pick up a deck shoe she'd stumbled out of as she reached the top of the stairs. "Welcome aboard."

"I thought I'd come a few minutes early in case there's anything you need help with," Karlie said.

Madison checked her watch. Great, four hours' sleep. She felt like shit and she knew she looked like shit. She smiled as she recalled the activities that had kept her up so late. The redhead had been worth every minute.

"Most of the hatches are open and the sails are ready," she said. "I just need to take us around to the marina and refill the tanks. We're not going to be that far out and we'll be under sail power most of the time, but I prefer being safe. I usually come out during the week and check everything. Only need to get some ice. Food is already aboard."

"Guess I don't need to worry about these extra bagels I bought, then."

"We'll eat them after we get out of the harbor into open water." Madison flashed her winning smile, surprised at the good mood she was in. She started the gas-powered engine and spoke above the noise. "Can you climb up on the dock and untie us? Just throw the ropes into the boat. I'll stay close enough for you to get back in."

Karlie didn't hesitate. She climbed up and deftly untied the boat's bow and aft lines then gingerly jumped back into the boat. Giving a thumbs-up sign, she proceeded to carefully roll the boat lines and stow them out of the way.

"Sailed before?" Madison asked, impressed with her neat precision.

"Some." Karlie climbed up into the bow and sat against the bulkhead, shivering. *Oh, goddess, why now?* She rested her head on knees she pulled tight to her chest as if, by sheer physical force, she could keep herself together and deny the pain in her heart. Madison's innocent comment had resurrected painful memories that threatened the calm she barely maintained. Random images flitted through her mind, of sailing with her husband in a happier time before he progressed to larger boats. She pushed the thoughts away, fighting the emotions that came with them.

Ten minutes later they were in the main channel headed out for open water.

"Can you put up the mainsail while I navigate?" Madison asked. "It's a simple operation and pretty much automatic." Putting the lock on the helm, she helped release the sail. Once Karlie was in position, she instructed, "Now just crank that gear and the sail will lift."

Madison carefully steered the boat until she had caught the wind and had a full sail. These were the times she loved. The sudden pull on the boat as the sail filled and the speed increased. She tightened the line on the boom to the metal tie down arch in front of her, making the sail strain as the boat maneuvered into a gentle heel. She was in control of every motion and zigzag. Madison Barnes versus the elements. And she would win. She always did. Momentarily everything else was forgotten except the feel of the boat under her feet and its tilt as it quietly slipped through the waves.

When sailing alone, she would go into a tight reach, testing the angle she could achieve and still maintain an upright position. It was one of the games she played with herself. She loved the risk.

"Coming about!" she shouted as she turned the sailboat and prepared to cross the wind.

She was finally in open water and felt free. The only calm and peace in her life were the hours she spent sailing. She smiled, focused on steering, and enjoyed the scent of the ocean, the sun beating down on her tanned body, and the power of control in her hands. Madison let her protective walls down on the water and allowed emotion into her life. This was her dream and her escape. She was one with her boat, while the water and wind were her lovers, caressing and challenging her.

When the boat was being built she'd made several visits to the Hunter Marine facility outside Gainesville. There she would run her hand over the teak, check seams and watch the boat take shape. Nothing missed her careful inspection. She had the craft outfitted with every possible electronic gadget, just in case. Not even Dee realized how important sailing had become to her, realized that sailing gave her life true joy.

She glanced at Karlie and was dismayed to see she'd withdrawn once more into the physical shell she'd occupied since they left the marina. Madison couldn't decide what to do. She'd never been good at touchy-feely, and Karlie looked barely under control. She hoped the rest of the day wasn't going to be like this, babysitting a PMS-ing, uptight straight woman who cried at sad movies. Shit. She ignored the emotions and did what she knew best—she took care of the business at hand.

Karlie ducked out of the way as the boom came across the deck. Once the sail filled, she moved further into the bow and stretched out, determined to relax. The problems she had left in New York were still there, but for this day, she was going to put them away and enjoy the feeling of freedom. She was allowed. The steady rocking of the boat as it slipped across the waves lulled her into a gentle torpor. Her legs and arms felt heavy, and for the first time in three weeks, she seemed to float above her emotions instead of being drowned by them.

Madison's voice disturbed her just as she was drifting into sleep. "You can stay here, but I need to get the jib up. I don't want you caught in the sheets or the sail."

Karlie watched, fascinated, as the jib moved into place. "I'd forgotten how much fun this is."

"I didn't know you sailed," Madison said.

"When Rob and I first started dating, he took me out on a small boat. He ended up with a twenty-seven-footer he practically lived on during the summer."

When will it stop hurting? This question plagued Karlie and threatened any peace she might have felt. No matter how much she tried to rationalize the direction her life had taken, she found no easy answers. Standing, she lifted the large bag she'd brought aboard and said, "I'll go down to the galley. I've got a thermos of coffee. I assume you have cups."

Laughter, warm and genuine, erupted from Madison. Karlie had almost forgotten how attractive she could be and how she'd even had a crush on Madison once.

"I've even got butter knives to use with those bagels. I prefer sailing to cooking, so I usually have food I can microwave, but I want it on real dishes with real silverware."

For the first time in the many years she had known this overbearing, aloof woman, Karlie was entertained. "You mean there's something you enjoy more than being a bitch?"

The question seemed to take Madison by surprise, but she recovered quickly. "If you tell anyone, I'll have to kill you."

Laughing with her, Karlie wondered why she'd never seen this side of her nemesis before. "If I told anyone, they wouldn't believe me anyway. What do you want in your coffee?"

"Just milk." As she stepped into the cabin below, Karlie was stunned at the beauty of the interior and all the modern conveniences. The wood surfaces gleamed, the teak radiating warmth and a sense of welcoming. The windows were tinted a delightful shade of green. There was plenty of room to move about the well-equipped galley. Opening a door, she found the head, which included a stand-up shower. Just beyond was the captain's quarters. The large bed was rumpled, and the clothes Madison had been wearing the previous night were thrown about. Karlie smiled and shook her head. *Everything your sister has ever said about you is probably true.* She found another stateroom at the opposite end, with sleeping space for two more people.

Karlie returned to the galley, poured coffee, and headed topside, fascinated by her explorations. She'd never pictured Madison as the type who would thrive on the solitary pleasures and dangers of sailing. Yet her boat was obviously much more than a toy or a status symbol. It was a home away from home, customized to her taste and personal requirements.

"Thought you might have fallen overboard," Madison said as she reached for her cup. "I'm not sure I could have performed an adequate rescue without sufficient caffeine."

"Didn't you get a chance to practice mouth-to-mouth last night with your friend from the café, or some other member of your harem?"

"Ouch." Coffee spewed over the deck as Madison coughed. Her blue eyes turned cold. "Karlie, why do you say things like that? You make me sound like some type of brigand."

"How appropriate for a sailor. Are you telling me you didn't spend the night? Excuse me, let me be more specific, Counselor. At least part of the night in some woman's bed? I forget how precise you attorneys are."

Madison locked the steering and walked over to her. "You have these preconceived ideas, but you don't know a damn thing about me. I worked hard in college and law school. I might not have had the grades you did, but I worked for every damn one of the A's I got. And when I got out, I hustled and worked for one of the busiest law firms in Dade County until I opened my own practice. No one handed anything to me. I worked eighty plus hours a week to build my practice."

"I'm sure you did. You still haven't answered my question, however. Is this an attorney's trick—ask questions or change the subject?" Karlie watched Madison's expression change from amused irritation to anger and calculation. There was something else, too, a flash of heat Karlie had seen before, but never directed at her. She decided she was mistaken. Madison didn't desire her; she was probably fantasizing about throwing her overboard.

"What difference does it make how I spend my time?" Madison said tersely. "I'm a fucking adult."

"Yes, you are." Karlie bit back her next comment. She'd goaded Madison enough, and hadn't she herself enjoyed sex just for sex?

Yes, but I grew up. Wanting to avoid that dreary path, she leaned against the low railing and looked out to sea, wondering why she'd set out to provoke Madison in the first place. They'd been having a pleasant time. Why sabotage it? The sun had warmed considerably and she was uncomfortable in her jeans.

"I'm going to put some shorts on," she said. "Can I get you anything while I'm below?"

"There isn't anything I need...or want." Madison's voice was cold, the courtroom voice her opponents no doubt dreaded.

"No, I guess not," Karlie threw over her shoulder as she again climbed down the ladder.

Why had she agreed to do this? Even more, why couldn't she just be polite to Madison for one day? Karlie sat in a chair near the table and wondered, as she often did, how Dee and Madison could be related. Madison represented everything she'd always disliked about rich, spoiled people. She was vain and egotistical and didn't care whom she hurt or walked on to get what she wanted. Power and money were her gods, and sex was just another power trip. She probably didn't even know how often Dee cried over some stupid, hurtful thing she'd said or done.

Karlie rationalized her anger toward Madison by thinking of

Dee. It was normal for anyone to feel protective of their best friend, wasn't it? She sipped her coffee and allowed the emptiness in her life to sweep over and claim her. What the hell was she doing here on a boat, taunting Madison Barnes instead of dealing with her own problems? Could anything else in my life get more fucked up? In that moment, she realized her anger with Rob had everything to do with her behavior. She was misdirecting her pent-up rage at Madison.

❖

Madison sat down on the deck and put her head in her hands. The peace she'd felt earlier was already slipping away. God, what a bitch that woman was. Probably a frigid bitch. A frustrated, resentful straight woman who wrote romances because she didn't have a clue what sex was all about. She felt the familiar desire to strangle Karlie, but this time the feeling caused dissonance with a different type of desire, flashes of attraction that unsettled her. Her reactions were purely physical. Still, she'd never felt anything like this for Karlie. Madison glanced toward the ladder and wished she'd asked Karlie to return with a cold drink. She was thirsty.

Checking that the boat was safely under sail, she headed below. As she reached the bottom step she stopped, uncomfortable with what she saw. Karlie sat huddled in one of the chairs, sobbing quietly, her arms wrapped around her legs. Madison paused, unsure of what to do. Anger, threats, these she could handle. Sexual behavior she could control. Crying women she avoided. Madison started to back up when a pair of red-rimmed eyes lifted and Karlie spotted her.

"I'm sorry. I'm just tired today." She quickly wiped her eyes.

Madison swallowed hard and went over to the cooler as if she hadn't noticed the tears. In the many years since she'd first met Karlie Henderson, she'd never thought of her as vulnerable. The image of her huddled on the chair crying didn't fit with the sarcastic, independent, dogmatic woman Madison knew. Troubled by the contrast, she pulled out an orange juice and returned topside.

When incongruities arose in her life, Madison inspected, dissected, and analyzed the evidence until she could arrive at a logical explanation. This new piece of information about Karlie would definitely take some time to interpret.

She studied the electronic navigation unit and modified her course slightly so they would be heading south, sailing along the Florida Keys. Performing the necessary course corrections put some semblance of order back into her life, and she felt a measure of calm returning.

The respite was all too brief. Karlie appeared after a few minutes with a tray of chips, salsa, and sodas. Her face was washed and she was wearing shorts and a long black T-shirt.

"Is everything okay?" Madison asked warily.

She was rewarded with a smile that didn't quite reach Karlie's eyes. "I'm fine. I'm sorry if I was grumpy. It's been a rough few weeks."

"Anything you want to talk about?" The thought of listening to husband troubles or "female problems" made Madison cringe, but she knew she should ask. She added quickly, hopefully, "We can head back to shore, if you prefer."

"No, I'm fine. Really." Karlie looked around. "Where are we?"

"We are near the northernmost of the Keys. I thought we might sail in there and get something to eat."

"Sounds good." Karlie drank some Coke and leaned back against the hull, apparently lost in thought.

Madison ate a few chips and tried to settle on a safe topic of conversation. "I was thinking about what you said last night. That you feel most romance novels are filled with overrated sex. How are yours different?"

The question was totally unexpected and immediately lightened Karlie's mood. "Well, I'm surprised you remembered any of our conversation, but I didn't say they were full of overrated sex, just that there's little or no seduction." Her emotions in a more neutral place at last, she said, "Those 'love at first sight' stories may be great romance, but in real life two people usually meet, date, find out they have some things in common, and love begins to grow. One day they wake up, look at each other, and realize they're in love.

Or maybe they're two people who don't really know each other, or can't stand each other, but then respect and admiration gradually build into passion."

"Like you and me?" Madison teased.

"What?" Stunned by the comment, Karlie filled with panic.

Madison laughed. "I meant the part about two people who don't really know each other or can't stand each other."

Karlie's pulse quickened. Grasping to maintain control of her voice, she said, "I've known you a long time."

"But do you *know* me?" Madison responded in a serious tone. "I've realized in the last twenty-four hours that there's a lot to you I don't know. That after all the years, I've seen you as a certain type of person and not gotten to know any more about you. That hasn't been fair."

An announcement that Madison was quitting her job and entering a convent couldn't have startled Karlie more. "Who are you and what have you done with Madison Barnes?"

"Touché." Madison laughed. "But I'm serious."

"Yeah, right, and there are snowmobile trails in the Everglades." Karlie quickly added, "I'm sorry. You're right. We really don't know each other. I guess I still remember your comment at Dee's wedding." Seeing Madison's puzzlement, she explained, "You told me the only reason you tolerated me was that Dee loved me. You said you didn't understand why, since you knew what kind of person I was. But obviously Dee saw me differently. Quote. Unquote."

The conversation was one Madison had regretted. She'd learned not to allow anyone to provoke her into statements she would later regret, but Karlie had pushed her that day. "I believe I said that you were not a nice person but that I was willing to accept your friendship with my sister."

Karlie rolled her eyes. "That's certainly an edited version of what you uttered through clenched teeth, but I don't want to argue with you. We really don't really know each other and neither of us has taken the time to challenge our assumptions." She stuck out her hand. "Do we still have a truce?"

Madison grasped the outstretched hand, enjoying the warmth

and the softness. She held it a little longer than usual before finally letting go. "Truce. And I would like to get to know you better. So, tell me more about your writing," she quietly requested. "What do you consider seduction? Is it the same thing as courtship?"

Karlie stretched her much paler legs out next to Madison's long, tanned ones and picked up the conversation. "I know that sounds kind of old-fashioned, but it can be. In our instant gratification society, we've forgotten about courting." Putting on her professorial cloak was easy and less threatening. She could discuss an intimate topic with academic detachment. "If it isn't mind-blowing sex right away, many people lose interest. Unfortunately, good sex can often take time to work out, but we're inundated with media telling us what sex should be like, and if it isn't, then someone must be at fault. Realistically, many of us have difficulty asking for what pleases us or encouraging our partners to try something different."

"Not all of us!"

"No, I'm sure you have no trouble getting what you want sexually." Karlie's exasperation leaked briefly before she returned to her academic tone. "But are you really satisfied? Or is it just release that you seek? A fuck." At Madison's wounded surprise, she wondered if she'd struck a familiar chord. Reminding herself to tread cautiously, she continued, "Making love is very different than fucking. The emotions make one more vulnerable. And that doesn't mean it's good or bad. It's just different."

"Love is overrated," Madison said. "A lover can never give me the satisfaction I have with my work. I never experience the high I feel when I win a case or tear apart an opposing attorney's case."

"Exactly. You just proved my point." Ignoring an astounded look, Karlie continued, "Winning has become everything to you, and in those situations you're never vulnerable. You're the conqueror. To allow someone to make love to you could make you vulnerable. And that can be dangerous for someone like you. Have you ever made love with someone and held her while she cried from the overwhelming feelings? Have you ever allowed someone to truly touch you? To know you and share who you are and to still allow them to say 'I love you'? To experience someone so totally that every breath you take, you can feel that person inside of you? Every beat of your heart echoes theirs. Every ounce of your being screams for that person to touch you, to taste you. To bring you to the edge of tears."

"I never cry," Madison interjected, recoiling at the thought.

Karlie stared at the smug woman. "No, I'm sure you don't. That takes trust and vulnerability. And most of us fear that type of vulnerability."

What a crock. You are so full of shit. Madison's thoughts came to a sudden halt as she realized no one had ever really touched her that way. Briefly she revisited a distant memory. Once, a long time ago, she'd given her heart to a woman who proceeded to trample it until it was no longer recognizable. She was young and naïve and foolish, and probably deserved the disillusionment. But never again. Her heart was not for sale. Only a vague memory of that pain remained and Madison put it back where it belonged, in the trash can near her heart. *Work always comes first,* she reminded herself. *Always.*

She felt the adrenaline as a nascent need to attack stirred. "Have you known that kind of love?" The question was both a challenge and a demand.

"Yes," Karlie whispered. At least, she thought she had, but that was a long time ago. She stared at her hands and was silent.

Watching her closely, Madison felt a turmoil of emotions. She wished she knew more about Karlie's husband. At the same time, she had an inexplicable animosity toward the stranger who shared Karlie's bed and heart. Feeling her control slipping, she asked, "How do you get from introduction to sex, then? Do you just hold hands for six months until you are ready to kiss?" As hard as she tried, she could not keep the sarcasm out of her voice. Or shut out the nagging thought of Karlie in love with someone.

"Hold that question," Karlie said. "I need a bathroom break."

When Karlie went below, Madison checked their location. They were near enough to Key Largo to make a course correction and head to the marina. Focusing on the screen in front of her, she worked on settling her unfamiliar emotions. The discussion had piqued her interest. Could there be emotions attached to sex, for her? Even more, why was she suddenly interested in what this sarcastic pain in the-butt had to say? Nothing Karlie had ever said mattered. Why now? She checked her equipment and maps. Navigation was a clean science; you were either on course, or not.

While the boat responded to her hand, she feared Karlie Henderson was another matter. She was definitely leading Madison off course.

Chapter Four

So tell me," Karlie moved the steering wheel a little, "how did you decide on Bali for your vacations? Why not Key West or Cancun?"

"I read some brochures when I was in law school and I decided to go there after I passed the bar. Seemed like a pretty good reward and not as easy as driving to the Keys." Madison stepped in closer. Here, I'll take over sailing."

Karlie gave up her position with a smile. She'd enjoyed her half hour at the wheel and was grateful that Madison had suggested they take turns. The task had been a welcome distraction, allowing her emotions to subside, which, she suspected, had been Madison's intention. If so, she was more considerate than Karlie could have guessed. Then again, the longer they were alone together, the harder it was to place Madison in the box she'd always occupied, that of the dragon lady.

When they'd first met, Karlie had found Madison intelligent, sharp-witted, attractive, and together. She'd accepted every invitation to spend time with the Barnes sisters. Before long, however, Madison's halo began to tarnish. As a nineteen-year-old sophomore, Karlie wasn't prepared for the put-downs and thoughtless comments Dee seemed to brush aside. In self-defense, she started throwing the pointed barbs back, and over time she did exactly what Dee had done; she built an emotional wall to protect herself. But Dee also loved Madison and saw a side of her Karlie never glimpsed and didn't think existed outside a younger sister's wishful thinking. Now she wasn't so certain.

Something else had changed, too. She didn't have the energy for those bruising skirmishes anymore. She didn't have to prove herself to Madison, so there was no point in picking fights. Besides, she had enough to deal with right now. She needed to focus on completing this day, and this coming week, then dealing with all she would face when she got back home. Just one day at a time, she reminded herself. She didn't have to fix anything or anyone. All she had to do was take care of herself and get through this period. She tuned back in to Madison's voice, hoping her inattention wasn't obvious.

"When I feel things are getting out of hand or too stressful, I only have to think about Bali and I relax."

"Is it only Bali that makes you feel that way? I would imagine there are similar beaches and waters in Mexico, or even Miami."

Madison chuckled. "And lots of people. There's something about the beauty of Bali. And the anonymity. No phones ringing. Not much on television. And the Balinese are incredibly hospitable and attentive."

"You wax almost poetical about the place."

Realizing she'd said too much about her sanctuary, Madison put on a staid countenance, ensuring her expression matched her words. "Not at all. Merely answering your question. Since you haven't been there but have chosen to write about it, I thought some firsthand knowledge might interest you."

"It does. Now I'm even more determined to get there someday soon." Karlie regarded her quizzically. "You must have a bladder the size of a football. How do you stay at the wheel for hours?"

Smiling, Madison replied, "Years of experience waiting on judges and juries. You learn to hold it and not give away that you can barely think because you've got to pee."

First shock and then amusement registered on Karlie's face. "I guess that's why lawyers have such poker faces."

"Either that or you wear rubber pants. And believe me, they can be quite noisy when you're walking back and forth in front of a jury making closing arguments."

Karlie's smile transformed her. Mesmerized, Madison stared down into eyes almost the color of the gulf on a sunny day. Gold speckled the sober gray as though radiating from deep within each iris. Light, small freckles dotted her upturned nose. A faint scar on her bottom lip hinted at some past recklessness. God, she was beautiful. How could they have known each other for so long without Madison ever noticing? The realization stunned and frightened her. Some embryonic emotion stirred, but she was neither ready nor willing to deal with it. How was it possible that she'd never really seen her? For someone trained to be an observer, this fact, this lack of recognition, dealt a serious blow to her ego.

"Now I know why you're such an excellent attorney. You can hand out the bullshit with the best of them." The words were said with gentle humor and not a trace of sarcasm.

For once, Madison just wanted to say thank you, but she played along with the mild banter. "I'm flattered."

"Be careful," Karlie warned playfully. "I might get started on some serious buttering up."

Reeling from the heat this woman was generating, Madison invited, "Try me. As you know, I have an ego."

Karlie laughed out loud, the kind of belly laugh she hadn't experienced in years. Good heavens, Madison Barnes had a sense of humor. Was she a split personality? Impulsively, Karlie said, "Thank you for suggesting this trip."

"You're welcome," was all Madison could think to say.

"I mean it," Karlie reiterated. "I know I'm not always…gracious to you, but today was exactly what I needed." She paused, reflecting on her good fortune to be here, floating far from her troubles and truly enjoying herself. "I'm sorry I haven't spent more time in Miami lately. I guess some things are meant to happen."

"I believe things happen because we make them happen."

"Yes, I am sure you do," Karlie replied. "Control is probably more important in your line of work than in mine."

Madison stared, taken aback. The comment could have been biting, but Karlie had spoken neutrally. Another barrier had come down. Impulsively, Madison said, "I have a question. What would your perfect date be? Where would you go? What would you do?"

Why do I care?

Leaning on the railing, Karlie looked out at the approaching land, masking her surprise at the personal question. She could easily change the subject and avoid it, but in her present mellow mood, she opted for honesty. "It is not so much 'what' as how. It could be an evening at home alone. We could go out to dinner after a day's sailing. Have a laugh and share the best moments from the day, taking turns listening and talking." She became lost in her vision. "I'd want to spend time touching. Not necessarily sexual, but sensual. Holding hands, playing with each other's fingers. Each one making the other feel like it matters…just being with each other."

Staring at Madison, she silently added, *Like now.* A strange fluttering sensation rose from her belly to the back of her throat as she waited for Madison to speak. They stared at each other for so long, she wondered if there'd been a reply and she simply hadn't heard it.

"What about you?" she prompted.

"The perfect date?" The controlled, always precise Madison didn't waste time on reflection. "Great sex, then I go home."

Karlie should have known better than to expect personal revelation. "Do you ever spend the night? Or just have time together without sex?"

The marina came up quickly, halting the conversation before Madison could make another glib reply. They busied themselves lowering sails and docking. Karlie went below to switch her shorts and top for a tidier outfit. As she slid on her bra she stood briefly in front of the mirror and looked at her body, first examining her breasts and then the curve of her waist and hips. Was she *that* different from the woman she was a few years ago? Was she so unattractive?

She felt tears threaten and immediately put on her shirt. Who was going to notice what she looked like anyway? Madison Barnes?

Her attempt to add humor to the situation did little to relieve the hollow ache that returned. She was tired of feeling empty.

"Are you hungry?" Madison stepped up onto the dock, offering her hand to Karlie. "Because this place not only has great food, they serve lots of it."

Smiling, Karlie said, "I'm starved. There is something about being out on the water. Let's go, Captain."

Tucking Karlie's hand in her arm, Madison teased back, "Okay, mate. Let's clean some plates." They arrived before the restaurant got crowded, and it was still early enough for them to sit on the patio and observe the boats. The meal was as delicious as promised and after they'd walked around looking at souvenirs, Madison made a quick decision.

"Since Dee won't be back until tomorrow afternoon, why don't we stay aboard the boat tonight? We can explore some of the reefs and then find a place to anchor and watch the sunset."

"Now that is on my list of romantic things." The words came out before Karlie had a chance to edit them. She could feel the growing warmth in her face and was certain, from Madison's smile, that she'd seen the blush. There was still time to decline the invitation but, incredibly, Karlie didn't want to. She loved the idea of lounging on the deck, watching the sun sink into the ocean, even with a woman who would probably ruin the ambience with a crass comment.

"Was that a yes?" Madison asked when Karlie released a long sigh.

Karlie nodded, ignoring the inner voice that warned: *This is trouble. You're making a mistake.*

❖

As the afternoon breeze picked up, Madison found herself absorbed in the delicate balance between getting the most out of her boat and losing control. It was a fragile line that could easily court disaster. Her gaze drifted to the sleeping figure lying on top of the cabin. Now *that* was a disaster in the making. Why was she so damn sexy? Breasts firm and full, begging to be touched. Hips slightly rounded, adding provocative shape to the lovely form. Toned legs that were turning bright pink. As the observation sank in, Madison cursed beneath her breath.

She hurried over to Karlie and shook her reddened shoulder gently. "Karlie, wake up. You're getting burned."

A pair of sleepy eyes blinked up at her. "What's the matter?"

"You need to put some sunscreen on or get into the shade. We're near some of the reefs I wanted to show you."

Karlie continued to stare, now wide awake.

Madison took her hand and pulled her up. "Come on. Let's get something on you before you look like a cooked lobster. Then I'm taking you to see the better part of the Keys, the underwater part." She led her to one of her stowage hatches and took out the sunblock. "Let me get your arms and back and you can take care of the rest."

Karlie inspected her limbs with dismay. "I should have been more careful."

She sat down and Madison began to apply the lotion. Her skin felt like it was on fire wherever Madison touched. *It must be the sunburn,* she tried to convince herself. But she couldn't believe how good it felt to have Madison touching her in such a sensuous manner.

"Does it usually take you this long to wake up?" Madison stroked cool lotion over Karlie's shoulders and neck, working the sunblock onto every inch of exposed skin before trailing slowly down her back.

"Sometimes," Karlie replied vaguely. The strokes continued until Madison was smoothing sunblock on her waist and lower back. The feel of the cool lotion on her warm skin was intoxicating. She wanted to prolong the contact for as long as she could.

Madison's throat was dry and she was having trouble swallowing. Her eyes were drawn to the soft, now moist skin below her fingers. She could feel every slight quiver, every breath drawn and released. Her senses were in overload and her hands screamed for a different kind of touch. Adding more lotion, she moved to the soft, graceful arms and just as tenderly coated them.

A sigh slipped from Karlie and she leaned back against Madison, eyes closed. "That felt wonderful," she murmured.

Madison stared down at her, wondering if she was imagining the undercurrent between them. *I want her. God, how I want her.* Whatever else happened, this was one of the most intense moments in her life and she was not willing to let it, or this woman, go. Shocked, she took a step back, breaking the spell. "There, no damage done."

Sitting up, Karlie said, "Thank you. I certainly want to be able to walk tomorrow and not look like some Yankee tourist." She batted her eyelashes teasingly and held out her hand for the sunblock. "I'll take care of the rest of me and then we can look at coral."

Madison continued to stare. She'd never wanted anyone or anything the way she wanted this woman at this moment. She reached up to rub a spot on Karlie's shoulder, explaining, "Too much sunblock."

She knew she was flirting and had no intention of stopping. Never one to analyze her interactions when it came to sex, Madison acted on whatever she felt and dealt with the consequences later. It was the one area of her life that avoided intense scrutiny. In half a day, Karlie had tilted her world and created such a hunger that Madison knew she would starve if she couldn't have her. Slowly she put her hand down and took a deep breath. *I will have her. I don't understand, nor do I care. I just want her.*

Karlie almost dropped the sunblock when she looked into Madison's eyes. Stunned by the intensity of emotion she saw there, she lowered her gaze immediately. Such rawness scared her. All too aware of her own arousal, she stood up and stepped away. "I think I better put a shirt on so I don't make this any worse."

Madison was on autopilot. She could not think, or reason, or understand. She was just raw desire, and she knew Karlie had sensed her tension and reacted to it. Maybe she'd even guessed the reason. She was straight, not stupid. "Yes, good idea." She could hear the strain in her voice. "Put a shirt on."

Karlie was standing inches away. With one swift movement, she could be resting in Madison's arms. A long silence stretched out between them like a bridge across the divide they'd never been able, or willing, to close. In that moment, Madison knew something had changed and neither of them could pretend otherwise. Karlie was the first to move, her body just brushing Madison's as she stepped past. Flinching from the brief contact, Madison sagged back against the hatch and released the breath she'd been holding. Her pulse was out of control. She wanted to possess Karlie, to take her and bring her to orgasm. *Forget it,* she warned herself. This woman was trouble. And straight.

But Madison was certain of one thing. Karlie had liked being touched, and if Madison wanted her she could probably have her.

❖

The time in the water reduced the tension, but the thread connecting the two of them remained taut. Madison pulled herself up on the dive platform at the back of the boat, removing her mask and snorkel as she did. "God, that was wonderful. I thought you were going to fly out of the water when that eel touched your leg."

"I'm still not sure that wasn't a water moccasin or some other deadly beast," Karlie replied, shaking water from her mask.

"Sorry, but there aren't any moccasins this far out. And you looked like you were ready to walk back."

"You were a lot of help. I think you drove it toward me deliberately." Karlie gave Madison's chest a playful shove, but her hand was caught as she tried to retreat.

"Not so fast." Madison clamped Karlie's hand to her chest. "I'll have you know I saved you down there. You would have passed out from hyperventilation if I hadn't brought you to the surface."

"Oh, please." Karlie's pulse raced at the feel of Madison's heart beating under her hand. Uncomfortable with the intensity of the emotion and the searing heat of the other woman's body, she tried to pull back but stronger hands held on to hers. Hesitantly, she looked up. Madison's smile had faded, replaced with a more serious expression. Karlie stood still. She knew she was going to be kissed and she was powerless to refuse. She wanted to be kissed.

Madison leaned down, gently brushing the lips she so desired. They were as soft as she'd imagined. Sensing no withdrawal, she drew the bottom lip into her mouth, stroking its length with her tongue. Salt and sun. Hmm, she could definitely get used to this. She caressed both lips and hesitated only briefly when she was given entrance. Feeling excitement build, she sent an exploring tongue into the dark heat, pressing their bodies together as she made her sensual assault.

Karlie was overwhelmed with emotion. It felt good to be wanted, to be the object of desire. Once, many years ago, she would have given anything to have Madison even acknowledge her. And now this. Her thoughts flew in so many directions. It had been a long time since anyone had wanted her the way Madison obviously did, and even longer since she'd had casual sex, and that's what this was. Lust, pure and simple. Her life was so screwed up, could this screw it up anymore? No one was making a commitment. After this weekend, things would go back to the way they were. Madison would have other women and this episode would be forgotten. A blast of fear made Karlie shrink back. She couldn't put her heart out there again and allow it to be bruised. She needed time to think.

Pushing her hands against Madison's chest, she said, "Please... hold on. This is happening too fast. I'm not sure what's going on."

"Look, I don't know what is going on either and I'm not going to try to understand. I just know I want you so much it hurts. Right now, I find you one of the most desirable women I've ever met." Madison stroked Karlie's palms with her thumbs. "I won't force you into anything you don't want." She reached up and moved a strand of hair behind Karlie's ear. "I just want you to know I find you incredibly sexy."

"Thank you." Karlie struggled to keep the tears from forming. God, how she'd wanted to be wanted. To be touched. Desired. To have Madison say those words made her weak with longing. She was well aware of the taut nipples close to her hands and how easily she could be caressing them. She didn't allow herself to think about where that would lead. She swallowed hard, then lightly kissed Madison on the cheek. "Let's back up and slow down. Please."

The words tore at Madison, but she nodded and let go of Karlie's hands. "Why don't you get into some dry clothes and I'll find us a spot to anchor. We can fix something to eat and watch the sunset."

She took several deep breaths as Karlie went below. She needed every ounce of reserve to not go down those stairs after her. Again checking her navigation system, she hoisted the jib and set her course, enjoying the challenge of handling the boat under full sail. When her heart rate finally returned to normal, she decided she'd had a lucky escape. She didn't have time in her busy life to deal with drama, and that was exactly what could happen if she had a fling with Karlie. She was Dee's best friend, for heaven's sake. And married. There was obviously something wrong in *that* relationship, if the kiss was any indication. Karlie certainly hadn't responded like a shocked heterosexual, happy with her husband.

This was about lust, Madison reminded herself. If she wanted sexual release, she could find it anywhere. She didn't have to risk Dee's anger or end up as the "other woman" in a divorce scenario. No way. Even mind-blowing sex wasn't worth it. She sighed. Would sex with Karlie be that good? Her body reacted damply to the idea, and Madison bent low over the wheel. This would pass, she told herself firmly. But she couldn't erase the taste of Karlie from her lips.

❖

Karlie grabbed a towel and stepped into the shower. She shampooed her hair and then washed off the salt from snorkeling. As she dried herself, she looked in the mirror and ran her fingers across her lips. She had enjoyed the kiss. Hell, if she was honest, she had more than enjoyed it. She really didn't want to stop. Once, many years ago, she would have done whatever Madison had asked.

Funny. Young, naïve Karlie had an incredible crush on Madison but was totally ignored by her, then teased and ridiculed when Madison finally noticed she existed. Karlie never forgot or forgave her for the pain and humiliation. But now...now Madison wanted her.

Why not? Karlie finally decided. It might even be fun. It wasn't as if either one of them wanted a long-term commitment. Surprised to find herself trying to justify a casual encounter, she carefully scrutinized her emotions. She was vulnerable and needy, and it *was* Madison Barnes. What a perfect revenge. She hated her guts, didn't she? A brief image crawled from the depths of her memories, another tall, dark-haired woman. A brief affair. Rebounding from Madison's rejection, Karlie had jumped at the overture. She relived the one night spent with that woman, and the pain she'd felt realizing it was the closest she would ever come to sleeping with Madison.

Until now.

She sighed and pulled out dry clothes. For once, she wanted to just do something because it felt good. Would she regret this? Probably. Damn, she was analyzing again. Maybe nothing would happen anyway. A part of her realized she was deceiving herself. No matter what was going on in her life, she tried to deal honestly. She took a deep breath and acknowledged that she wanted something to happen. She'd always wanted it. But with Madison, not just any woman.

She dressed in shorts and an oversized T-shirt. When she returned to the deck, she found Madison staring up at the sails. "What's so interesting up there?"

"Sorry, I didn't hear you. I'm watching the edge of the sails. The wind keeps changing direction. I'm trying to keep the sails from luffing too badly and ending up dead in the water." She offered a smile that seemed far too seductive for a discussion about sailing technique. "I can always get us going again but we'd lose some of the momentum."

"O Captain, my Captain, I have no doubts about your sailing abilities. Or other skills."

This drew a laugh. "Ah, the real Karlie is back. I was afraid she'd swallowed too much sun and surf."

"Mmm. I don't think she ever went away. Just choosing her battles."

"Ah, a contest. You know how I love challenges. I find them very…stimulating." The smirk was classic Madison. "And I always win," she added in a lower, sensual voice.

"Maybe in the courtroom," Karlie said. "But not necessarily here."

"A worthy opponent." Madison touched Karlie's nose. "I can see we're well matched."

"Let's just say this will be an interesting challenge." Her own audacity surprised Karlie. She couldn't believe she was blatantly flirting with her nemesis and first crush. But the bantering was pleasant and suggestive, and she couldn't summon any desire to end the game. She reached up and moved the ebony hair away from Madison's face. "Besides, you definitely need some lessons in"—she waited as Madison held her breath—"humility."

"I'm devastated." Madison placed a hand across her chest and feigned being wounded. "I thought I was perfect. And it's not easy being humble under those circumstances, by the way."

Karlie grimaced. "No wonder you don't have long-term relationships. That ego. Nobody is strong enough to feed it except you."

"Ouch." Madison's wounded gaze became even more plaintive.

"Give it up," Karlie advised. "That look may work with your ninety-minute wonders, but it doesn't cut it with me."

"You are definitely going to be a challenge. Come on. Why don't you take the helm for a while?" Madison pulled Karlie in front of her and gave her control of the sailboat.

She slipped her arms around Karlie's waist and enjoyed the full body contact. They stood close for some time. Madison would whisper small sailing corrections and then watch as they were accurately and competently carried out. As the time slipped by, the shadows deepened and color began to bleed from the sky. Reluctantly, she released Karlie and said, "I'm going to lower the sail. We can anchor out here. We're not that far from the coast. Once it gets dark you will see the lights."

Karlie nodded, instantly missing the warmth of Madison's body and the security of her arms. She watched her lower the anchor and wait for it to catch. "We make a good team," she said.

Madison returned and put an arm around her waist. "Let's get some warmer clothes on before the sun goes down."

Leaning into the strong body, Karlie said, "Good idea. We can eat later."

"I'll get a blanket in case the wind picks up while we sit out here."

Madison looked into the slate-colored eyes that constantly drew her own and saw only a steady, sure gaze. The thread between them tightened and the outcome of the evening was suddenly in no doubt. All she thought she knew about Karlie lay in shreds, and she kept making choices she would normally run from. For once she wasn't orchestrating every moment, focused on her goal. She wasn't even sure what her goal was anymore. She was used to controlling her sexual encounters, but she had to admit, a little unpredictability added to the anticipation.

The course was not unfettered with peril. Like any journey, this one had already brought surprises and there would be more to come. Madison couldn't remember ever feeling the mixture of relief, comfort, and excitement she felt now, thinking about the possibilities. Waiting for Karlie was like waiting to see land, after a long, barren voyage.

CHAPTER FIVE

As the sun began to set, Madison reached tentatively for Karlie's hand. For most of her adult life, she'd gone after whatever she wanted. Once her decision was made, she felt she was merely claiming her prize. The rules were different now. She needed to be on firmer ground.

"Is this okay?" she asked, nodding toward their entwined hands.

Karlie was touched by the reluctant vulnerability she heard in Madison's voice. Who was this woman? She smiled and leaned into her. "Yes, it's okay."

It was more than okay. Karlie found swallowing difficult and tears near. It had been nearly a year since Rob had touched her, other than in the most casual way. She pushed thoughts of her husband aside and watched the horizon, enjoying the heat radiating from the body next to hers. She repositioned herself so that she was sitting between Madison's long legs, her back against Madison's chest. Strong arms encircled her and she felt herself melting into Madison's warm body.

"You smell good." Madison leaned into Karlie's neck, breathing in the perfume she always associated with her. Remnants of the slightly floral scent were evident on the shirt she wore. "You've worn that fragrance for some time. At least since Dee's wedding. I like it."

"Why, Madison, I didn't know you were aware of anything about me except my troublemaking ways."

Had there always been this undercurrent in their teasing, or was there something new in Karlie's tone of voice? Madison was unsure. Everything about Karlie now seemed uncharted territory. "Surely you're aware of the keen powers of observation I possess," she said. "That's part of what makes me such a great lawyer. And it is part of my charm."

"Uh-oh. So is the ego." Karlie tried to keep the amusement from her voice. "No wonder you enjoy being on the water. You can stay outside where there's plenty of room for your head."

"Don't you find me charming?" Madison purred into the ear next to her lips. She couldn't remember the last time she'd just held a woman this way. Once the sex was over, she left her companion's bed. She never brought anyone to her territory. That would be a problem. She glanced around the boat. There was nowhere to go.

A chill of awareness ran through Karlie as she contemplated Madison's question. *Charming?* Yes. And as desirable as hell, and probably as dangerous. "I find you...hmm." The longer she hesitated, the more tension she felt in the arms around her. Enjoying the game, she said, "I find you...nice."

"Nice?" Madison couldn't believe what she heard. "Christ, Karlie, nice is for old ladies and babies."

Laughing, Karlie ran her hands softly along the arms linked around her waist. "Well, that's an improvement from earlier, when I thought you were a bitch."

"But I am a bitch. Actually, around Miami I think the more appropriate title is 'blood-sucking barracuda bitch.' Aren't you frightened, little girl? I'm told I'm quite dangerous."

The sensuous voice sent sparks dancing throughout her body, but Karlie wasn't ready to give into the desire she felt building. "Puh-lease. When has anything you ever said or done scared me?" She lifted one of Madison's hands and heard a sharp intake of air as she ran her tongue across the palm. Her brazen behavior amazed her, but she wasn't planning on stopping. "I've known you too long, Madison. Save your bitch behavior for someone who'll appreciate it."

This woman is killing me. Madison leaned down and ran kisses along Karlie's neck and shoulders. She was going to explode if she couldn't have her soon. "Are you sure I don't scare you just a little?"

"Actually, I think you should be more frightened of me than I of you."

"And why is that?" Madison whispered, continuing her kisses. The woman in her arms felt as if she belonged there. Her hair smelled clean and warm like the sun.

"Because you can't get up and leave in the middle of the night," Karlie replied. "And because I'm not willing to give you total control over what will happen." The kissing stopped and the body behind her stiffened. Ignoring the inner voice screaming at her, asking her what the hell she was doing, Karlie continued, "This is not just about sex. This is about seduction. So, relax, hot stuff. We have no place to go. Enjoy the sunset."

Had she been on shore, Madison knew she would have seriously considered getting up and going home. It took several deep breaths before she felt herself begin to relax. The sun had reached the horizon and the golden orb rested on the earth's edge. She contented herself with watching the sky transform.

"Safe" was not a word she linked to other women, yet she felt safe with Karlie in her arms. She also felt aroused and challenged. She tried to not think about the other emotions roiling beneath the surface. *Act, don't think.* That had always been her motto. No one had ever stirred her the way Karlie did, but if she thought about this too much, she would probably change her mind. She tightened her embrace, reveling in the unspoken promises, yet overwhelmed at the emotions threatening to take possession of her, body and soul. *Above all else, don't lose control,* she reminded herself. She could have what she wanted without taking unnecessary risks. The sky wasn't going to fall if she slept with a woman all night.

They sat silently, bodies entwined, until the sun disappeared and the sky completed its journey from fiery red to gold to azure and then darkness. And still they sat, the two former sparring partners poised on the brink of a change that seemed unavoidable. Karlie accepted this quiet interlude as a bridge between her life as it had been to what she knew awaited her. A time of exploration and sensation. Healing and vulnerability. Passion and hope. She hated to break the silence, but she was finally ready.

"It's getting chilly." She stood up and extended her hand to Madison. "Let's go below and get something to eat. I can't have you wasting away."

She was nervous. No, aroused. *Get a grip, old girl. This is just sex.* Even as she heard these words in her head, her heart rejected them. Once below, she took command, pushing Madison down onto the couch.

"I'll fix us something to eat. Stay."

Madison smiled and leaned back, crossing her legs. "Am I your pet dog?"

"Heavens, no. My pet dog is well mannered and behaves."

"Oh, I'm crushed." Madison lifted one brow, charmed. She wondered again how she could have known this woman for so long and not known her at all. There were too many questions, and she feared most of the answers. The one question she knew she wouldn't ask, couldn't ask, was what tonight meant to the woman fixing food for her in the galley.

Karlie hummed as she cut fruit and vegetables into bite-sized chunks. Madison had brought along enough supplies to last several weeks, if they happened to find themselves lost at sea for a while. The idea made her smile briefly, before her thoughts returned to the present situation. Could she go through with this? And with this woman? Karlie rationalized that she had nothing to lose. She needed someone to want her, and that was okay. Besides, the encounter wouldn't mean anything to Madison, and maybe that was a good thing. Karlie didn't need complications in her life either. She knew what she needed and she was pretty certain she could find it in Madison's bed. Resolutely, she found the chilled French wine and carried the bottle to Madison to be opened.

While Madison removed the cork and poured the wine, Karlie placed some chopped fruit on a small table nearby and settled on the couch with her legs folded under her. As she watched Madison, she realized she could no longer be objective. Her heart pounded and she felt a tingling between her legs. She sighed. *I want to make love with her.* Stunned, she hastily corrected herself. *I want to have sex with her.*

A smooth velvety voice interrupted her thoughts, the invitation as clear as the wine Madison offered. "To what shall we drink?"

Karlie hesitated only briefly. "To time standing still. To getting to experience each other. To passion."

The last words caused a stirring sensation in Madison's stomach. Already she could feel the heat between her legs. Controlling her building need was going to be difficult around Karlie. She raised her glass and sipped. She wanted to be sober, but her throat was drier than a Southwestern desert. She finished off the glass and poured another.

Karlie was surprised by the discomfort she could see. This was an area in which the unflappable Madison had greater familiarity and experience. What was she so nervous about? Karlie put her glass down and moved closer. "You're tense. Turn around and I'll rub your shoulders while you finish your wine."

She moved to her knees to reach Madison's tight shoulders. Slowly and gently she began kneading the neck muscles and then moved down, gradually increasing the intensity of her strokes until she could feel the deep tension ebbing away.

"That feels great," Madison said. "I hope you're not trying to put me to sleep." She leaned back against the body of her tormentor. The breasts she'd been admiring were close to her head. She groaned and moved her cheek lightly against them.

"Never," Karlie answered quickly. Too late she realized she'd finished her second glass of wine. She chose a small piece of apple and placed it in Madison's mouth, teasing, "Just to keep your energy levels up."

Madison reached up and drew the body behind hers even closer. Slowly and deeply she inhaled Karlie's distinctive scent once more. "I'm rather known for my…stamina."

"You are such an egotist." Karlie ran a hand through Madison's thick, short hair before sliding out of her grasp.

"Oh, no you don't." Madison was on her feet in a split second. "Do you really think you can tease me like that and get away with it?"

Her voice was husky with desire and the eyes raking Karlie made her skin burn. Foolishly, she couldn't resist a taunt. "What are you going to do about it? I'm not one of those women who fall at your feet, so grateful they do exactly what you want."

Madison's eyes glittered with intent. "Really? You seem to be having trouble keeping your hands off me so far."

"God, how do all those women you go through put up with that ego?" Karlie muttered. Years of pent-up anger suddenly consumed her. Even as she spoke, she knew her insecurities dictated every sarcastic word. She was sabotaging herself, and the wine didn't help her judgment. "I mean, do you ask them to rate you after you fuck them?"

The retort only served to ignite Madison's temper. "I don't need scorecards. Who, when, and how I choose to have sex is between me and another consenting adult. Women have sex with me because they want to, and I make sure they enjoy themselves."

"How would you know? You don't care a flying fuck about anyone but yourself."

"Damn it, Karlie. How do you come off being the fucking expert on my personal life? I haven't had any complaints."

Karlie stopped and stared, completely incredulous. "You actually think you're doing them a favor, don't you?"

"You have no idea what you're talking about."

"I guess you have someplace where you carve another notch for every victory?" Karlie continued, ignoring Madison's narrowed gaze. "Is that what I am?"

Madison gripped her arms, forcing her face-to-face. Her voice was low and ominous. "You tell me. Because right now you're not making much sense. Are you intentionally trying to pick a fight?" She paused, then insisted, "Look at me and listen if you can. I want you, Karlie. I want you so much it hurts. But I don't think you know what the hell you want. Maybe you write your bullshit books because it's safer than real life. Maybe you thought you'd experiment with me because you can't enjoy sex. I wouldn't be surprised if that husband of yours has some girlfriend on the side."

The words pierced an angry, ugly wound and sparked a rage so deep it triggered a response completely unexpected. Before she had time to think, Karlie slapped the smug face inches from her own. Madison reacted quickly, grabbing her wrist in midair. Her eyes were cold and dark, daring her to make another wrong decision.

"Do that again and I'll charge you with battery." She released Karlie's wrist, and as she did, she leaned into her and captured the lips she'd wanted ever since that first intoxicating kiss. This time the kiss was one of possession. No trace of the earlier tenderness. She claimed the woman who had taunted and teased her, who had caused her body to reach almost painful levels of arousal. And only after she'd thoroughly staked her claim did she pause, resting her forehead against Karlie's.

"Karlie, this is about fucking," she whispered. "I want to fuck you. If you don't want the same thing, then say something now, because in thirty seconds I won't be willing to stop."

Without a word, Karlie gave her answer. She backed Madison onto the couch and straddled her lap. Facing her, she slowly lifted her own shirt over her head. Madison stared at the tempting breasts inches from her mouth. Her imagination had not prepared her for the reality of Karlie's breasts or the feel of the hardened nipples in her mouth. She sucked one breast, biting into the nipple that lay hard against her tongue. A pulsing started at her core and Madison knew she would have trouble controlling her own orgasm.

Karlie leaned into the caress, her wetness flowing. Strong fingers played up and down her back as Madison alternated between sucking and biting each tender nipple. Needing relief, Karlie begged, "Please, Madison. Please fuck me."

She gasped as Madison rose and wrapped her arms and legs tightly around her. Once in her cabin, Madison lowered her to the bed and knelt between her thighs. Never breaking eye contact, she loosened Karlie's shorts and slid them down. Still kneeling, she removed her own clothes, throwing them on the floor next to the bed.

As she lowered herself, Madison felt the heat between her own legs begin to soar. *Fuck, not yet.* She positioned herself so her clitoris was exposed and rubbing against Karlie's and gave in to the sensation. Her orgasm was quick. Eyes closed, head back, she moved her hips rhythmically until the last spasms subsided.

The pulsing she felt from the woman riding her aroused Karlie more than anything. Aching with desire, she wrapped her legs around Madison's slender hips and began to push against her. Madison moved faster, stirring even deeper passion.

"Come for me, Karlie. I want you to come for me."

The words were like pouring gasoline on an already out-of-control fire. Desperate for release from this physical prison, Karlie moaned and lifted her hips. "Oh, God, you're so hot and hard. Please, I need you inside me. Please, Madison, fuck me. I need to feel you in me. Please."

Madison's hand found her dripping center. "You're so wet, baby. You make me hot, feeling how wet you are." Her fingers teased and taunted. Moving in and then pulling out, never going deep.

"I need you in me, please. Please, Madison." Karlie tried to push the teasing hand into her.

"Impatient? Tell me. Tell me what you want me to do."

"Fuck me. Now."

With that Madison plunged deep inside.

"Yes. Don't stop." Karlie gasped as each thrust brought her closer to release.

When she finally felt herself spasm around Madison's hand, she gave in to the profound shudders with a deep cry of release. Madison continued, slowing her movements until the shudders dwindled to a barely perceptible pulsing. Karlie finally opened her eyes. She wanted to speak but was unsure of what to say to this woman who had so skillfully taken her. As her rapidly beating heart began to slow, she said, "That was a good start."

Madison wanted to laugh. "You're such a smart-ass."

Before Karlie could answer, she placed a series of kisses around her neck and shoulders and began to move down her sweat-covered body. By the time she reached the wet heat, she found Karlie close to orgasm again. This time Madison took possession with her mouth and gloried in the taste of Karlie coming. Then, for the next two hours, she repeatedly brought her to the precipice, dangled her over its edge, and finally helped her across. Only when she was again close to orgasm did she ask or allow Karlie to bring her home also.

For a long while they lay spent in each other's arms. Then, when she felt Madison's breathing slow, Karlie eased gently from her embrace and slid her feet onto the floor. For several minutes she stood at the side of the bed, staring down at the face that had sometimes seemed etched in her mind's eye. She pushed aside strands of dark hair and let her thumbs play at the edges of Madison's lips until a smile crossed them. *I want to fuck you and make you feel all the things I did*, she thought. *Where do I begin?*

Holding a finger across the lips she wanted to kiss, she said, "We don't know jack shit about each other, but I know something about passion and I'm willing to share." She kissed one corner of the tempting mouth. "At least for today." She ran her tongue along the bottom lip and heard Madison groan. "Stay here, and wait, please."

"As if I could move." Madison smiled languidly.

Karlie went into the galley and got a small bowl of fruit and a glass of wine. After climbing back into bed, she grabbed a strawberry and dipped it into the wine, instructing, "Open your mouth." When Madison complied, she placed the strawberry between her own lips before transferring it to Madison's.

The mixture of taste and sensation, and the feel of Karlie's tongue, sent sparks sliding through Madison. While she savored the taste of strawberry, Karlie began a detailed exploration of her face, kissing the brows before sliding down to the eyes closed with pleasure. Soft kisses slid across them and toward Madison's ear, where a warm tongue probed, followed quickly by an even warmer breath.

"Mmm. You taste salty."

Karlie's breathy words made themselves felt between Madison's legs. A moan began deep inside her and struggled to the surface. "I'm not sure I can wait. I'm hot with wanting you now."

Karlie nipped down Madison's jawline until she reached her

chin, then headed south to the tanned neck. She continued to explore until she found a spot that drew another soft moan. She focused on that spot while she ran her hands through Madison's hair. "I have to defend my honor. I want to see if you still think what I write is bullshit."

Madison groaned. Was this woman intent on driving her crazy or was this some stupid contest? She could feel her own arousal and knew she was wet with anticipation. She traced her hands up Karlie's back only to find her wrists caught.

"Hold on, hot stuff. I'm not done with you." Karlie pushed Madison's hands away.

Sitting up, she examined the very familiar face. Madison's blue eyes were dark and glazed. Her breathing had changed. Karlie ran her hands over Madison's chest, enjoying the contrast of strength and softness. She leaned in and began to nibble at her exposed neck while playing with Madison's small, firm breasts. The softness of her skin amazed and stirred Karlie. The taste and feel of her was different from anyone else. She continued to kiss and bite until Madison's moans got louder.

"I'm not sure how long I can hold on." Madison groaned.

"Oh, you will. And so will I."

Madison laughed. Sex had never been funny, but now she was aroused and laughing. "God, you're driving me crazy. You know that, don't you?"

Karlie slid a finger across one of the darkened, aroused nipples before gathering it in her mouth and gently biting down. When she lifted her head, she wore an innocent smile. "You seem to be breathing heavy, and I don't want you to get dry mouth." She stood up and poured a glass of wine. "Maybe we should slow down. Have some wine and something to eat."

Madison could only think of one thing she wanted to eat. She took the wine and dragged Karlie across her lap. Her kiss was commanding this time. She was in charge. "I have an appetite," she whispered when she paused for breath. "And I know how to satisfy it."

Karlie dipped her fingers into the wine and traced one wetly across Madison's lips before slipping it into her mouth. Madison sucked.

"Tell me what you like," Karlie requested. The light blue eyes staring back at her filled with desire. She let Madison take another wine-covered finger into her mouth. The sucking sensation made a direct connection to the warm, damp place between her own legs.

"I like...breasts," Madison said. "I like the feel of the nipple getting hard in my mouth. I like being inside someone and feeling her come."

Karlie tilted forward and cupped one breast to Madison's mouth. "Suck me, baby. Please. I need to feel you sucking my breast." As her nipples stiffened to the pleasure and pain of Madison's teeth, she urged, "Yes, baby. That's good. I need to feel you touching me. I want your mouth on my breasts. I want your hands on me. I want you to take me."

Madison slid between Karlie's legs and began to rub her clit against Karlie's hard center. "Oh, Karlie, I want you. You're so wet, baby. I can feel how excited you are. Help me, baby."

Karlie slid her hands down Madison's back to her narrow hips. Wrapping her legs around Madison, she lifted her hips in tempo to Madison's rocking. A slow fire burned from her belly to her chest. Its warmth infused her limbs, making them weak and heavy. She needed more. "Don't stop. I need to feel you in me. I need you to fuck me."

The words brought Madison close to orgasm. She slid one, then two fingers inside and began a steady dance, stimulating Karlie's hardened clitoris while her fingers plunged deeper. The tempo grew and sounds of pleasure encouraged her. Her efforts took on a new intensity. She felt the first spasms begin around her hand and rode the waves. "Come for me, sweetheart. Come for me."

"Please don't stop." Karlie's voice rose and became tight. "Baby, please. Omigod. Don't stop. Fuck me, Madison. Yesss!"

Madison stared down at the look of exquisite pleasure and moved deeper inside until she thought she would be swallowed. She led Karlie on the journey to orgasm, her own body quivering in anticipation. As Karlie's fingernails raked across her back she moved her hips swiftly to release the pent-up tension. And she continued to stroke until at last, Karlie lay quiet beneath her.

"Want more?" Madison asked after their panting subsided.

"Yes. Now." The hunger in Karlie's voice brought Madison back to the brink of ecstasy.

"Tell me what you want."

"I want you to take me with your mouth again." The words spilled out as though they'd been trapped in the back of Karlie's throat for an eternity. "And I want you to wait to go inside until I'm almost ready to come. I want to come hard with you."

Madison gathered Karlie in her arms and kissed her eyes, then her nose, and finally her lips. An unfamiliar emotion threatened to dislodge itself and she fought to keep her reserve in place. She kissed a path past the breasts she'd so recently tasted, down Karlie's stomach to her inner thighs. Placing kisses along the silky flesh, she absorbed the scent of Karlie's sex. Rubbing her own swollen clit on the bed, she leaned in and licked at the well dripping before her. The first taste of her lover's clit almost sent her over the edge.

"Wait for me, baby." Karlie was rubbing herself and encouraging Madison to continue. "In me, Madison. Now. Please."

Madison shoved her fingers inside and this time she rode toward the edge with Karlie. The first contractions around her fingers brought on hard spasms of her own. She thrust her hips until the last of the orgasm dissipated. At the same time she felt Karlie's grip around her fingers tighten.

"Oh, God," Madison cried, drenched and exhausted. It had been some time since she'd experienced such a hard orgasm. She shifted up next to Karlie and gently stroked her face. "How are you?"

"Mmm, good. How about you?"

"Wonderful. Exhausted."

"Think you've got one more in you?"

Madison stared in disbelief. "Don't tell me you want more?"

Karlie smiled. "This time you can lie there and watch me. You can join in anytime."

She placed an extra pillow under Madison's head, then lay back down, one hand on her breast, the other between her legs. Madison watched. This was new to her. She started to sit up but Karlie pushed her back down with her foot.

Her voice heavy with want, she said, "Not yet. You aren't ready yet."

Madison groaned but leaned back to watch. Karlie continued to play, teasing her nipples into knots and parting herself so that Madison had an unrestrained view. She ached to touch the enlarged, wet clitoris she could see nestled in the damp curls. Karlie smiled as she dipped her hand and slowly withdrew to inspect the moisture coating her fingers.

"Want to taste?"

Madison could only nod.

Karlie climbed on her lap and straddled her. When she lifted her hand, Madison tried to pull it into her mouth.

"Not so fast." Karlie only allowed her to lick one finger at a time.

The taste of Karlie in her mouth, the wetness dripping onto her lap, the heat from the aroused body drew Madison into a trance of tension and desire so powerful she could not move. Another finger slipped between her lips and played with her tongue. Madison thought it was impossible to feel this aroused and not implode. "I need to fuck you again," she whispered. "Please."

The slow smile Karlie flashed back deepened her desire. God, she was incredible. Taking Madison's face between her hands, she gently kissed her. "Together this time," she murmured.

Madison nodded, knowing she would agree to anything. Karlie's fingers entwined in hers and she drew their joined hands down. At the same time she explored Madison's wet center with her free hand and began to stroke in the rhythm Madison initiated. Their breathing became labored. Their entwined hands pumped and stroked Karlie's center until, with a loud cry, she exploded. Quickly Madison followed, calling out Karlie's name as wave after wave of pleasure flowed through her. Basking in the smell of sex, they lay still for several minutes, their enjoined fingers still deep within Karlie. Then Karlie began to giggle.

"What's so funny?" Madison asked.

"I just feel wonderful."

Madison didn't bother to contain a huge grin. She knew she was good. And they still had tomorrow. And Karlie wasn't leaving for a few more days. This could be a very good week. Pulling Karlie close to her, she settled in, ready for a deep sleep. The uncharacteristic behavior made her anxious for a moment, but something had shifted and her reaction seemed out of step with the new reality. So Madison let her eyes close. The heart and the head could not agree on everything, she reflected as she drifted into tranquility. With a cloud forming over the future, wasn't it wise to make the most of the present sunshine?

Chapter Six

Very slowly and gently Karlie moved a stray lock of hair away from Madison's handsome face. She was beautiful and, in her sleep, innocent looking. Karlie nearly laughed out loud at that thought because she didn't remember Madison ever looking innocent. She studied the face, amazed at how familiar and yet new it seemed. What the hell was she doing? This was Dee's sister. And Karlie was still married. These thoughts and the urgent need to use the bathroom pulled her out of Madison's bed. Putting on a baggy T-shirt, she visited the head, then grabbed a blanket and went topside.

The stars were magnificent. Wrapping herself in the blanket, she sat on the deck and leaned back against the cabin. She could see the distant lights of the city and they were equally spectacular. Her heartbeat slowed and a calmness settled within her. For the first time in weeks, she felt whole. But she'd just made love with her friend's sister. Not love, sex. This was just about sex. Right?

She didn't know how to answer that question. What she'd experienced in Madison's arms was foreign. The total abandonment and the complete vulnerability. Just thinking about it made her shiver with desire.

As if silently summoned, a dark figure appeared on deck, wrapped only in a blanket. "I wondered where you were. I missed you."

"You were asleep," Karlie said. "I didn't want to disturb you."

Madison sat down and pulled her close, drawing their blankets together. They sat watching the city lights, neither speaking for some time. It was Madison who broke the companionable silence. "God, I can't believe how I want you again. You're so beautiful." She leaned down and kissed Karlie's lips. "I don't know which I enjoy kissing more, your lips or your breasts." She laughed as she moved down to take an erect nipple in her mouth.

The pleasure of Madison's mouth on her breast mixed with some deep sadness. A gasp escaped Karlie, followed by tears. She didn't want to think about Rob, or the mess of her life, and she couldn't believe she was allowing those thoughts to interfere with this moment.

Madison heard the sob and immediately moved her attention from Karlie's breast to her face. Kissing away the tears, she asked, "What's the matter? Did I do something?" She couldn't remember ever being this concerned about another person, especially when it came to her sexual encounters. This was foreign territory, but she wanted to fix whatever bothered the woman in her arms. An unfamiliar ache sparked in a dark place in her heart. "Please talk to me."

"It's nothing, really," Karlie lied. "I was just overwhelmed for a moment." Trying to smile, she reached up and caressed the handsome face. "If you stop now, however, you will have a very frustrated woman on your hands."

"Hmm, that wouldn't be good for my reputation."

"I wouldn't want to ruin your bad reputation." Karlie leaned down and nibbled on the beautiful neck. When Madison reached for her, she pushed her hands away. "Slow down. Let me make you feel good. Just relax and enjoy."

Madison put her hands under her head and closed her eyes. Karlie's hands seemed to be everywhere and Madison could feel a tender mouth on her breast. The wetness between Karlie's legs spread across Madison's stomach. So many sensations. Madison thought she would come without being touched. She took a deep breath and tried to slow herself down.

"Open your eyes, Madison, please."

Hearing Karlie call her by name reached a place inside her that seemed completely untouched. Surprised, Madison did as requested and Karlie leaned in and began to expertly kiss her. Madison was having trouble breathing. Already she felt herself moving toward orgasm. "I need you to fuck me, Karlie."

Preferring to prolong the teasing a little longer, Karlie continued to kiss her, taking Madison's lower lip into her mouth and brushing it with her tongue. She trailed small bites down Madison's neck and chest. When she reached a taut nipple, she took it in her mouth and sucked hard. She was rewarded with a moan from Madison, who was struggling under her. She slid one hand down to the opened legs and found the engorged shaft, barely touching.

"Karlie, you're killing me. I need you to fuck me now."

Ignoring the pleas, Karlie continued her gentle stroking, occasionally running her hand along Madison's inner thighs. She began to kiss down the tense abdomen until she was lying between Madison's legs. She breathed in her heady scent and found herself completely aroused. She put her head down and had her first taste. It was more than she could have ever imagined. She sank her tongue into the damp heat and drank of life, filling the cold, empty places within, where hope had shriveled. She needed to feel alive and Madison had given her that gift. Karlie knew memory of this moment would sustain her when Madison was no longer around.

She moved her hand up and pushed into that wetness, and felt Madison begin to move against her. She continued to drink at Madison's well while she rapidly moved in and out, until she heard a cry so arousing she felt herself spasm in response. Moments later Madison held Karlie close, almost afraid to look at her, not because of what she might see in her face, but what Karlie might see in hers. She'd opened herself and allowed Karlie to arouse intense passion, and more. She'd surrendered control, and it scared the shit out of her.

"That was a great good morning," she said when she finally felt safe enough to speak. Trying to lighten the mood, and fearing her control was still too fragile, she said, "Maybe I should start reading your books and taking some lessons."

Karlie tried to emulate the playful mood, but she was struggling with her own demons. "What should we do for an encore?"

"Well, since it looks like the sun will be up soon, we should probably go below."

"Good idea. I don't plan on demonstrating my writing to the public." Karlie stood up, pulling her blanket back around her. As she glanced down at Madison's long, lanky, nude body she realized she wanted her again. Extending her hand, she said, "Come on, before we have the Coast Guard and the Miami police arresting you for indecent exposure."

Madison smiled. "I'm sure plenty of my colleagues would pay for the opportunity to sit in the courtroom during that hearing."

Ten minutes later as she cracked eggs into a bowl, Madison was honest enough to admit that she didn't want their day to end. Another wave of desire flowed through her as she watched Karlie search for her clothes. Fuck, she could come just looking at her. She had to have her again.

"What can I do?" Karlie asked, glancing at the breakfast preparations.

Every fiber in her body screamed *Let me fuck you!* Madison swallowed and forced herself to answer calmly, "The coffeepot is under the counter. How about some fresh coffee?" She could almost swear she could see the small mole on Karlie's left breast through the cotton shirt. And she was almost sure she smelled the desire oozing from Karlie. "Then have a seat and let me feed you." She flashed her most seductive smile.

Karlie laughed. "You never stop, do you?"

"What are you talking about? I'm just offering to fix you breakfast."

"You must be a damn good attorney."

"Of course. You have any doubts?"

This brought genuine laughter from Karlie. "No, I'm sure you're everything your PR says you are."

Madison was about to respond when her marine phone interrupted. She put the omelet in the pan and turned down the heat. Picking up the phone, she barked, "Barnes. This better be good."

Karlie watched the transformation in Madison with amazement and fear. The laughing lover had changed into an angry predator. Her voice chilled the cabin.

"Why does he have to see me? Can't you bail him out and tell him I will see him tomorrow?" Madison's expression became glacial. "You better be at my office at two thirty. I won't wait. Do you understand?" She began to pace in the small cooking area. "I don't give a rat's ass. You be there or get another attorney. I don't need your fucking money." Fury blazed from eyes almost black with rage. Her next words were spoken in a low, measured voice, "Don't you ever, do you hear, *ever* threaten me again." She slammed the phone down.

"Problem?" Karlie asked carefully.

"I need to get back a little early." Seeing her breakfast special about to burn, Madison removed the omelet. "Damn. My first weekend off in months and that prick has to go pull a stupid stunt and get arrested." She smiled and, as if in a reversing metamorphosis, became calm. Her darkened eyes were blue again but held no warmth. Charm had once again become Madison's garment, but Karlie now knew how deadly that cloak could be. If she hadn't witnessed the whole interchange, she would have doubted such a thing possible.

They carried their breakfasts up on the deck in the shadow of their recent sexual encounter. "Look, I'm sorry about this," Madison said. "I was looking forward to spending most of the day with you."

"Don't apologize. This gives me a chance to change clothes and get cleaned up before I meet Dee and Jim."

"No, I'm sorry. Really. I was hoping we could have dinner." Madison smiled and ran one hand up the inside of Karlie's thigh. Rule number one had always been *Never bring anyone home,* but Madison was so intent on recapturing her prize she ignored her usual code. She also felt disturbed at the emotional distance Karlie was placing between them. "I can order something in. We could experiment." She left no doubt that food was the least important item on the experimental list.

Karlie stared down at the hand playing the tender tissue on her leg, gradually moving closer to the source of her incessant heat. She closed her eyes, forcing the rising passion into a manageable place. Her body was at war with her head, rendering her incapable of clear thought. Reality had intruded on the idyllic twenty-four hours she'd spent aboard the sailboat. She had only one choice. Marshalling the remnants of her self-respect and logic, she stilled Madison's hand, briefly covering it with her own. "Thank you for the lovely weekend, but I am going to be busy the rest of the week."

"Look, we're both busy," Madison said. "I really enjoyed this weekend and I know you did, too. How about an encore at least once before you leave?" The lifted eyebrow and the familiar smirk too easily filled the attractive face.

Anger joined the battle between logic and desire. For once Karlie was more angry with herself than with Madison. Trying not to reflect her inner turmoil, she replied, "I thought you never had repeat performances."

"Oh, for chrissakes, I'm not asking you to marry me." No warmth had returned to Madison's eyes. "You're already married and I'm definitely not into that type of knot-tying. What's wrong with another night of just great sex?"

Karlie stood. "No," she said calmly. "I don't think that's a good idea."

Madison stood up. Her voice almost a purr, she said, "You know you want me as much as I want you. We're good together. Why get uptight now and deny yourself something you really want?"

Karlie stiffened. "What part of no do you not understand?"

"What is this? Some kind of tease?"

Karlie stared into taunting blue eyes filled with desire. "That's something I would expect a man to say. I would not have expected that, even from you. You disappoint me."

"I disappoint you? Christ, I don't believe this. Is that how you make it easier to deny what your body wants? Throw in feminist garbage?"

"There's no need to raise your voice. My heart and my head and my soul are saying no. The last time I checked, they're the important parts of who I am. I don't go round having mindless sex out of some strange drive to fulfill a bodily need."

Madison slammed her hand on the cabin. "What the hell was going on this weekend, then?"

Karlie fought back a tear. "I don't know. I thought I did, but I was wrong." Looking away, she went below.

"How the hell did this day fall apart?" Madison asked an uncaring ocean. Inside her stomach a small, barely noticeable gnawing had begun. "Great. A fucking ulcer," she declared.

A measure of calm infused her by the time she was in sight of the marina. She realized as she began to lower the sails that the joy of sailing was as much her ability to sail the boat without any help as it was anything more existential. She was her own person. She was free to come and go. She needed no one.

Arriving in the opening to the bay, she turned on her engine and guided the boat into the dock. As she pulled alongside, a tawny head appeared out of the forward hatch and Karlie jumped to the dock without saying a word.

After she helped secure the boat, she asked, barely making eye contact, "What else can I help with?"

"Nothing." Madison's tone was flat and icy. "Go get my sister and her bonehead husband." As she begun the process of securing her sails and placing the covers over them, she did the same for her emotions. Control, that was what she needed. Was it only a few hours ago that they were lying on the deck fucking? What the hell happened? Her body recalled in detail the softness, the warmth, the hot wetness. A groan escaped.

"If you want, I can get the hatches."

"No, I'll stay aboard tonight and clean up."

"I don't mind," Karlie offered once more.

Madison looked up. "What part of no don't you understand?"

"Touché." Karlie felt the sting. Looking up, she watched Madison's adept hands securing the ties on the sails. Just as expertly those hands had played her body. Shivering, she tried to make amends. "Look, I'm sorry. I did have a good time."

Madison stopped and coldly stared. A brief question formed on her face and then was replaced by the flat expression of her courtroom persona. "No complaints, then?" The jibe was unmistakable.

Karlie swallowed a sob, picked up her gym bag and left. It was easier this way, she thought as she threw her stuff in the back of the silver Subaru. She leaned her head on the hot roof and thought about her tenured position at the university and her once-neat life now in shambles. Then there was her best friend. Dee had always believed in her and trusted her, and now she'd royally fucked up. How was she going to explain what had happened?

Great, now she was beginning to obsess over a woman with a monumental ego who wouldn't even remember her in two weeks, if that long. Something about that assumption bothered her. In some corner of her heart she wanted Madison to miss her, to hunger for her, but she was a realist, and why did she even care? That question haunted and challenged her. For a brief time, Madison had really mattered to her, but that was so long ago, she couldn't even dredge up those memories.

And now? She tried to banish the images that instantly rolled through her mind, but she couldn't escape the raw, sensuous Madison she'd discovered in the past twenty-four hours. Perhaps she never would.

CHAPTER SEVEN

Madison worked hard and deserved the perks. Her office overlooking Biscayne Bay provided not only the prestige of its location but also allowed her to enjoy the view. Today she saw only the threatening clouds. Lawrence Hidalgo, immaculately dressed, a grin wide across his darkly handsome face, stood in front of her desk.

"You are one stupid prick," she began. "What the hell were you and Ramon doing in that strip bar with pot in your possession?"

"Look, you bitch, remember who you work for." He stretched to every inch of his five-foot-seven frame and still was three inches shorter than her. "Your job is to keep us out of trouble."

Cold fury consumed Madison. She leaned against her desk and folded her arms to keep from strangling the man in front of her. These assholes had ruined her weekend and probably any future opportunity for sex with Karlie, if there ever was a possibility. They refused to listen to her advice. Now, when they were in trouble, she was supposed to fix it. Not anymore.

"No, my job is to deal with your fuckups," she said. "You and your pea-brained brother can't seem to get it through your thick, empty heads that possession, of any amount, is illegal. Well, you know what, I think Ramon needs some time to improve his understanding. Maybe we'll just leave him to cool off for twenty-four hours."

"Don't mess with me," Lawrence Hidalgo warned. "We pay you big bucks. You better get my brother out now."

Madison stalked toward him, forcing him to step back. "Listen, you little fart. You don't pay me enough to ruin my day and then come tell me how to run my business. It's Sunday. They're busy in the holding cells. I'll get your brother out of jail when I'm damned good and ready. After that you can go find yourselves another attorney, because I quit."

A disbelieving expression slipped across Hidalgo's face. "You can't quit. We own you, you stupid bitch. No one ever quits the family."

"Get out of my sight," Madison said. "And just remember, this is my pond, friend, and you're a small fish. I have much bigger fish who will eat you if anything happens to me."

Hidalgo left, grateful he still had his balls intact. *Fucking bitch. First he would convince Papa not to do business with that barracuda anymore. Then he'd take care of her himself. Whatever it took, however long it took, he would make her pay.*

❖

"What have you done with Madison and who's living in her body?" Jim Sanderson asked after the waiter had served their meals.

With a guilty start, Karlie asked, "What do you mean?"

Jim chuckled. "Well, you're still alive."

Dee looked her up and down. "I don't see any missing body parts. So, tell me. How was it?"

Karlie's heart raced. *She's just asking.* She struggled to keep from choking. "We got along…quite well, actually. We discovered we both enjoy being out on the water. We didn't once even attempt to throw the other off the boat."

Jim held his steak knife poised. "Are you trying to tell us Madison behaved?"

How was she going to answer that? *She was so good, actually, I was begging for more.* Feeling the blush crawl up her neck, Karlie was thankful for the low lighting in the Cuban restaurant. Her mind flew through a variety of responses before landing on one she thought wouldn't hang her. "We had some interesting conversations…about writing and relationships and sailing. And yes. I guess you could say she was…well behaved."

"I hope you like the food," Dee said, glancing at Karlie's untouched meal. "This place is one of Madison's favorites."

Karlie said something positive and desperately hoped they could get through the rest of the evening with minimal mention of Madison. Time and distance would dissipate the awkwardness, she reassured herself. And the want. Raising her glass of Peruvian Cabernet, she distracted her companions with a toast. "To friends."

Jim and Dee raised their glasses in salute. Dee smiled and added, "And to health and happiness."

Karlie had not even swallowed her first sip of wine when a familiar voice made her throat seize. "Welcome home, sis. How was your trip?"

Dee jumped up and hugged the tall woman standing at their table. "Please join us."

Madison looked into Karlie's eyes. "Do you mind?"

Immediately Karlie's pulse quickened and she could feel the subtle tension building between her legs. *There goes forgetting about her.* She could not pull her gaze away. Softly she answered, "No, not at all."

Madison took the seat next to her and across from Dee and Jim. "Well, you two obviously didn't get arrested."

Mild laughter followed, providing merciful cover for Karlie's downcast eyes and rapid breathing. Madison ordered something from the menu and insisted they continue with their meals.

"This food is terrific," Jim said. "At this rate, they'll have to roll me out of here and into bed."

"Just as long you don't roll out with anyone but me," Dee teased.

"I don't know. I may have to find out more about the cook," Jim threw back.

"*His* name is Gutierrez," Madison said.

Dee laughed heartily. "Darling, is there something you want to tell me? Because after this weekend, I'm going to be one surprised woman."

"Guess I walked into that." Jim didn't seem bothered by the laughter at his expense.

"I think I have exclusive claim to queerness in this family," Madison said softly.

Her comment thrust into Karlie's consciousness. *Am I queer?* She had to stop herself. Madison wasn't the first women she'd slept with, but she was the only person, male or female, who had aroused her so completely.

"And I've already warned you. You better not hurt my sister." Madison reached across and tapped her brother-in-law lightly on the forehead.

The warmth and affection in her voice made Karlie tremble. Only hours before, that voice had caressed her, and it still sent her pulse out of control. This was ridiculous. She tried to focus on the angry Madison rather than the passionate one, and consciously slowed her breathing.

"Remind me to make sure our insurance is paid up." Jim put his arm around Dee and leaned his head against hers. His cell phone went off and he complained, "No one knows we're back." After checking the caller ID, he flipped the phone open and listened, the concern on his face evident.

"What's going on?" Dee asked.

"We need to get going," he said, ending the call. "Cindy has to bring the kids home early. Her granny has had a stroke."

"Oh, no. Is it serious?"

"She doesn't know yet. The entire family is headed to the hospital."

Dee began to gather her belongings. "I hate doing this to you two, but if you don't mind bringing our food in takeout boxes, I'll be eternally in your debt. I haven't eaten all day."

"Of course." Karlie's emotions surged like a tidal pool. She was going to be left alone with either a generous lover or a calculating lawyer.

"Is there anything else we can do?" Madison asked.

"No." Dee was on her feet. "Take your time. Enjoy your meals."

"We'll catch up with you," Madison said.

Moments later they found themselves awkwardly alone. Unable to stand the tension, Karlie said, "Once we have the takeout boxes, I can catch a cab. You don't need to drive me back."

"Do you really hate being around me that much?"

Karlie looked into the intense blue eyes and feared they were boring into her soul. She wanted to deny the attraction that squeezed the air from her lungs. She wanted to fall back on easy disdain. She wanted to fall into Madison's arms. "No. Not at all."

Madison covered Karlie's hand with her own. "I'm glad, because I'm not ready to let you go."

"Miss Barnes, how nice to see you again." A lightly accented voice made Madison's body stiffen, and the hand on Karlie's fell away.

"Hello, Lawrence." Madison's voice was emotionless.

"You haven't introduced your attractive friend." The man stepped toward Karlie, openly appraising her breasts. "Lawrence Hidalgo. And you are?"

"Not talking to you," Madison completed. In a guttural growl, she said, "Now leave."

The approach of their waiter stopped further conversation. He placed Madison's meal in front of her.

"A moment." Madison said. "We'd like to have all four meals to go." She handed her Amex card to him.

"Maybe your friend prefers more pleasant entertainment," Hidalgo said in a virulent whisper. "Or is she a pervert like you?"

Leaping to her feet, Madison knocked over her chair, causing conversation in the restaurant to stop. She grabbed the man's shirt and leaned into his face. "If you say another word, you'll be singing the castrato part in your church choir. Do you understand?"

"Señorita, is there a problem?" An attractive, plump, gray-haired man came up to the table and Hidalgo quickly moved away.

"No, everything's okay, Luis. You have to be careful about some of the riffraff you allow in here." Madison smiled at the confused-looking owner. "I'm sorry if we caused a stir."

"It's nothing, señorita. There is always a table here for you."

After Karlie finished transferring the food into the takeout cartons, they left the restaurant and waited until they reached Madison's car before speaking.

"Do you always handle problems with threats of violence?" Karlie asked, astounded by Madison's behavior.

"No." Madison held the passenger door for her. "I'd rather be a lover than a fighter." She settled into the driver's seat and stared straight ahead.

All day she'd tried to deny it, but Madison's physical presence pulled at Karlie in ways she could not have imagined. No one had ever affected her so much. She wanted Madison more than she wanted to breathe. Common sense and self-protection cautioned her to get away from her as quickly as possible. But her body had its own agenda. She thought about the harsh words she'd used earlier and knew she'd rejected Madison because she was afraid.

Trembling, she said, "Madison, about what happened—"

"We don't need to talk about it. He's a dirty little man."

"No, that wasn't—" But her words were cut off by Madison's lips. The merest touch sent a jolt of raw desire coursing through her body and she leaned helplessly into the kiss.

"My place is only ten minutes from here," Madison said, pausing in her passionate assault. "Come with me, even if only for a little while."

It was more a command than a request. Karlie reached out and placed her hand on Madison's lean, muscular thigh. Heat rushed through her body. She wanted Madison and she couldn't pretend to resist. Looking into her eyes, she nodded. There was something so compelling in the hunger she saw there, she felt light-headed. "Hurry."

Madison's eyes darkened. "I've thought all evening of things I want to do to your body. Right now, I think all I need is for you to touch me and I'll explode."

Karlie trailed her hand slowly up and down the warm thigh, sensing waves of desire that matched her own. She couldn't believe she had the power to arouse Madison this way, but looking at that beautiful, familiar face, she saw her desire reflected back. "I want you," she said. "I've wanted you all day."

❖

Clothes strewn from the entrance of the house to the bedroom were evidence of the failure of control. Madison's barely contained arousal demanded immediate attention. Having swiftly removed her clothes, she helped Karlie undress, desperately trying to keep from damaging garments in her haste. Her hands burned to touch the familiar curves. Only the taste of those generous breasts would slake her thirst. Only Karlie could reduce the fire in her body.

"God, I haven't stopped wanting you," she whispered as she leaned over the now nude woman. As soon as her body covered the full curves and soft flesh, she felt her orgasm take control. Not even her formidable willpower prevented the inevitable as Karlie gently stroked her.

"Come, Madison. Come for me." Her fingers dug into Madison's buttocks. "Come for me, Madison."

And she did. Her breathing ragged, she exploded hard and fast before collapsing on the bed. Quivering, she ordered her body to obey her head. The head had reigned over her professional and personal life for so long she was nearly incapacitated as chaos threatened to usurp her usual self-possession.

"I'm a little chagrined," she confessed to the woman next to her. "I don't usually come that fast." She was rewarded with a magnificent smile. "God, you're beautiful." She caressed Karlie's gently curving stomach. "I love touching you. You're soft in all the right places."

She continued the gentle meandering, establishing a pattern, claiming each parcel of skin. In her wildest fantasies, Karlie had never anticipated the intensity and uncontrolled desire she felt with Madison. In recognizing the power she had over this strong-willed woman, she drew a sense of strength and confidence she hadn't felt in years. "Madison, I want you. And I'm going to make you want me more than you want anything."

She pushed a hand up into the dark, short hair, pulling Madison down into a kiss of passion and control. They lost themselves in a give-and-take Karlie had never known before. By the time they drew back, breathing hard, she felt her boundaries had become fluid. She no longer knew exactly where they were or why she had them.

Leaning up on one elbow, Madison continued to stroke the slightly rounded stomach. Her eyes never left Karlie. "I want to get something. I have a harness with a dildo on it. We don't have to use it unless you want to."

Too stunned to answer, Karlie tried to imagine what it would be like. Her senses went into overload. She needed Madison inside her, and soon.

Not waiting for an answer, Madison went on, "One end will be inside me while the other slips into you. Every time I thrust into you, you'll be pushing into me. I'll feel your excitement and it will heighten mine."

Karlie's breathing changed. Wetness dripped down her thighs. Staring into Madison's eyes, she was barely able to whisper, "Yes." More begging than an acknowledgment. She knew then that, at that moment, she would do anything Madison asked. She hated such powerlessness, yet she could not deny any of Madison's requests. "Please, yes," she repeated.

Madison reached into the bedside drawer and pulled out the harness. She had Karlie help with fastening it, then said, "I want you to put this in me so you'll know how I am feeling as I'm inside you." Smiling, she placed the shorter end of the dildo into Karlie's shaking hand and guided it down. "See how wet I am for you? You do this to me, Karlie." Spreading her legs, she allowed Karlie to explore. "Just rub it around my opening."

Once again the feelings of power returned, infusing Karlie with a sense of adventure and excitement. She rubbed the dildo into the dripping crease of flesh and was rewarded with a groan.

"That's so exciting," Madison gasped out. "I'm almost coming."

Oh, yes. This was good. Karlie continued to stroke, circling, gently entering, and then easing back. She lost all sense of her surroundings except for the breathing of the woman next to her. She could hear the sharp intake of air every time she dipped into Madison's heat. She loved the power she had. Finally looking up into eyes filled with want, she asked, "Do you want me in you? Do you want to feel me pushing this in?"

Madison nodded. Her own struggle to deny her rising tide precluded much thought. She opened her eyes, placed her hand on Karlie's, and then plunged the smaller end into her own center. "Yesss. Now, baby, just hold still until I can breathe a little better." She felt her walls accept the object and let herself acknowledge that it was Karlie. Once relaxed, she rolled over and straddled Karlie's body. "Are you sure?" she asked as she pushed the soft thighs apart.

Karlie's eyes never faltered. Opening her legs wider, she urged, "Yes."

"I'm just going to moisten the tip, as you did." Madison moved the smooth head around Karlie's opening. She never bothered to explain to other women. She just told them to spread their legs and they gladly accepted her. Usually she just took them from the rear. With Karlie, she wanted to take her time and watch herself being accepted. She wanted to see Karlie's face resplendent in orgasm. "I'm going to slide into you slowly just so you can feel what it is like to have me inside you. God, Karlie, you feel wonderful."

Karlie lifted her hips as the cock slid inside her. Any hesitations were quickly forgotten as the friction built inside her. Pumping against her lover, her legs encircling Madison's waist, she urged, "Fuck me. Now, baby. Please." The long, swift plunges increased in tempo, and Karlie's breathing seemed to stop as she began the primal dance of orgasm. "Oh, yes. Please, Madison."

Karlie's excitement served as an incendiary, pushing Madison ever closer to the edge. She could smell Karlie's desire. As she pushed down, she felt the wetness flow up to meet her. "Karlie, come with me. I'm going to come." She increased her rhythm, lost in sheer pleasure. "Tell me what you want." She wanted desperately to wait for this woman who could control her as no one had. "Tell me, Karlie."

"You, Madison. I want you. I want you to fuck me."

No further words were needed as body and soul created a language of their own, the language of passion. Karlie's orgasm hit with such force she felt every cell explode. She held on desperately as they made the journey their bodies found so familiar.

Her cries cracked Madison's walls and she surrendered to an orgasm that drained every ounce of reserve. Her heart pounded as the crest dashed against her body. Burying her head in Karlie's soft, golden hair, she whispered, "Karlie, I need you."

Her vulnerability had forced the truth out, but her pride demanded it be denied. Holding Karlie tightly, Madison tried to find a follow-up retort to lessen the intensity of the moment. *I don't need anyone.* As their breathing returned to normal, she gently withdrew and lay on top of Karlie, her body covered in sweat. If some emotions other than satisfaction had been stirred, she didn't acknowledge them. She just basked in the glow and the warmth.

Karlie held Madison tightly against her, tears threatening. If she let go, she felt that some part of her would vanish, and she wasn't prepared for the loss. She replayed the whisper she'd heard as Madison shuddered against her. *I need you.* What the hell should she do now?

"What time is it?" she asked, dragging herself back to reality. Dee and Jim were waiting for their meals.

Madison rolled off her. She gently placed one hand over Karlie's mouth and whispered, "Stay?" Rule number two was in danger: *Never spend the night.* The boat didn't count, she reminded herself.

Karlie shut her eyes and breathed in the now familiar scent of Madison's perfume mixed in with sex. She would always remember that smell. "I can't. I have class tomorrow. And your sister needs to eat."

"I can have food delivered," Madison said dismissively. "I'll take you to my sister's in the morning."

"I don't think that's a good idea. Just give me a couple of minutes and I'll get dressed."

"Don't go." This time it was a command. The perfect moment was gone. The old antagonists were now vying for dominance. This was the more familiar territory.

Karlie sat up. "I can't stay. We both know that."

"Never thought you were the love 'em and leave 'em type," Madison stood and looked for her clothes. Walking out of the bedroom, she found them tossed across the living room. "Fuck, can't wear these," she muttered as she found jeans and a clean shirt to put on.

"Never thought you were the spend-the-night type," Karlie whispered and walked into the bathroom to repair the damage of the hastily arranged encounter.

Tumultuous emotions racked her mind and spirit. She splashed water on her face and rinsed her mouth. She didn't want to see the eyes that stared back at her from the mirror, so she turned off the light. When she felt composed, she followed the trail of clothing into the living room. She'd never been to Madison's house. The room was magnificent. White leather furniture, black and chrome tables and accessories. Elegant, tidy and sterile. Definitely like Madison. Staring at the white walls, she noticed a familiar painting. It was one Dee had done during their junior year.

"How did you get this painting?" she asked as she zipped her jeans.

"I bought it."

Looking around the room, she saw several more of Dee's paintings. "And those?"

"I bought them, too."

For most of her adult life, Karlie had one well-defined image of Madison. In two short days, she'd discovered how little she knew of this enigmatic woman. "Why?"

Slipping her sneakers on, Madison replied, "Why not? They're actually good, and Dee will have her own exhibition in the spring.

Besides, they're a great investment. They're already worth twice what I paid for them."

Karlie ran one hand through her hair in frustration. "You know, just about the time I think you're a decent person, you do or say something that jolts me back into reality. I'm ready to go."

Distant eyes surveyed her. "Maybe it comes from you spending too much time in fantasy in those romance stories you write." Madison's words were harsh. "The world is not a nice place and I'm not a nice person. Let's go."

The drive across the city was a silent one. Karlie could feel a simmering rage emanating from Madison. Fear and her own anger kept her quiet. "I'll walk you in," Madison said as she turned into the Sandersons' driveway.

"It's not necessary," Karlie snapped. "I can manage."

"I don't doubt it, but I want to see my sister. You can stay out here if you want. I don't really care just as long as you are not in my car when it's time for me to leave."

"You are a piece of work. You don't care about anyone or anything, unless that person, or thing, meets your needs. You're a user. You definitely march to your own drummer."

"No," Madison's words were out with venomous bite, "I march to my own orchestra." She was already at the door when Karlie lifted the food out of the car.

Dee waited to greet her, hugging her warmly. "Karlie, I'm sorry if Madison's given you a hard time. I know she can be…difficult."

Handing the dinners to her, Karlie quickly brushed moisture away from her eyes and followed her inside. Jim and Madison sat at the kitchen table quietly talking. Karlie wanted to run out of the room but couldn't come up with an excuse to explain such rude behavior. She leaned against a counter and remained silent.

"Jim just told me about the command performance." Madison looked up at Dee. "What are we being put on exhibition for this time?"

"They're in town for the next two weeks and they're having a few friends over."

"A few or few thousand?" Bitterness filled Madison's words.

"Madison, our parents just want to have a small get-together."

"I've got a busy week."

Their parents spent most of the year traveling. Usually these rare get-togethers were intended to announce that the Barnes family would be returning to Miami's social scene. The successful, wealthy, beautiful Barnes sisters were sought after guests in their own right, so Madison and Dee served as accoutrements for their parents, validating that they were indeed leading lights in Dade County society.

"Madison, please. They'll be back here for the winter season in another few weeks. Let's try to start this one off on a better note." Turning to Karlie, Dee said, "They've asked if you would join us. Mother went on and on about seeing you on *Nancy Grace* and *Today*. I wouldn't be surprised if this party is for you."

Karlie hesitated. She often felt uncomfortable and excluded around Mrs. Barnes. She didn't think she was imagining the older woman's condescension and the excuses she made for insignificant lapses in the social graces. The thought of spending an evening trying to keep her composure around Madison in a social setting was daunting in itself, without the fault-finding scrutiny of Deirdre Barnes.

Dee interpreted her silence correctly. Drawing her aside, she said, "I know you're not in the mood for socializing, but please come. It's always such a relief when you're there. You help me stay sane."

Dee was hard to resist, and Karlie felt she owed her a measure of support. They'd always been there for each other. "Okay. What is the dress for the occasion? I'm sure my jeans won't do."

"I must admit that would create quite a stir." Dee laughed and hugged her. "I'll call Mother and find out how formal this is going to be. If necessary we can go out and get you something to wear." Turning to her sister, she asked, "Well, Madison, will you put aside the war for this one evening?"

Madison's dislike for her parents' soirees warred with her desire to see Karlie again. She hesitated, not wanting to give in to the desire nor willing to completely release her anger. Still, she refused to admit there was anything she could not control. "I need to do some rescheduling. Let me see what I can do tomorrow. I'll let you know." She rose and kissed Dee on the cheek. "I need to go. I'll call you later."

With that she headed out the door and stalked to her Lexus. She was so aggravated as she accelerated away that she almost hit a dark Lincoln, parked a few yards from the driveway.

❖

As the Lexus sped past, Lawrence Hidalgo said, "Take that film and get the pictures developed. I want to know who the blonde is and who lives in that house. Madison Barnes will pay, little brother."

"Dad's going to fire her after my case. Why don't you drop it?"

"The barracuda needs to learn respect. She has not yet learned her place, little brother. She has tried my patience, and now it is time she learns. Respect, Ramon. Remember that. Without respect you are nothing."

Ramon Hidalgo was surprised at the hatred filling his older brother's face. He nodded and sat quietly. He'd always feared his brother's wrath. Lawrence took things personally and bore grudges. Ramon felt sorry for the lawyer. Whatever she'd done, Lawrence would not let it go until he'd hurt her.

Chapter Eight

K arlie felt the forced smile was permanently plastered on her face. She'd answered the same questions for the twentieth time. Turning to Dee, she whispered, "How do you stand these things? What a fawning group of sycophants."

"They adore you," Dee said. "you're a star."

"Oh, please. I can't believe they have such little knowledge of the publishing industry or how much money is made from the sale of a *New York Times* best seller. How condescending. And I can't believe you talked me into buying this dress. It's so expensive."

"You look stunning in that shade of green. Almost a jade color. It makes your eyes look green instead of gray. Besides, it's the kind of dress you can wear to lots of occasions."

"Sure, it would be perfect for a faculty senate meeting. Or maybe a book reading at the local writer's group. The low back won't cause anyone heartburn."

"You look elegant," Dee responded. "You're one of the most beautiful women here, *and* you haven't had plastic surgery. Besides, it's only money."

"Well, I never thought I would be on the Barneses' A-list. Your mother was actually warm to me. I guess I'm socially acceptable now."

"You've always been on this person's A-list, Karlie," Jim responded. "I'm not sure I would be on the Barnes A-list, even married to Dee, if one, my father wasn't chair of the Dade County

Republican Party when I married Dee. And two, he wasn't a former diplomat. And three, my mother wasn't from a long line of English nobility."

"You make my parents sound awful," Dee said. "You and Madison."

"Well, at least there's something the two of us agree on." Jim looked around. "I thought she'd be here by now. Uh-oh, here comes Randall Beckett."

The eighty-year-old philanthropist walked over and pinched Karlie's cheek, making a remark about beauty and talent. Karlie quickly moved out of reach, stunned at the rude behavior of the aging Casanova. Thankfully Jim took his arm and insisted he had someone desperate to meet him.

"I haven't read any of your novels." Beckett wagged a finger at Karlie. "But I hear the housewives are eating them up. Imagine that."

Allowing her frustration to seek some relief, Karlie muttered, "I love how people like him think there's nothing to it. Sure, I've gotten great advances, but I work hard on those damn books."

Dee smiled. "Writing, I'm afraid, dear friend, is not considered real work. You, however, have become a familiar name in many households. These people are always in awe of name recognition. Tomorrow they'll be telling everyone they had dinner with Karlie Henderson. They will either detail what you look like and how you dressed and one or two gentlemen will hint at some type of flirtation or they will say you swore them to secrecy and then hint that your fiction is actually based on personal experience. After all, you do write rather graphically. Or you'll be decried as a snob and barely literate. They'll say someone else has actually written your books and the picture on the cover is some bimbo model from New York, hired to add sex appeal."

Clutching her wineglass, Karlie stared in horror. "I have a damn PhD in literature. My novels have received critical acclaim. The reviewer from the *New York Times* loved my last book."

"Karlie, these people don't care. They're just here because

they want to say they were at the Barneses' party and they met that Henderson woman."

"It's weird," Karlie said. "I wonder what they expect."

"Well, if they've actually read any of the spicy stuff in your books, they probably expect some kind of panting sexpot."

"What did I miss?" came a familiar voice from behind her. Madison gave Dee a hug. "The sexpot, where is she?"

Karlie kept her face neutral. "Don't you have some kind of radar? A homing device that leads you to women with one thing on their minds?"

"Ouch! Why do you always think the worst of me?" Madison clutched her chest and feigned pain. "You hurt me, Karlie." Smiling, she whispered in a voice only for Karlie, "You look wonderful. Good enough to eat."

Karlie let herself meet Madison's dancing eyes. "You clean up well, too." Deciding to avoid anything more personal, she asked, "How was court?"

"Grueling. I'm in the middle of a nasty trial and I probably should be working tonight. But a command performance is a command performance." Madison indicated Karlie's empty glass. "Want another drink?"

"No, thanks." Karlie definitely wanted to keep her head clear tonight.

"You sure? I just automatically assume this will be a three scotch night." Finishing off the drink in her hand, she said, "I need a refill. Dee, want anything?"

"I'll come with you," Dee said, giving Karlie's hand a squeeze. "It's time I rescued Jim from that awful man."

As they strolled away, Karlie was surrounded by another group of people who treated her like a celebrity. She played the role, using it as a buffer for the emotions threatening her calm. Madison caused too many memories to surface. Karlie hoped her feelings weren't written all over her face.

❖

Dinner proved to be a test in tolerance. Liberals, intellectuals, Democrats, and the media were all fair game for the wealthy conservatives around the table. Fitting into all four categories, Karlie wondered what insanity had caused her to agree to this fête. Seeing Dee smiling feebly at some inane comment from a local politician, she realized she was not alone in her suffering.

"Carolyn, Dee tells us you're working on another book," an elegantly coifed older woman to her right said. "Do we get a sneak preview?"

Karlie wondered if she ever read anything, much less a mainstream novel. An insidious thought crept through her brain as she smiled at her well-dressed dining companion. *Actually, I wonder what she considers romance. No, I don't want to go there. Too boring.* Refraining from laughing nearly caused her to choke on the water she had been drinking.

Putting a more serious expression on her face, she finally replied, "My editor won't let me discuss the book with anyone. The publishing business is so competitive that if anyone knew my plot, he would have to have them killed."

The rapid intake of breath was followed by a look of curious disdain. "Is that an example of New York humor?"

Karlie's retort was cut short by their hosts rising and inviting the crowd into the large sitting area for coffee and dessert. Seeing her chance to escape, she went up to Dee's parents and quickly made her excuses. They were polite and proper, just enough smiling to make people feel there was some sincerity, but enough distance to always make them wonder.

"We hoped you could stay longer," Deirdre Barnes said. "But thank you for joining us. The Braithwaites will be livid when I tell them you were our dinner guest. We'll let them know you may join us sometime when we're back in New York. In the meantime, do come again. Dee says you often visit."

"Thank you. As always, I've enjoyed your hospitality. I'm afraid it will be a while before I am back visiting, but I appreciate the invitation." She hesitated, then politeness forced her to add. "I'll certainly call upon you when you're in New York."

"How gracious of you. We've always been delighted you and Dee have been such good friends." *Smarmy*, Karlie decided, was the only word to describe Deirdre Barnes. "We look forward to seeing you again. Perhaps you and your husband could join us for dinner one evening."

The emphasis on "husband" was not lost. Smiling and controlling her retort, Karlie nodded. "Of course." She quickly excused herself and went in search of her friends. Finding Dee and Madison in the kitchen in heated conversation, she started to back out of the room but Dee saw her.

"Karlie, is everything okay?"

"I just wanted to say good night. I need to go back and prepare for tomorrow's class. I only have two more to teach, the exam, and then this will be over." She gave Dee a quick hug.

"We'll be home late, I'm afraid," Dee said. "Let's talk in the morning."

"Don't I get a hug, too?" Madison asked with a faint, taunting edge.

Putting out her hand, Karlie answered, "Good night, Madison. And I guess I might as well say good-bye. I'll be leaving on Saturday. Thank you for the wonderful outing on your boat. I'll always remember last weekend and you."

Before the stunned Madison could respond, Karlie planted a kiss on her cheek, turned, and headed out into the crowd. She was almost to Dee's car when she heard her name being called.

"That was a quick exit." Madison approached with the overconfidence of a woman accustomed to meeting very little resistance. "Could I persuade you to stop by for a nightcap?"

"I try to limit what I drink, especially when I have to teach the next day."

"I'm sure there are other things we can do besides drink." Madison's voice was husky and full of promise. "Come on. It's still early and it may be a while before we see each other. How about a farewell fuck?"

Karlie swallowed several retorts. The unabashed cockiness, the unrestrained assurance with which Madison spoke rankled her.

"You have court, and I need to get ready for class and begin to pack."

Apparently believing she wanted to be convinced, Madison stepped in to her and slid her arms around her waist. Karlie did not resist, but she did not participate, when Madison's lips brushed hers. Madison let go.

"What's wrong? I thought you'd enjoy one last fling."

She'd chosen the wrong words. "No, *you* want one last fling." Karlie spat the last word out like sour milk. "I've told you what I want, but you don't seem to be listening."

A hand encircled Karlie's wrist, stopping any forward movement. "I want to see you before you go." A hint of pleading hung on the statement.

Something inside Karlie shifted at the desire that glimmered in Madison's eyes, but her resolve remained firm. She needed to get on with her life in New York. "I think it's best we leave things as they are."

"How is that?" Madison asked softly.

"We had a great weekend. We got to know each other a little better and maybe we won't be so antagonistic. But as you said, it was a fling and it's time to go on."

"Suppose I don't want it to be over?"

Karlie searched Madison's blank face. "We're two very different people," she said sadly. "You like your life the way it is and I like mine. You need nothing and no one and your job comes first. I distinctly remember you saying that on many occasions." She lifted a hand to Madison's tanned cheek in a fleeting caress. "I, on the other hand, need to be needed. You don't want complications. And, this weekend excepted, I don't want flings. I want a permanent someone in my life, and if I can't have that, then I'll spend my life alone, enjoying each day." She paused. "But I will not be second place in anyone's life ever again."

The tenderness of that brief touch caused Madison to hold her breath. "How do you know that this is just a fling?" She surprised herself with the question.

"Oh, Madison." Karlie leaned into her for moment, then stepped back. "Are you telling me it isn't?"

No answer.

Karlie shrugged. She would have been stunned if any answer were given. Too much of a commitment in either direction. "Take care of yourself."

"Why do you have to define this?" Madison asked. "Why can't we just enjoy what we have? See where it goes."

Karlie almost laughed. "Because I'm beginning to care. And I've already told you I want more." She stared up at Madison. "Seriously, do you want a relationship?" Reading her hesitance, she acknowledged, "I didn't think so. Be happy and thank you for what we shared. I'll miss you."

She placed a tender kiss on Madison's lips and walked away. From the woman and the unsettling emotions.

Madison carefully coiled another rope and tied it off. The gleaming metal bird lifting off from the Miami airport banked and turned north. She looked up and again wondered if Karlie was aboard this one. For the past hour she'd asked herself the same question about each plane. Realizing she had no idea what time or what airline Karlie was on only made the watching more frustrating. Why the hell did she care? The answer danced in her body. Her hands ached to touch. Her lips hungered to taste. She could close her eyes and feel a firm nipple in her mouth.

All night she kept hearing Karlie's moans and cries and seeing her flushed face and swollen lips until she ached for relief. Unable to sleep, she'd driven to the marina at dawn. For the last hour she had been staring at the departing planes wondering which one was carrying Karlie back to New York and away from her.

Fuck her. Anger and lack of sleep prevented any logical thinking. Madison swore beneath her breath. She had better things to do than worry about some married bitch she probably wouldn't see again for another ten years. She put the ropes into the storage locker and closed it. The next several weeks would be demanding, and she doubted she'd have time for anything but work. Methodically she closed hatches and secured the boat. It would be a while before she could come aboard and not think of a certain blonde.

As she secured her prize possession, she refastened the lock on her heart. No one was going to tamper with that, least of all Karlie Henderson.

CHAPTER NINE

"What do you mean he wants more money? He earns four to five times what I do." Karlie paced the length of Garrison Snyder's office, furious.

Her divorce attorney opened a folder of financial statements. "He's claiming that his income is down significantly and that he has rather large debts. I must admit I'm surprised. For as many years as he's worked on Wall Street, he should have amassed considerable capital. His debt, however…"

"Debts?" Rob had paid cash for a new car every two years. He used to walk in with a bonus check and flaunt the amount. "The house he's living in is almost paid for. I know because I used most of the royalties from my first book to pay off the mortgage."

"According to his financial statement, there is a mortgage of over a million dollars on that property," Garrison said.

"That can't be possible. He couldn't have borrowed against the house without my knowing. Or could he?" Karlie sat and folded her hands in front of her, staring at her entwined fingers. "I just don't know anymore. I didn't believe he was unfaithful even after he admitted there were other women." She looked up. "What does he want?"

Garrison leafed through some papers, summarizing. "Half of all community property including the advance on your next two novels, half of all royalties on books completed during the marriage, and half on books in process."

"Books in process? He knows I haven't worked on anything in over a year."

"He claims that you do significant research on novels before you actually write and that you're working on two or three ideas at present."

"What a crock."

"Obviously this is a blatant attempt to extort more money from you," Garrison said. "His people are hoping we'll negotiate some type of settlement. If it's all right with you, I'll put an investigator on Mr. Stockard's financials. Based on what you're saying, if we can prove something illegal, your husband's claim can be significantly reduced."

Sighing and wondering what else could go wrong this week, Karlie agreed. She still couldn't believe she was sitting here listening to an attorney reduce her marriage to little more than a bad financial transaction, one for which she was probably going to pick up the tab. How could she have lived with someone that long and not known who he really was?

❖

Madison was working as many hours as she had when she first opened her own practice. The recent illnesses aboard some of the cruise lines leaving out of Miami had resulted in very angry patrons, including some of her parents' friends. These wealthy and well-connected people knew she would demand large settlements for their pains, and Madison knew their discomfort would result in large attorney's fees for her.

"Look, my clients are not interested in another discounted or free trip." She drew lines on her pad as she listened to the attorney on the other end of the phone. "They're traumatized. One had to be taken by helicopter from the ship to a hospital. She never travels by air. One couple celebrated their anniversary with food poisoning. Do you think they want to get aboard any one of your ships and be reminded of how dreadful that experience was?" She paused to listen to more offers. Tiring of the boring refrain, she interrupted.

"Mr. Townsend, my clients are not people who've put their whole life savings into one trip. Obviously you don't want to settle, so we will see you in court."

She slammed the receiver down and called her clerk in. Throwing papers across her desk, she barked, "File these before the end of the day. Get over to the courthouse now. I want each claim to be filed individually. We're going to make life miserable for those bastards at the cruise line. We'll nitpick and make them respond to every single complaint." She walked around the desk and stood in front of her clerk. "Do not come back until each suit has been filed. Understand?"

He nodded, grabbed the papers, and darted back out the door, passing Lawrence Hidalgo, who strolled into the office unannounced. A grin plastered his dark, attractive face and he wore a deep navy blue silk suit and a flamboyant tie with a huge knot. "My brother has been calling and you fucking don't return his calls. That's not very polite."

Remaining standing, Madison answered, "I've already told you and your brother that I don't have anything to say to either of you. I will let him know when his court date is set. He doesn't need to call every fifteen minutes to tell me how to do my job. And you"—restraining her anger, she looked at her watch—"you have fifteen seconds and then I call security."

Reaching inside his coat pocket, Hidalgo pulled several photographs out. "Such a lovely woman," he said before tossing them on the desk. "I just wanted to give you these. You seem… attached to her."

The pictures were taken at the entrance to Madison's place. A telephoto lens showed her kissing Karlie. They were taken the night she'd seen Hidalgo at the Cuban restaurant. He must have followed her when she left with Karlie.

"Dr. Henderson is an attractive woman. And married, even though she doesn't use the name of her husband." Hidalgo sneered over this pronouncement. "If these pictures fall into Mr. Stockard's hands, I wonder what he will do."

Madison struggled with her anger. Karlie didn't need a dirtbag like Hidalgo harassing her, so she tried to play down the problem. "Get off it. No one cares whether or not a couple of women kiss each other on a doorstep."

"But your special lady friend is getting a divorce." Hidalgo obviously thought he'd struck gold. "I bet her husband would like these pictures." Madison pictured a divorce lawyer licking his lips over juicy proof of infidelity. If that's what their encounter was. Or maybe the separation had already happened. She thought about the sadness she'd detected in Karlie. The mood swings and irrational anger. Dee hadn't said a word about a divorce. Neither had Karlie. *Yeah, and you're her best friend. She would tell you everything.*

Madison contemplated the best strategy. It would be a mistake to allow Hidalgo to think she cared. With a dismissive shrug, she said, "I personally don't give a rat's ass what you do with the photos, since I'll never see that bitch again. But when you come to my office and threaten me, it pisses me off. Do you understand?"

A grin of evil pleasure slid across Hidalgo's face. "I understand that your sister is very good friends with Dr. Henderson."

"And your point?"

"Does she know you treat her friends like your whores?"

Restraint was gone. Madison lunged forward, grabbing Hidalgo and causing him to wince. "You can't stand the fact that I get more women than you do." A forceful jabbing finger in his chest emphasized each word. "But if you don't get out now, I will personally make sure your wife becomes a wealthy widow."

Fending off Madison's hands, Hidalgo extracted himself, straightened his suit, and replied, "Your threats do not help the situation. My family owns you and we expect loyalty. Do you think we will forget your disrespect?"

Not waiting for an answer, he left quickly, avoiding the book Madison hurled at the closing door. She picked up the phone and instructed her receptionist to keep a careful log of all calls and messages from members of the Hidalgo family. Then she called Dee.

"Do you know how to get in touch with Karlie?" she asked after some general chatter. "I just thought I would say hi."

"Maybe it's not such a good idea to call her right now." Dee sounded awkward. "She has a lot going on."

Madison waited for Dee to expand, but there was no mention of divorce and she didn't want to give the impression she was interested enough to snoop. "That's fine. Just tell her I said hello and was wondering how she was doing. And tell the folks I'll be at their dinner party Saturday night. Thanks."

Fuck, now what? She could call her at work. Madison tried to find some justification for making contact, but nothing rational came to mind. She stared again at the pictures. How could he have gotten that close? It was incredible to think that she was so wrapped up in kissing Karlie, she hadn't noticed they were being watched. Hidalgo wouldn't dare do anything, she rationalized. He was all macho bluster, and she knew too much about him and his family for them to risk making an enemy of her. She had to hang on to that belief.

❖

"You're losing weight. You're getting depressed. And I know there's something bothering you," Sandy said over lunch. "Want to talk about it?"

Karlie's thoughts strayed to Madison, as they had constantly ever since she came back to New York. But she wasn't ready to discuss what had happened. It still felt too raw. Instead she played it safe with the topic she knew Sandy was expecting.

"How the hell did I live with Rob for so long a time and not have a clue what a bastard he was? I don't think of myself as naïve or gullible, but he's gone through over a million dollars in the last year. A million!"

"Karlie, Rob is a charmer. He can look at you and declare all innocence and you want to believe him, probably because you loved him. Besides, he convinced you to let him handle all the household finances. I'm glad you put the proceeds from your last three books into a separate account."

"Me, too. Thank you for talking me into setting up a retirement account. With all the money Rob had coming in—or at least, what he said he made—I figured that would be a nice nest egg in case I ever needed it. Right now, I'm living off what my parents left me. Never thought I would need it.

"Sounds like your parents wanted to make sure you were taken care of," Sandy said.

"They had my name on their accounts, and the money has been collecting interest all this time." Karlie swallowed with difficulty. She felt empty, reviewing the losses in her life. "I still miss them. I'm so glad I kept their house after they died or I wouldn't have a place to live. Housing is so damn expensive and I couldn't afford a house, or an apartment, only on my salary."

"What about your writing money? You still have that private account?"

"Yeah. You know, I felt so guilty when I opened it. I justified it by saying I could put money away in case we had kids or to get special presents for him or use it for retirement." She wiped away the tears in the corners of her eyes.

"Has Rob been involved in anything illegal? Is there any possibility he could be gambling or doing drugs?"

"I don't know. At this point anything is possible."

"Karlie?" A man several tables away stood up and strolled over to her. "My God, you sure aren't taking care of yourself."

She stiffened and bit back an angry retort. After a cursory appraisal, she said, "Hello, Rob. You're looking like you usually do. A shit. Aren't you working? Oh, I forgot, you're hoping your ex-wife can support you."

"You always had a smart mouth. I'm just getting what I'm entitled to."

"Entitled? You're not entitled to *my* money. What did you do with your own? You always reminded me of how much you made and how you could spend it any way you wanted." She felt the bile rising. "I'll see you in hell before I give you another dime."

Rob straightened his tie and stood taller. "There's not a damn thing you can do. I'm entitled to half of community property. So take some advice and pay up like a good girl."

She cast a contemptuous look at the man who had betrayed her and was now trying to steal from her as well. "You bastard. One of us will be dead before you get my money. And it won't be me." Shaking with rage, she turned to Sandy. "Come on. Let's get out of here."

As they left the restaurant, Sandy said, "Don't let him get to you. He's always been an asshole, and he's being cocky now because he thinks he has the upper hand."

It was good advice but Karlie was so angry she couldn't maintain an intellectual distance. This was her life. "I just want to take a two-by-four and smack him. He's always been so sure of himself. I used to love that about him." She took a deep breath. "Now I detest it...and him."

She'd been completely blind. And not just about Rob. There was plenty she hadn't recognized about herself.

"Karlie, I know this has been a rough time for you." Sandy seemed to be choosing her words carefully. "Is there anything else that's bothering you besides Rob and the divorce? I don't mean to pry, but you've been depressed and jumpy. I'm a good listener."

Karlie took a deep breath. "I'm just not a good talker, well, at least about some things." She sighed and collected her thoughts. "When I was down in Miami something happened. You know I've talked about Dee's sister, Madison."

"As I remember you wax rather fiercely about her outstanding qualities," Sandy said. "Morals of a rabbit, incapable of committing to anything that's not green and has at least three zeros after the first digit. I could go on..."

"It's okay. I get it." Karlie grimaced. She knew all too well the comments she'd made about Madison. "I was wrong about some of those things I said."

"Oh?"

"I told you that I spent a weekend sailing with her and we didn't kill each other. Well..." Karlie struggled for courage. "We... oh, shit!"

"Something happened between the two of you?" Sandy asked, leaning against her car.

Karlie nodded and turned red.

"No. You didn't? You…you and Madison?"

"It was just sex. There's no emotional commitment."

Sandy looked stunned. "Okay. Had sex. No commitment. Just what the hell happened?"

"It was the most intense experience I've ever had."

"With Madison?"

"I know. At times, I have trouble believing it, but, yes, with Madison."

"What happened?" Sandy leaned forward eagerly. "Wait, I don't think I want details, but how did this happen?"

"I'm still trying to figure that one out. One minute we're talking about my writing and the next we're kissing. The funny thing is that I wanted her to kiss me. Maybe I should say I wanted to kiss her. I was sure I wanted to be sexual with her. Most of all I didn't want to stop. She probably thinks I'm some type of sex maniac, but it was an incredibly intense experience."

"This is the Madison who goes through women like golfers through tees? Use 'em and lose 'em."

"Believe me, I've remembered all the things I've said about her. I feel foolish." Looking down at her hands, Karlie recalled the feel as she stroked Madison's glorious body. "And I miss her."

"I don't believe this."

"I have trouble believing it, too."

"No, I mean, I can't believe you didn't say something sooner. How did things end? Will you two see each other?"

"The last time I saw her she wanted to continue our…encounters. When I asked her if she was making a commitment, she looked at me as if I was asking her to cut off her right hand." Karlie made an even harder admission. "I think I was falling in love with her."

"Sounds like this woman is an incredible lover." Sandy rested a hand on her arm. "I'm sorry things didn't end well. Have you tried calling her? Maybe she feels something for you, too."

Karlie wiped the tears and gave a short laugh. "That's an empty road I don't want to go down. She could have called me and hasn't."

"Does she know how to get in touch with you? Does she have your phone number?"

Karlie thought for a moment. "She could get it from Dee. And she's an attorney. They can find people's phone numbers."

"Maybe she thinks you wouldn't want to talk."

"That's possible," Karlie conceded. "I was pretty clear about saying good-bye."

Sandy played absently with the car keys in her hand. "Did you talk with Dee about this?"

"Not yet."

Karlie had started to several times, but she didn't want to get between the two sisters. She was pretty sure Madison hadn't said anything, either. She was always so sure of herself that Karlie couldn't imagine her being hesitant about telling Dee. Or calling, if she wanted to talk. Was it possible that she didn't have her number? Madison would never admit she needed anyone or anything. Yes, and that's why she would never ask Dee for a phone number. Karlie briefly allowed herself to feel some hope.

"I don't know what to do," she told Sandy.

Her friend nodded thoughtfully. "Give it some time. You have a jerk to divorce."

❖

"Your Honor, my client is a reputable citizen of Dade County." Madison managed to speak with breathtaking sincerity. "He's an honor student at Miami-Dade Community College and works part time to pay for school. The day in question he had gone out with a few friends. One of the young men was celebrating his twenty-first birthday and that was the reason he was in the strip club."

She always tried to paint the best possible picture of her client. In this case she could argue that Ramon was being victimized because of his family's unsavory reputation, but she didn't play that card immediately. She might need it later.

"Your Honor, Mr. Hidalgo is twenty-eight years old and taking one course. The police did not report any marijuana in Mr. Hidalgo's possession until *after* he was booked. How is it that there was no evidence of an illegal substance until he arrived at the jail?"

The judge looked at the district attorney. "Is that true?"

The assistant DA had to know this was the weak part of his case, but he was obviously determined to fry some member of the Hidalgo family. Madison encountered the same attitude every time she defended one of them. The charges were usually dropped.

"Your Honor, we believe that it was a mistake in the written report," the assistant DA said. "The arresting officers assure us that Ramon Hidalgo had the marijuana in his possession at the club."

The judge looked through the papers on his desk, shaking his head in frustration. "Their report does not indicate taking possession of any substance until after he was booked. There is no direct chain of evidence linking it to Mr. Hidalgo and there is no justification for his arrest. You are going to have to do a better job. I'm dismissing all charges against Ramon Hidalgo. And don't bring his brother before me, either. Case dismissed."

Madison put her papers into a folder, disgusted with her client and his brother. She was glad the whole thing was over and she could walk away from this slime. As she prepared to leave the courtroom, the assistant DA walked over.

"How can you sleep at night? Even for you this is a new low. Sooner or later, you'll slip. I just want to be there."

"Don't hold your breath," Madison advised. "How can you even bring a case like this to court? I'm not the one making you look like a fool. You do fine by yourself." Laughter at her side drew her attention. "What are you laughing at? You ought to be grateful someone made a typing error."

"Chill out." Ramon was obnoxious now that he was free. "You'll get paid, and there's lots more."

"What part of no do you not understand? When I walk out of this courtroom I don't want to see your face or your brother's, or any of your family. Do you understand? This was the last time I represent you."

"Look, bitch." Lawrence Hidalgo had walked up behind his

younger brother. "I've already explained that we hired you and we will decide when you are no longer needed."

"And I've told you I decide whom I will represent. Don't call. I won't answer. Don't come by. I'm not there." She left the two brothers glaring at her back. "Assholes," she whispered as she headed out of the building.

Chapter Ten

Karlie's sleep was deep and untroubled. She was rested and feeling well when she awoke. All the household tasks she'd put off since the beginning of the semester seemed doable. Tackling one item at a time, she found enough energy to get several done. "Well, it's finally looking livable," she said, smiling.

The smile lasted all week and she was reminded of her thoughts about calling Madison. Picking up her phone, she was surprised at how readily the number came to mind. *Why do I have trouble remembering my number but I can so easily recall Madison's?*

On the other end she could hear the phone ringing. She waited and counted, finally a familiar voice answered, but it was the voice mail system. Disappointment almost made her hang up, but she decided to at least leave a message. "Hello, Madison. This is Karlie...I wanted to say hi."

She put the phone down quickly, regretting that she'd called and that she'd left evidence of that call. Sadness filled her and she went to bed, dousing her pillow in tears of loneliness.

Saturday morning started much earlier than she planned. She still felt like shit. The loud knocking pulled her from a sound sleep. "Hang on! Damn, I'm coming."

Opening the door, Karlie was confronted by two men flashing police badges. "Mrs. Stockard? May we come in?"

Pulling her robe closer, she stepped aside, asking, "What's wrong? Is there a problem?"

"Ma'am, is there anyone else here?" When Karlie shook her

head, confused, he asked, "Is there someone you would like to call and come over?"

"Why? What happened? Did I get a speeding ticket? I'm not losing my driver's license? I rarely drive anymore." Her head ached and she was sure she looked like a mess. She couldn't remember how long she'd cried, but she knew it was very late when she finally fell asleep.

The two detectives looked at each other and the older of the two spoke. "No, ma'am. I'm Detective Rush and this is Detective Marks. We're not from traffic. We're from homicide."

"Homicide?" Panic dragged Karlie down a dark road.

"I'm sorry, but this is about your husband. He was found murdered early this morning."

Stunned, Karlie leaned against the back of the couch, "Rob? Rob's dead?" Any sense of reasoning abandoned her as she struggled with what she'd just heard. "Are you sure?"

"Yes, ma'am. We had a call from your home in the Hamptons this morning. A team responded. Your husband had his wallet with him and the housekeeper identified him." The detective took out a notepad, then asked, "What time did you get home last night? Did you see or talk to anyone after you got home?"

"No, I was tired and went to bed early. Rob's dead?" What little she had eaten was quickly rushing up for an exit. "I'm sorry. I'm not feeling well." She ran from the living room and barely made it into the bathroom.

"She doesn't look well," she heard the younger detective comment as she slowly made her way back. "Should we get an ambulance?"

"That won't be necessary." Feeling light-headed and clammy, Karlie leaned against the door frame.

"I'm sorry." Detective Rush said. "Would you like to sit down?"

Karlie nodded and walked unsteadily to the couch. The detectives sat across from her. She was vaguely aware that they were speaking. The only words she heard were the ones echoing inside her head: *Rob's dead.* Almost a mantra, the refrain played over and over, finally forcing her to understand.

"No, there must be some mistake," she said, fighting the reality of the words. "There has to be some explanation. He probably lost his wallet. It must be someone else you found. I'm sure he's at his apartment. He has an apartment in the city."

She picked up the phone and began to dial. One of the officers walked over and gently took the phone and put it back in its cradle. "Ma'am, we have officers there now. Can you tell us what time you got home?"

Reality hit hard and Karlie sank back into the soft cushions. Emotions moved from one extreme to another. She had once loved Rob and had thought their world perfect. Now she hated him for his lies and deceit. *Sure, I've wanted to strangle him...* Tears spilled as she mourned a love that had once filled her life.

Finally realizing they were questioning her, she hesitated. "Why are you asking me these questions?" Nausea was again threatening. She willed it back down.

"We understand that your husband had a restraining order filed against you."

"I think I better call my lawyer." With that, Karlie put herself into her analytic mode, finding her attorney's number, calling, and leaving a message with his answering service. The absurdity of the situation amazed her. She had wished Rob dead in an angry retort, but those were just words. She couldn't believe anyone thought she was capable of such mayhem. The two officers did not move as she made the call. One took notes.

As soon as she hung up, Karlie dialed Sandy and said, "Look, there are two police officers here. It seems something happened to Rob and he's dead. Would you mind coming over? I've called my attorney and I'm waiting for him to call me back."

"Mrs. Stockard, we have some questions," Detective Rush said.

"Is this where you say 'We need to take you in for questioning' and I go with you?"

"No, ma'am. You can come down to the station later today. We just need to know who'll be making funeral arrangements for Mr. Stockard. The medical examiner needs to know what arrangements will be made after the autopsy."

Great. Even in death, she had to take care of everything. "He wanted to be cremated. His parents are deceased and his sister lives in Paris. Oh, God. He's really dead? I can't believe this."

"He died sometime overnight, ma'am." Detective Rush studied her face with visible concern. "Can I get you a glass of water?"

She shook her head and felt sadness for the abrupt end to her husband's life. Tears again uncontrollably flowed and she struggled as she spoke. "Where is he? Can you tell me what happened?"

The detectives had just finished providing an abbreviated account of the housekeeper finding Rob's body when Sandy arrived.

Detective Rush stepped forward as Sandy placed a supporting arm around Karlie. "Here's my card. Call me later today and let me know when you can come down. Arrangements also need to be made for the body after the coroner releases it."

"The body. My God, that sounds so impersonal."

"I'm sorry, Mrs. Stockard. We'll let ourselves out. Call me later." With brief nods to both women, the officers left.

"Christ." Sandy led Karlie back to the couch. "What happened?"

"I don't know. They said they were sure it was Rob. He could be such a bastard, but still, I can't imagine anyone wanting to kill him."

"Kill him? He was murdered?"

"Yes, but who? Why?"

Trying to lighten the mood, Sandy said, "How about me?"

Karlie couldn't hide her shock. "Sandy, don't even say that in jest. Someone might believe you. God, they could even suspect me." She grasped Sandy's hand. "Isn't the surviving spouse the usual suspect?"

"There's no way they could suspect you. Come on. Let me

make you some coffee." Pouring water into the coffeepot, Sandy asked, "Do you think we should call your lawyer again?"

"If he doesn't call in the next thirty minutes or so, I'll try again," she answered as she sat at the table. "I'm beginning to feel like I've stepped into someone else's life. What else can happen this year?"

Setting two cups of coffee down on the table, Sandy said lightly, "Careful about what you ask for, you may get it."

It was noon before her attorney returned her call. Apologetic for not responding sooner, he was shocked when he learned the reason for the call. "Meet me in my office in an hour," he urged.

"Do you think I have something to worry about?"

"I don't know, but I think it's best we meet."

❖

"I'm not a criminal lawyer, Karlie," Garrison Snyder reminded his client, "but we have one of the best in our firm." He walked across the conference room to the coffeepot. "I've taken the liberty of calling him, and he should be joining us shortly. Can I get either of you some coffee?" Seeing the nod, he asked, "How would you like it?"

By the time they were seated and drinking coffee, an attractive, thirtysomething attorney walked in.

"Good morning," he said, extending his hand. "I'm Leland Roberts. Mr. Snyder told me you may have some legal problems." Wearing jeans and a gray Harvard sweatshirt, he did not fit Karlie's expectations of what a criminal lawyer would look like. "While I get some coffee, why don't you tell me what's going on?"

Leland Roberts was thorough. Karlie felt her reserve fading. After two hours of questioning, she was no longer able to focus. "Is there anything else we should know?" he asked.

Sandy jumped in. "I think Rob may have been trying to kill Karlie."

"What are you talking about" Karlie asked.

"Those accidents you told me about. I thought they seemed too much like coincidence."

"Sandy, I stumbled on the sidewalk and almost fell into traffic. Then someone banged into me and I almost fell down the stairs at school. But nothing happened."

"Karlie just thinks it was an accident," Sandy added. "But I didn't believe it at the time, and now I'm more convinced."

"Is this true?" Leland Roberts asked.

"Yes. They were accidents caused by my own clumsiness and not feeling well. Rob wouldn't do something like that." She paused because her belief systems were slowly being shredded. She closed her eyes and took in a slow, deep breath. "Right now, Mr. Roberts, I'm feeling tired and emotionally drained. I don't think I could answer one more question."

"I suggest you go home and rest. I'll call and arrange a time for you to meet with the police."

Karlie nodded.

While Sandy was not surprised by her friend's resilience, she was dumbfounded by Karlie's reluctance to acknowledge the falls. "I'll take her home and make sure she's ready."

"Good idea. I'll see you later this afternoon, then."

Sandy waited until they were nearly back to Sandy's place before speaking. "Why won't you at least consider that those falls weren't accidents? I wouldn't put that past Rob." She put her hand up to halt Karlie's protest. "I'm sorry, but I never trusted the man. He came back begging to reconcile. He needed money, remember?"

"I remember." Karlie felt emotionally beaten down. Reaching across and touching her friend's arm, she continued, "I just hate to think that I married someone that…evil."

❖

"Dee, phone for you." Jim put the phone on the kitchen counter as he grabbed a beer.

Picking up the phone in her office, Dee Sanderson tried to juggle the call with assembling her portfolio. "Hello."

"Dee, this is Sandra Bailey. I don't know if you remember me. We met a couple of weeks ago when you were here in New York. I'm a friend of Karlie's."

"Sandy. Of course I remember. How are you? What a nice surprise." Dee struggled to match a face with the voice and name. Gradually an image of a fortysomething, graying, thin woman came into focus. A quiet, intelligent woman with an easy smile. "Is this about Karlie? Is she okay? I was just there. She seemed fine."

"She's fine, but something's come up that could be a problem. Rob's dead."

Relief briefly engulfed Dee before the full impact of the comment penetrated. "Good heavens, what happened?"

"The police came by this morning. They said he was murdered."

"The police? Murdered. The bastard deserved to die." Realizing how callous she sounded, she quickly said, "I'm sorry. That sounded awful. I was afraid you were calling to say something had happened to Karlie. I'm not sorry he's dead."

"I agree with you, but that's not why I'm calling. When the police were here, I had the feeling they think Karlie may have had something to do with his death. They didn't have a lot of information, but it was the questions they were asking."

"My God. I can't believe this. I guess I better be careful of what I say or I'll be investigated. What makes them think Karlie had anything to do with it? How is she doing?"

"We don't know. Karlie is sleeping right now. She's going down to the station in a little while with her attorney. They want to question her and get her statement later this afternoon."

"A statement? They can't think she had anything to do with it."

"There's no way she could have, but there is no telling what the police will come up with. There's something else." Sandy hesitated but needed to share her fears. "You remember when Karlie nearly fell into traffic? I didn't think it was an accident. Something similar happened at the university. We were walking down the stairs and some guy rushed by us. Karlie stumbled and would have gone flying down the stairs if I hadn't grabbed her. She refused to think it was anything but a student in a hurry, but there weren't any other people on the stairs. He had plenty of room to go around."

"Did you see what he looked like?" Dee asked.

"Short, dark hair? About my height. You know, I wouldn't put it past Rob to hire someone. He's acquired some rather unsavory friends lately. Karlie had a run-in with him recently and it was obvious he was just after her money."

The enormity of the situation hit Dee full force. "Rob was an asshole. He always had some scheme to make money. Or spend it. Where the hell is that money he supposedly made?" Focusing back on the death, she continued, "There must be a dozen people who would have stronger motives. Surely they can't believe Karlie would be involved." She hesitated. "She isn't, is she?"

"No, I'm sure she isn't," Sandy said. "The problem, I'm afraid, is that there are a lot of people who heard Karlie threaten him about a week ago. She explained that to her lawyer, but it still may make her a suspect. Dee, she's physically and emotionally exhausted without this. I don't know how she is going to survive. I'm worried about her."

"Should I fly up?"

"I don't know. You know how she is, not wanting to ask for help."

"Next to my sister, she's one of the most independent people I know. Won't ask for help even if her life depends on it." Dee put her glasses on the desk and thought back to all the years and memories she shared with Karlie. She realized that Karlie was more than a friend. They had been each other's confidante, cheerleader, and sounding board. As much as she loved her sister Madison, she felt closer to Karlie. "Sandy, is there anything I can do?"

"Not that I know of, but Karlie is going to need her friends. I know Madison is a lawyer. Maybe she has some suggestions. Would she be willing to help?"

"I don't know. They have had a strained relationship, but I kind of sense that may be changing. I'll talk to her. Call me if you find out anything." Placing the phone in the cradle, Dee felt a need to do something. She just didn't know what. She picked up the phone and called the airlines.

❖

It was nearly two in the morning when the phone in Lawrence Hidalgo's bedroom rang. "Hello," he answered groggily.

His brother responded, "There was a slight change of plans and we ended up destroying another package. You will receive full details in the morning. Your original package, however, will be taken care of shortly. We look forward to continuing our business relationship."

Now fully awake, Hidalgo slammed the phone down. His brother should already be back. He quickly dialed. Before his brother had a chance to answer, Lawrence Hidalgo barked, "What the hell is going on? I just got a call from New York about another package. What have you two been up to?"

"Calm, brother. You will not believe how good our fortune is and how grateful our New York friends are. The bitch will suffer."

Not sure what was going on, Lawrence decided not to go into detail on a phone that could have other ears listening. "I will meet you for breakfast. You know where. This better be good." He hung up wondering if his little brother would ever follow directions. Ramon's escapades had brought attention to the family, and the family businesses, too many times. It was time for the younger brother to grow up.

❖

Madison was exhausted. *She's insatiable! I don't think I can move.* She arose slowly from the bed and tried to think of a graceful way to exit. "I've got to go to the bathroom."

"Better hurry. I can still feel you fucking me."

"Hmm, hurrying," Madison muttered as she removed the harness and looked at the blonde. She couldn't even remember the younger woman's name. She walked into the bathroom, closed the door, and leaned against it. How the hell did she get into this? Briefly she recalled meeting the attractive stranger a few hours earlier and buying a drink for her. It wasn't long before they were at the woman's apartment and in bed. After four hours of intense sex, Madison was ready for sleep. Grabbing her clothes off the floor, she dressed quickly and stepped out.

The blonde sat up quickly. "You're dressed. I get it." She crawled across the bed and tried to reach for her departing guest. "You want me to undress you again?"

The look of lust startled Madison. Staring at the swaying, pendulous breasts, she could feel the nipples in her mouth. The young woman had been amazing, both in her stamina and her willingness to experiment, but now Madison wanted to go home. "Sorry, but I've got to go."

The aroused woman pouted and leaned back on the bed, her legs spread. "Can't I persuade you to stay? Surely whatever it is can wait?" She put her hand between her legs and gently stroked herself. "I'm still wet. You can't leave me like this." The voice purred sexual intent and left little doubt as to what the owner wanted.

Damn, she's hot. Madison could feel desire rising. She'd enjoyed fucking the tight ass and hearing the moans of the woman encouraging her to fuck her harder. *She does have an amazing tongue, too.* Madison felt wetness spreading between her legs. Just the memory brought her close to orgasm. Her resolve was weakening, but she realized she had already stayed much longer than she intended.

She shook her head, kissed the woman, and said, "If I stayed, you would be the only thing I would get done. Good night."

Forcing herself not to look back she quickly exited and left the building, looking for her car. She knew she would be sore in the morning, but eagerly admitted she had enjoyed the variety of dildoes and leather harnesses her sex partner provided. Her thoughts turned to another blonde. No matter how she tried, Karlie haunted her.

"Fuck her. I hope she's miserable."

CHAPTER ELEVEN

Sunday was the one day Madison could go into the office and get work done. No one else would be there. She put her coffee on her desk and went through her messages. As she went through the slips, she stopped on one. "Fuck," she groaned. "I thought I'd gotten rid of that bastard."

She went to the next one and saw the same name. Her morning had just turned sour. What did he want now? She wadded all four pieces of paper and threw them in the trash, then walked over to the window and looked out. Time passed and she continued to glare out the window, not noticing the beautiful Miami morning growing outside. No matter how much she tried, every memory, every thought seemed to end in the same place: Karlie. After her sister had given her the message that Karlie had said hello, Madison had finally asked for Karlie's phone numbers. Since then, she'd picked up the phone a dozen times to call but had not dialed the number. What the hell was wrong with her? Since when was she reluctant to call any woman?

Finally the sun's glare forced her to move away and try to concentrate on the paperwork on her desk. A little before noon her cell phone rang. Seeing her sister's phone number, she answered, "Hi, little sister."

"Hello, older sister."

Madison laughed. This was an exchange that had become more

frequent. Dee enjoyed reminding Madison that she was approaching forty. Giving her usual response, she replied, "Ah, but, like fine wine, I'm getting better. What's up? What are you folks up to?"

"Mother called." Dee hesitated. "They'll be arriving this week. This time staying for the season. Mad, they want us to have lunch with them next weekend, probably Saturday. Can you break away for an hour? Before you say no, I promise you won't have to stay more than an hour."

Madison hesitated. She enjoyed the time she spent with her sister and her family and missed Dee when she didn't get to see her. Her parents were not, however, even blips on Madison's personal radar. "I feel like a zoo animal being put on parade for Miami-Dade's cotillion crowd. Maybe I should bring my latest fuck toy along and give them a show. Then I won't have to worry about ever getting invited back." Madison paused in her tirade only long enough to take a sip out of her coffee cup. "I have better things to do."

"Madison, your language has really been in the toilet lately. Your behavior hasn't been much better."

"I could apologize, but it wouldn't change the way I feel."

"That still doesn't explain your behavior. The last few weeks you've been hanging around with some…rough-looking women. I've stayed out of your personal life, but when you brought that woman to lunch the other day, I'm sorry, but I was embarrassed by the two of you. I've got to ask you to not bring any of those women around the kids. Jim and I wanted to invite you to go to dinner with us Saturday night, but we didn't want the kids around your friend."

Madison's rising anger took a sudden turn. She adored Dee's kids. Never had she even considered the consequences of her behavior on her family. Suddenly her thoughts were filled with the image of her impressionable young niece. That kid looked up to her. What kind of example was she setting?

Not getting a response, Dee continued, "You seem to be going through more women than usual and your language is worse than I've ever heard."

Angry at herself, Madison became defensive. "My life is my

own. I go in to work every day and I haven't missed an appointment or court date. So give it a rest."

Dee could not remember a time when she and Madison had argued so much. Something was going on. She'd learned long ago that Madison was not the kind of sister to share her deepest feelings when something was bothering her. As frustrated as she was with her present behavior, Dee wasn't willing to create a chasm between them. Taking a deep breath, she said, "Fine. Just put time in your calendar next Saturday."

"You sure are asking a lot." Relenting, Madison said, "Tell Jim he better be there or I'll strangle him the next time I see him."

Laughter finally slipped from Dee. "You know how much he looks forward to these outings. He wouldn't miss it for anything. Besides, he said the same thing about you. See you Saturday. As soon as I know where, I'll let you know. And, Madison, thank you. I love you."

The words were frequently spoken over the many years. This time they reached deep and lit a spark in Madison's otherwise controlled heart. "Yeah, me, too. Take care, DeeDee. And tell Bonehead and the kids I love them, too."

The depth of feeling as Madison spoke surprised Dee. *Something is definitely going on. Sooner or later I'll find out. Give her some space.* Instead Dee said, "They know and love you, too. See you Saturday."

Madison placed the phone down and grabbed her PDA. She didn't want to deal with the emotions. Data was easier to handle. Turning on the PDA, she was again grateful for modern electronics. In her calendar she reluctantly entered the luncheon date with her family. Without thinking, she went to Karlie's name and phone number. She stared at it as she had so many times and then turned the device off. "Well, it's been downhill all morning."

She had just put away the PDA when her office phone rang. Thinking her brother-in-law was calling to make sure she showed up next week, she answered, "You better be there, you weasel."

A male voice replied, "If you are going to be there, I wouldn't miss it. Just tell me where and when."

"Tell me why I should spend another thirty seconds talking to you." The sound of Lawrence Hidalgo's voice triggered an irrational rage. Madison wanted to strangle the creep.

"As our attorney, our well-paid attorney, I remind you, you have severely neglected us, not answered our phone calls, and refused to see any member of my family. You continue to dishonor us and neglect your responsibilities, Ms. Barnes."

"I no longer represent you. You have received written notice of the termination of our professional relationship. We have nothing more to discuss." Before she had a chance to hang up, she heard Hidalgo's maniacal laugh. "What the hell is so funny?"

"You will come back. No one, and I mean no one, walks away from my family without my permission. Your stupid pride will be your downfall and the source of pain to others. Maybe you should find out what your little bitch has been up to. I will expect your call."

The click on the phone irritated her. "What the hell does that mean, you asshole?" Looking at the clock on her bookcase, she decided to give up on her work and get some lunch. Afterward, she might need to schedule another session of sex. The blonde liked being fucked and preferred her sex a little rough. Madison was definitely in the mood. She needed to fuck someone.

❖

"Oh, baby," the blonde whispered. "That was the best yet. Let me get my breath and then we can do it again."

Without saying a word, Madison thrust her hips, hearing the cry of pleasure from the woman underneath her. "Can't wait? Oh, baby, you're hot tonight. I can't get enough of you." Madison continued for a few seconds more and then cried out in release.

"That one was good," the woman gasped. "Sure you've never done BDSM before? You're a natural. Oh, baby, you are good." Finally she asked, "What now, master?"

Suddenly Madison felt empty. What now? *Yeah, what now?*

Time to go home. Madison slowly pulled herself out and rubbed the firm flesh in front of her. *What a great ass...and tits.* She lifted herself off. "Enough, baby, you've pleased me." She removed the harness, stretched, reached for her clothes, and began to dress.

Stunned at Madison's sudden decision to leave, the woman carefully inched forward. "Baby, you can't leave now. I need to finish you."

"No." Realizing she had spoken harshly, Madison began again. "No, you've given me more pleasure than you can know, but I do have to go. I have an early day tomorrow. She leaned over and kissed the young woman's cheek. "Get some rest."

"Will I see you again?"

"Maybe."

"You've got my number," she offered.

Laughing, Madison noticed for the first time that the woman was attractive, but young. "How old are you?" she asked.

"Twenty-six. How about you, you stud?"

Madison laughed. "An old stud." *God, she's twelve years younger. I need to get out of here and quickly.* "We've been at this for hours and tomorrow is a work day. If I keep this up, I won't be walking." The woman was not easily dissuaded and tried her best to keep her sex partner in her bed. Madison finished dressing and left. All earlier anger was gone. She was empty again. She needed to be alone.

As she started her car and headed for home, she was overwhelmed by her own smell. Sweat and sex. Whew. And she still didn't know her name. Unexpected waves of incapacitating emptiness washed over her, causing tears to swell. Damn it all to hell. she didn't cry. Wiping the small amounts of moisture at the corners of her eyes, she said, "Christ, I can't keep doing this."

She put her head in hands and leaned on the steering wheel, trying to control the intense extremes of emotions battling within her. For the first time in her adult life she felt lonely. The more she used sex to feed her needs, the hungrier she felt. And the more alone. With some semblance of control returning, she decided she was tired and needed a vacation. *I need a fucking break. Why don't I give myself a fucking break and call Karlie? I need to call her like I need...need what? I need a vacation.*

It was already well after the time when she usually made reservations for her annual trip to Bali, and as of yet, she hadn't finalized her holiday plans. She made a mental note to make that a priority when she got to work. Maybe she just needed some time away from all of this.

❖

Tuesday Karlie sat in her office trying to prepare exams for her classes and wishing it was closer to winter break. Her head resting in her hands, she didn't notice the two police officers entering.

"Dr. Henderson?" She looked up and nodded. She recognized one as the man who had informed her of Rob's death. "Dr. Henderson, we have a warrant for your arrest in the death of Robert Stockard."

Stunned, she sat staring until the second officer came over and pulled her out of her seat. "You have the right to remain silent. You have the right..."

The words faded as numbness set in. "I don't understand. There must be some mistake."

"What the hell is going on?" Sandy asked. "What do you think you're doing?"

The graying officer cautioned, "We have a warrant for Mrs. Stockard's arrest. Please move aside or we'll have to arrest you. That won't help her."

"The hell you will," Sandy bit back.

The younger officer pleaded with Sandy. "Please, ma'am. You can help a lot more if you call her attorney. Here's my card."

"I'll call Leland and we'll have you out in no time," Sandy said. Helplessness and anger filled her, and only the look of despair on Karlie's face as she was led away kept Sandy from screaming.

Once back in her office, Sandy quickly located the attorney's number and dialed it as other faculty and staff began to gather in her office asking questions. After passing on the necessary information to Leland's secretary, she slammed the phone down.

"Shit!" she uttered as she drove toward the police station. She quickly put in a call to her partner and they tried to figure out how to help.

By midnight, Leland Roberts had managed to get a judge to set bail. The attorney used both Karlie's impeccable reputation as well as her ties to the community to persuade the judge to release her. Sandy made a couple of calls and used the escrow in her house for the bail. Neither woman spoke until they were back at Karlie's house.

"How the hell can they think I could kill Rob?" Karlie asked. "Even more, how the hell am I going to convince them I'm innocent? I mean, yes, I was angry at Rob, but kill him? I'm sorry, but I'm beginning to wonder how much more I can cope with."

CHAPTER TWELVE

Madison was dreading her parents' party, but socializing had never been her forte. Her parents' gatherings only reinforced her distaste for attempting conversation in large group settings. As a family, they had never celebrated holidays or birthdays unless it served as a means of gathering the elite of Miami's social scene. Madison hated being put on display and pretending to be interested in whatever her parents' friends had to say.

"I think I'll just have a liquid dinner tonight," she muttered, "and then I can put up with all the shit." She stared at the image in the mirror and realized she needed sleep. The clock said it was nearly noon. She dialed Dee. No one answered. "Where the fuck is everybody?" Giving up on doing anything she considered constructive, she drove to her sister's house.

"How's my favorite brother-in-law?" she yelled as she exited the Lexus.

"Your only brother-in-law," Jim answered.

"Where are the kids? It's too quiet."

"At the movies." Jim took pride in his vehicles. Keeping them clean and running gave him immense satisfaction. Kept him connected, he liked to say.

"With Dee?"

"Nope, Cindy. The nanny." He pulled the small hand vacuum into the van and climbed in.

"You sure are full of conversation. I guess I'll go in and talk to my sister, then."

"You'll have to talk loud. She's in New York."

"New York. What's she doing in New York? Skipping the party?"

"That's what I accused her of." Having moved the middle seats, Jim pulled out the debris left from recent trips with the kids in the van. "Nope, she went up to see Karlie." Holding up the small plastic trash container filled with fast food bags, coffee cups, and other detritus, he continued, "Can you believe how much junk we end up throwing away? We rarely make it past a McDonald's without having to stop."

Leaning on her car, Madison tried to act indifferent. "What's she doing up there?"

Karlie again. *Damn, why can't I get away from her?* Karlie haunted her thoughts when awake and her dreams when asleep. The woman was driving her crazy and had become an unrelenting hunger.

Jim seemed hesitant. "It's a private matter."

"Are you and Dee okay? You're not fooling around on my sister, are you?"

"Chill out. We're fine. It's not us." Several moments passed before he continued, "Madison, I know you never cared for Karlie, but she's having a rough time. Please don't pick on Dee or Karlie. I won't allow it."

"Why the sudden protectiveness?" Something was wrong. She could feel it. Her skin began to crawl, always an early warning sign for her. "Come on, Jim, give. What's up?"

"Karlie's husband's been murdered and she's been arrested."

"What the fuck? That's not very funny." Madison jabbed a finger at his chest. "That's not funny at all."

"You're right, it's not funny at all. Dee got a call yesterday from some friend of Karlie's and we got her on a flight this morning. This friend also said she thought someone had tried to kill Karlie, more than once. They're not sure if it was Karlie or her husband they wanted. The police are only interested in Karlie right now."

"She's not capable of killing anyone. It's obviously a mistake. How can they arrest her?"

Jim shrugged. "I don't know. I'm not a lawyer."

"Well, I am. Why the hell didn't someone call me?" Hidalgo's threats bounced around in her head. This wasn't fucking happening. If Hidalgo was involved...yeah, then what? Then it was her fucking fault Karlie's life was fucked up. She was responsible.

Jim's words were spoken softly, but they hit hard and hurt. "Madison, why should anyone call you? Why would anyone even think you were interested? You've made it clear how you feel about Karlie. The last thing Dee needs right now are some smug comments from you when she's frantic about her best friend."

Swallowing was difficult. Yeah, what difference did it make? So what if she bagged the bozo? What if she was being set up? As hard as she tried, one thought intruded: *I don't want to lose her.* Lose her? Hell, she didn't have any claim on her. When she was asked, she'd just stood there and said nothing. She'd never wanted any permanent involvement before. Why now? What was different? And what made her think Karlie would want her popping in now? Madison had more questions than answers, but she knew one thing. She needed to fix this.

"Does Dee have her cell phone with her?"

"Yes, but I'm warning you, Mad, I don't want you upsetting her."

"Upset her, Jesus, you make me sound like some ogre. I love Dee and would do anything for her."

"If you're in a good mood."

"What the hell does that mean?"

"It means you do whatever is convenient...for you."

"Fuck off!" Madison shouted. She walked to her car and started to open the door.

Turning to make a final comment, she saw Jim glaring at her, his fists clenched. Jim Sanderson was not only loving and devoted to Dee, he had been a good, loyal friend to Madison. Her behavior might not have always been above reproach, but she wanted to keep Dee and Jim an important part of her life.

"I'm sorry, Jim. Believe it or not, I really don't want anything bad to happen to Karlie, and I would never intentionally hurt Dee. Promise."

"Mad, the problem isn't your intentions. It's your actions."

"What's that supposed to mean?" Her voice was challenging but concern was written across her face. She didn't have a clue what Jim was talking about.

"I don't think you realize how many times you've hurt someone and never even thought about it. You do things, like the Saturday you brought some woman to lunch and, from what Dee said, the two of you, well, embarrass is too kind a word. She came home in tears. Then you constantly trash Karlie in front of her and she has to choose between the sister, her only sister, and her best friend. You put her in the middle every time your parents plan some event. She's left to explain and clean up. I know you never intended to hurt Dee, but still you did."

Madison was speechless. The picture Jim painted wasn't a pleasant one, and Madison had no way to defend herself. Too many emotions tore at her. Dealing with all the accusations was more than she was ready to tackle at this point. Focusing back on her original task, she said, "You don't know what you're talking about. Right now I just need to know how to get in touch with my sister. That's all."

"She's got her cell phone," Jim repeated. "She got there about two hours ago."

"I'm…thanks." She tried to make amends, but gratitude was not a familiar characteristic. She quickly climbed into her car and started her drive home. Pulling out her cell phone, she hit a speed-dial number.

❖

"Madison!" Surprise was evident in her sister's voice. "I'm kind of busy right now. Can I call you later?"

"Dee, I know where you are. Can I speak to Karlie? Is she there?"

"Madison, please. Don't start something. She's had a rough day."

"Let me talk to Karlie!" Madison tried to maintain a neutral voice but found herself becoming frustrated.

"No. Madison, for once I am not going to let you hurt my friend. Not now."

"Give me a fucking break." Her patience, limited in the best of times, was stretched now. "I'm not some unfeeling monster. Just let me talk to her."

"No, Madison, you're not a monster. You just don't consider others when you do things. I don't think you realize how sarcastic you can be, especially to Karlie. I'm not going to put up with it anymore."

A second reminder of her being inconsiderate pissed her off. "Just give her the goddamn phone."

"No." The word was carefully articulated.

Taking a slow deep breath, Madison counted to ten before speaking, trying to defuse the growing tension, "Dee, believe me, this time I just want to talk to her." Lowering her voice so that she was once again calm, Madison continued, "Please let me talk to Karlie. Please."

Madison never said "please." Too stunned to speak, Dee passed her cell phone to Karlie.

❖

The voice still caused chills. Karlie listened, unable to speak.

Madison carefully chose her words. "Karlie, are you okay? Look, I think…"

"Hello?" Karlie took a deep breath, closed her eyes, and tried to slow her rapidly beating heart. "You think? That's scary."

"Shit, Karlie…you can be such a bitch." Then, remembering the comments of both her brother-in-law and sister, she silently chastised herself. "I'm sorry. I need to talk to you."

"Oh, and to what specifically do I owe the honor of this call? And the lovely salutation?"

"If the shoe fits." Madison stopped, frustration growing along with an increasing awareness of her own role in this now chronic animosity. Taking a deep breath, she tried again. "I didn't call to argue with you. I called to offer my assistance."

"Why? Why now? Why haven't you called before?"

Surprised by the question, Madison found no easy answer. *I don't know. I wish I had. How about you may be in trouble and I can help? How about I can't concentrate, thinking only of you? How about I was afraid to pick up the phone and call? How about I don't fucking know!*

"I heard what happened and believe it or not, I don't want anything to happen to you. Please, Karlie, baby, I want to help. I'm an attorney. I'll get you the best in New York. Don't worry about money. We can get you the…"

"Very touching, but very out of character." This was not a response Karlie expected or knew how to handle. "I'd feel more comfortable if you were calling to gloat. I would trust that. I would understand that." Feeling the need to gain some semblance of balance, she said, "Thanks, but I'm fine."

Controlling her rising frustration, Madison continued, "I'm sure you're fantastic, which is why you were arrested. Now cut the bullshit. You obviously have an attorney. Is she someone with criminal experience? Don't worry about the cost."

Why did this woman always bring out the worst in her? Karlie just wanted to…to what? "I have a very experienced lawyer who does only criminal law, and he's very professional."

The tone was sharp, taunting. It was all Madison could do to not slam the phone down. "And I'm not? What the hell am I? Just some friendly fuck?"

The woman on the other end of the phone thought of a multitude of sharp retorts but in the end simply asked, "What do you want?"

"I told you," Madison shot back. "I really want to help." Changing her voice to one more conciliatory, she said, "Karlie, I've made a lot of money. I can afford anything. Do you hear? Let me help."

"Yes, you already said that, and I've already told you no. I don't know what it is with you and money, but I'm no longer the poor scholarship student hanging around with rich kids. Thank you for the offer. Good-bye."

Karlie handed the phone back to Dee and walked out of the room. She didn't want to explore any feelings, for anyone, least of all Madison.

❖

"Mad, I'll talk to you later." There was no mistaking the anger in her sister's voice. "I need to talk to Karlie."

"Why? Once she's made her mind up, dynamite up her ass couldn't move her."

"Madison!"

"Dee, I'm sorry. Karlie's in trouble and all I want to do is help. She won't even let me try."

"You may be accustomed to most people doing whatever you want, but there isn't anything you can do. You offered. She's refused. Accept it and forget it. I'll talk to you when I get home." Without waiting for a reply, Dee hung up on her sister, thinking, *What the hell is going on?* Since when did Madison care about Karlie?

Madison was furious. An unsuspecting driver who pulled in front of her received a sharp horn blast. "Stupid bastard, move!"

She swerved and drove quickly around him, nearly forcing the smaller sedan off the road. Disregarding posted limits, she pushed her Lexus and arrived at her office in near record time. Her mind was in turmoil. The recent conversations with Lawrence Hidalgo grew more ominous. If that bastard had anything to do with this, she would personally cut his balls off and shove them down his slimy throat.

Opening her office door, she realized she had to do something. At this point it didn't matter what. If she had to personally kill the Hidalgo brothers, she didn't care. Dialing a number she had memorized, she waited for an answer.

"Hi, this is Madison Barnes. I need a favor. Can you meet me in the office in an hour? Thanks."

Two more calls netted two more affirmative replies. As she looked over her phone list, she realized she had represented both the wealthy and the wicked. It was the darker side of her client list that at times had provided services she could not legitimately solicit. As she waited for her guests, she turned on her computer and searched the Internet for information about Karlie and her husband.

By the time her first visitor arrived, Madison had pages of notes. Unfortunately there were still too many loose ends and unanswered questions. She greeted her former client, offering him something to drink.

Carlton Best was a tall, well-built man in his late forties. He'd been in the army many years before joining the police. Most of those years were spent either in specialized ranger units or in covert operations. The years of special forces training had become ingrained and he maintained both his physical fitness and his wariness. He'd been a respected police officer until he was accused of laundering drugs.

Madison had gotten the charges dismissed, but Carl had been forced to resign. She'd helped him set up his own business as a private investigator and used his services whenever she needed specialized help with cases.

"Good to see you, Carl. How's it going?" Neither was much for small chat, so they quickly moved to the purpose of the visit. "I need for you to run an intensive background check on this guy." She tossed a stack of papers down in front of him. "This will give you a start. I'm not as much interested in the obvious as I am in some possible link to the Hidalgo family."

"Hidalgo? Lawrence Hidalgo? The piece of shit that planted drugs in my car and turned me? What does he have to do with this?"

"I don't know. He's made some threats and I think he may be responsible for a friend being in trouble. You need to be discreet. You more than anyone know how dangerous he can be." Pointing to the sheets on the table, she continued, "This guy Rob Stockard is dead. His wife's been charged, but I think Hidalgo had something to do with it. You've got to help me find the link. I don't care how much it costs."

"This must be a good friend." Refusing to acknowledge how close the comment struck, Madison answered, "She's actually my sister's best friend, but I've known her a long time. She's incapable of harming anyone." As she said those words, she mentally added, *Unlike me*. Reaching for another file, she continued, "I have two people coming in shortly who can help you. They used to be part of Hidalgo's family until he set them up. They both owe me and they both hate Hidalgo and will do whatever we ask."

Forty minutes later Madison found herself alone again, but at least she had put a plan into motion. Her office line rang. "Madison."

"Working on a Sunday? You still aren't returning my calls."

She needed information. "Well, if it isn't Miami's dumbest piece of shit. What do I have to do to get you to go away?"

"You're the dumb one. You'll be singing a different tune when you hear about your little blonde."

"Which one?" Her hands were clenched, but her voice remained cold and detached.

"You won't be laughing when your girlfriend is as dead as her husband. Show a little respect and maybe we can help you save her pretty neck, and ass."

Careful with her reply, Madison answered, "I guess I finally found something big about you. Your ego. It sure isn't your brain... or your dick. I don't have any girlfriends. It's a waste of time. You should understand. Why keep drinking at the same well when there are so many other drinking sources? Besides, I'm too busy trying to avoid talking to idiots like you. Now, go find a sewer to play in. I've got better ways to spend my time."

"Come on, I saw you with her. Let's see, what's her name? Oh, yeah, that writer. Karlyn Henderson."

"Hidalgo, I'm hanging up. Don't ever call me again. Do you understand? If this woman is in some trouble, it has nothing to do with me. So fuck off."

"You are one coldhearted bitch. You should join me. We could make a good team." Madison snorted. "Maybe this whore doesn't mean anything to you, but she does to your sister. You listen to me now or regret it later."

"No, you bastard, you listen. This is between you and me. If anything, and I mean anything, happens to my family, if my sister even breaks a fingernail, I will personally bury you." No longer able to control her fury, she hung up. "I'm going to have to kill that bastard myself."

❖

After spending nearly two hours in tears, Karlie rejoined Dee in the kitchen. She spoke hesitantly. "I'm sorry. I don't know what's wrong with me. I seem to be on an emotional roller coaster."

"Karlie, don't apologize. I can't even begin to imagine what you're going through." They sat at the kitchen table. "Remember when we used to stay up late talking? Just sitting in the kitchen and drinking hot tea. I guess that's why the kitchen has always been my favorite room in the house." Having elicited a hesitant smile, Dee reached for Karlie's hand. "I'm sorry about Madison. When she called, I was so surprised and she sounded genuinely concerned. I didn't know what to do."

Karlie turned away and pretended to stare out the window. "Don't apologize." She wanted to hide her own confusion. Attacking was one way. "I find it hard to imagine her caring about anyone but herself. I'm sorry, Dee. Maybe a better answer is that I don't trust her."

"She's my sister, Karlie, and she's really not a bad person."

"I know," Karlie whispered as she stood and walked over to stare out the window over the sink. "I have no doubt she deeply cares about you. Yet I think there's a part of her that sees everything only as it relates to her own life. You may even be an extension of her own sense of self, her own identity. Whatever it is, I would imagine she is extremely protective of what's hers."

"That's unfair. Madison is very capable of loving."

Smiling, Karlie said, "Life isn't fair. I believe that's one of Madison's favorite quotes." Realizing her best friend was again in the middle, Karlie walked over and sat next to Dee. "God, I'm sorry. It's my turn to apologize. Again. I'm not being fair. You're my best and oldest friend. Madison is your sister. I shouldn't take out my own frustration with Madison on you. You're right, she does have a good side." She wanted to find a dark hole to hide in, as far from the feelings and events that kept her life in an uncontrolled spiral.

Dee reached for Karlie's hand. "I don't want to spend our time talking about my sister because I love you both and I've never understood this tension between you two. Sometimes I wonder if…" She looked away, thought carefully about what she was going to say, then decided to continue. "Karlie, did anything ever happen between the two of you?"

A small knot in the pit of her stomach threatened to explode. Karlie stared into trusting blue eyes. "You two look so much alike and yet you're so different. How did that happen?" Lying would put a wedge between them that nothing would change. Telling the truth could do the same thing. "What do you mean, happen?"

"Come on, Karlie, I'm not that naïve. It was obvious you once had a crush on my sister. Our freshman year you turned red every time she was around. You were always asking about her. At the time I didn't think much about it because you were dating guys. I figured it was the same type of hero worship I had for Mad. But the two of you were always sniping at each other. I never figured out what happened."

Relief washed over Karlie and she used the temporary reprieve to breathe again. "I don't think your sister ever really liked me. At first she barely tolerated me. I wanted to be liked and be accepted so badly I was willing to do anything to have her like me and not stop you from being my friend. After we were arrested in college, I guess she figured she had free rein to attack. Our sophomore year, I felt like a huge open scab. Then I guess I decided to be more assertive." She grudgingly acknowledged the reality. "Okay, so I began to attack back. I don't know how it happened, but I got tired of the constant sniping. Maybe I felt rejected, but at the time I didn't think about why. I just reacted. You know, she's the only person I react to that way. Whenever Madison says something, I can't seem to control myself. I want to hurt her. I'm sorry, I guess I hadn't realized how bad things had gotten."

"Oh, Karlie, I never realized how much you must have loved her."

Pulling her hand back, Karlie felt as if she had been slapped. "Love? I had to care for her enough first. She never gave me the time or encouragement to even think of her as human." *Until this summer.* She amended her previous statement. "I'm doing it again. I'm so sorry. I'm trying to change, honestly. We actually spent nearly forty-eight hours together without killing each other."

"Then what's going on now? Why the reaction to the call?"

"I guess old habits die hard."

"Are you sure that's all?"

"I can't really say."

CHAPTER THIRTEEN

As usual, Carlton Best was thorough. "Your friend is in big trouble. There's been a contract out on Rob Stockard for some time. My informants tell me it was just supposed to be some serious roughing up. He owes a lot of money to some not so nice people. Betting, coke, some illegal property transfers. He may have even lifted money from work. Not long ago a stranger pops into town trying to arrange a hit on Stockard's wife for a huge chunk of change. Word on the street was that some low-level punk took the contract. There were a couple of badly botched attempts and then more money was offered."

"Hidalgo. That vermin." She wanted to punch something, she didn't care what. She allowed the cold fury of revenge to fill her. "Go ahead. I'm listening."

"The only thing I could definitely find out about the buyer was that he was Latin and from out of state. The description I got sounds like Ramon Hidalgo. I can't prove it, but I'd bet my retirement on it." Carl twisted his coffee cup around. He had a history with the Hidalgo family that was longer than Madison's. "The man who took the second contract broke into the house expecting to find Dr. Stockard and ran into Mr. Stockard. Apparently Stockard may have recognized the intruder who was forced to take him out. It gets kind of fuzzy here. My contacts say the hit man can't keep his mouth shut so a lot of this is from gossip on the street, probably from the source. The hit man did some fancy talking and convinced everybody he could frame Karlie Henderson for the killing. Or get her out of the way, too."

"So he gets money from two sources," Madison concluded.

"And also takes care of a problem for his organization and develops a rep for himself." Carl finished his coffee and set the mug aside. "The rumor is that if she hadn't gotten arrested, they were going to arrange a suicide."

Madison felt an uneasy blackness descend over her. It had skirted the edges of her existence, growing stronger with time. Now it was consuming her. She wanted revenge.

"The police just want a quick conviction. They're building a circumstantial case, strong on motive."

"Jesus. Doesn't anyone care that she might be innocent?"

"I have a buddy in the NYPD. It sounds like someone could have been paid off to not look deeper. There's a state task force looking into police corruption charges in some of the communities outside New York City. That's the good news. The bad news is that it won't happen fast enough for Dr. Stockard."

"Are you telling me there's nothing we can do?" Having been in control for so much of her life, the possibility of sitting by while Karlie was in danger was beyond credulity.

"No, I'm just saying we may have to take care of this ourselves. Even if they found out who actually killed Stockard, the contract on the wife is still out there."

"So, what now?" Madison stared down at her untouched coffee.

Her life had been one of control and order. The study of law, and its practice, required it. With startling clarity, she recognized how slowly, but steadily, she had been slipping away from that pristine order. As a result she no longer knew black and white. She'd gotten rich by bending rules and occupying gray areas. She could get anything she wanted. Cars, travel, sex. And at no personal cost. Or so she had thought. Now two people she cared about were threatened.

"The way I see it, we've got two jobs," Carl said. "First, we have to figure out how to get the charges against Dr. Henderson dropped. Then we have to get rid of the Hidalgo brothers without any fingers pointing to us."

Carl smiled. "Next to my wife agreeing to marry me, that's the nicest thing any woman has said to me."

"I have some thoughts," Madison said.

The plan was deceptively simple and risky. And the personal cost could be prohibitive. She would have to embrace the darkness. Aware of the path she was taking, she measured her words. "Carl, I can't ask you to continue. Your wife would kill me if anything happened to you, and if this plan doesn't work..." She hesitated briefly. "Then one of two things will happen. The Hidalgos will come after us, or I will have to go after them."

The ex-cop owed his life and everything he now had to the dark-haired woman sitting across the table. At the end of his trial, he had silently pledged to do whatever he could to repay her. "Boss, there's no way I would miss this," Carl said. "You may be a great lawyer, but you're out of your league when it comes to dealing with this type of operation. I'll take care of it. You're the one who needs to stay clean."

Madison had already made her decision. She always solved her own problems. "I can handle myself. I've been shooting since I was a kid. I used to compete in tournaments. I've done self-defense and I work out."

"You're full of surprises. I don't doubt your fitness, but this is not a civilian situation."

"Carl, I'm not stopping until Karlie is cleared of this mess and the Hidalgos are no longer a threat. If you choose to continue, I'll be very grateful for any help you can give."

"And as I said, I owe you. Besides, I want them even more than you do. I'm in."

Loyalty had not been part of her vocabulary and, with rare exceptions, certainly wasn't a characteristic she could claim. Power had been her only god and motivator. But she valued Carl's commitment and understood the reasons for it. They were at an impasse. Putting out her hand, she said, "I guess we're both in, then. Thank you."

Carl shook her hand. "I never imagined I'd have this opportunity. Thank you."

"What do you need?" Madison got down to business. "What do I need to do? I'm a fast learner."

"There are some things we'll need, and it is best I get them here. I'll drive up to New York with our supplies. No one checking luggage that way. Your job is to register in an expensive hotel and make sure they notice you're there. Get two rooms. Register as Mr. and Mrs. Jacob Smith and family."

Madison nodded. "You're right. No one would ever be looking for a family."

"I'll check in and pay for the rooms," Carl said. "I'm going to pick up disposable cell phones for us to use. We'll take out the trace chips. Everything else will be taken care of when I get to New York."

"I'll leave for New York today. How do I get cash to you?"

"You do catch on fast." Carl smiled. He outlined the financial arrangements he wanted. "When I was in special ops we used to kid that our goal was to leave no footprint, but if we did, leave it as small as possible so that anyone finding it would think elves existed."

"I'm beginning to believe in elves myself," Madison said. "How are the two guys I introduced to you doing?"

"They hate the Hidalgos enough to take any risk. It's also an honor thing with them. They are already headed to New York, by way of St. Louis and Chicago. They won't arrive until day after tomorrow."

"Carl, thanks." She put out her hand. He readily took it. "Anything else?"

"Just get me the information that everything's set as quickly as possible so that I'm not sitting around here."

As soon as he was gone, Madison got on the phone and made the travel arrangements. She knew she was going to need a gun but would have to rely on Carl to get it. It would be too easily remembered if she tried to fly with one. She went home to pack and catch a short nap. She was on the red-eye to New York.

❖

"Hello?" Dee said, not checking the display before she answered her cell phone.

"Don't hang up. I need to talk to you and to Karlie."

"Damn it, Madison. She doesn't want to talk to you. Please, don't call."

"Okay, then I'll sit out here and ring this damn bell until someone lets me in."

In spite of the warning, the sight of her grinning sister standing in the doorway shocked Dee. "What are you doing here?"

"Who's at the door?" Karlie stopped. Too many times she had dreamed of this moment, both hoping and dreading it.

Madison was unprepared for the sight of the woman who had walked into the room. She was barely recognizable. Dark circles underscored haunted eyes. Her long golden hair was listless. In a matter of weeks her soft curves had been traded for gaunt angles. Her clothes hung on a fragile frame. Madison's mouth dried. Watching her sister and her best friend, Dee slowly recognized that the tension between the two had somehow changed. It had to have happened the weekend she had been out of town. Feeling guilty for her role in whatever had occurred, she backed out of the room. "I'll be in the kitchen." She doubted either woman heard her.

"Why are you here?" Karlie asked her one-time adversary.

Madison remained silent for a few seconds, just staring, before she answered absently, "I told you. I want to help." She put up her hand. "Wait, hear me out. It's important." She moved in close and touched Karlie's sallow cheek.

Karlie hated the pity she thought she saw in those blue eyes. She grasped for a reply. "Gee, it's good to see you, too, Madison. Now what the hell do you want?"

Madison took a hesitant step even closer and felt her smooth veneer stripped layer by layer, leaving her naked and vulnerable. She hated it. Her voice soft and low, she began, "Karlie, I…fuck." She started to raise her hand to touch the full lips. Trying to remain calm, she whispered, "Karlie, baby, what's going on? Is this because of what's happened?"

Each syllable fired a nerve, reviving memories of this magnificent woman touching her, kissing her, arousing her. The endearment only reaffirmed the depth of her feeling for Madison. Karlie clutched her arms tightly around her body, fighting the emotions enveloping her. She turned away before replying, "I needed a change. Obviously I wasn't attracting enough attention. Don't you think the anorexic look is much more in today? I'm getting all kinds of attention."

Madison briefly questioned why she had bothered to come, then acknowledged the stress Karlie was under. She was facing murder charges, for God's sake. Madison knew what she needed to do. "Karlie, can we start over? I need to talk to you and your attorney. You're in danger."

"No kidding." Karlie gathered her dignity and poise around her, determined to make the best of this awkward situation. "Come on, Madison. Isn't it a bit dramatic, riding in on your white horse to rescue me?"

"I didn't think so."

"Well, sorry, Lancelot, I'm not impressed, and I assure you my lawyer is perfectly capable of keeping me out of prison. Right now, I think the only danger is you."

Madison sighed with frustration. "Damn it, Karlie, as soon as I found out what was going on, I rearranged my whole schedule. I flew from Miami naïvely thinking I could help, and you're being a bitch."

"I don't remember inviting you or asking you for help. So you and your white horse can leave on the plane you flew in on." With as much of her pride intact as possible, she walked away from Madison.

"Sometimes you're a real pain in the ass," Madison said, following her. Standing behind the exhausted woman, she reached for the too-thin arms and felt her hands burn with the touch.

Turning abruptly, Karlie, looking up into the blue eyes she felt she could never escape. Madison's gaze was with her night and day, and sometimes she even woke in the morning as though being stared at. Reeling from the intensity of her touch, she shook herself free. "Don't," she softly pleaded.

Madison couldn't decide whether to grab her and shake her or hold on to her tightly. "Don't? Karlie, I can't help myself. I need you." Staring up at the clock, she realized how much time had passed. "Look, I've got to run. Please."

She tentatively reached for Karlie's hand. "I just need to talk to you. Give me some time tonight. Give me fifteen minutes. Then if you still want me to go away, I'll leave you alone. I promise."

Karlie held her gaze. "Fifteen minutes," she agreed wearily. "Then you have to stop whatever game you're playing."

Carl drove into the city. He was familiar enough with the route to get them quickly to their destination. "I've contacted an old friend. He's reliable and can help. He knows who, where, and how. In the last ten years there have been an increasing number of crime organizations competing for whatever turf they can steal, buy, or kill for. Many years ago it was just the Mafia. They were organized, large, and absolute power rested in few hands. There was a strange code of honor that everyone adhered to. Today these groups don't even trust members of their own organizations. That can work for us."

Madison nodded, half listening. Karlie's drastically changed appearance still haunted her. There was little of the life and spark in the woman she had seen earlier. Her mind was filled with the barely recognizable form. Gone were the soft curves she had enjoyed exploring, the soft tawny hair that aroused her at the merest touch. What was left was a shell. Madison didn't care. Somewhere, in a small part of her heart, a dim light struggled for life. Regardless of what the outside looked like, Karlie was the source of the light. Madison needed the warmth and brightness the flame provided.

The car stopping brought her back to the present. "Just wait for me," Carl instructed.

Thirty minutes later they were headed back toward their hotel, this time armed with handguns and ammunition. The weapons would be difficult to trace or link back to them. Madison dropped Carl off at the hotel, reset the GPS, and headed toward the woman she needed to see. Whatever happened in the next few days, she needed to maintain her concentration. Right now, her mind awhirl, she was unsure of how to even talk to Karlie. She knocked on her door and leaned against the frame, trying on her best cocky smile.

Karlie tried to close the door as soon as she opened it. "Ah, the bad penny. I'm sorry, but I'm not up to another ten rounds with you right now."

"You promised me fifteen minutes." Madison walked past her into the living room. "Where's my sister?"

"She ran to the store but should be back shortly." Karlie remained near the door, stubbornly declaring her opposition to Madison's presence.

Plopping herself down into the nearest chair, Madison made herself comfortable. The scenario she'd vividly replayed during her flight to New York would have landed them in bed by this point, with Karlie happy to see her after a few prickly minutes, and Madison sharing her concerns and confused feelings. So far, the scenario fell far short of the one she had pictured.

Acknowledging her untenable position, Karlie took a seat across from her and checked her watch. She folded her arms across her chest, put her feet up on the coffee table, and said, "Go. Fifteen minutes."

Madison took careful inventory of Karlie's appearance and strayed from her initial plan to get straight to the point. "Karlie, what's going on for you?" Putting up her hand to forestall any flippant answers, she said, "Look, I don't want to go back to this little war. I'm here to help, whether you believe me or not. But I'm worried. You look...ill."

Unwilling to discuss what was stressing her as much as being arrested, Karlie procrastinated. "Fourteen minutes."

"Jesus, can we have a serious conversation?"

"Thirteen minutes and thirty seconds."

Madison walked over and knelt in front of her taunter. "Look at me." She reached for Karlie's hands, "Karlie, I've missed you. I can't tell you how many times I've thought of you."

Caught off guard, Karlie was unsure how to respond. This larger-than-life woman had invaded more than her physical space. She took a deep breath and struggled to keep her hands from shaking. As she stared into Madison's disconcerting blue eyes, she felt her world tilt. *Damn you, Madison, why couldn't you just stay away? I don't want to think about you.*

Her feelings in tumult, she said, "I'm honored, and surprised, that you've thought about me at all. I doubt if it was always flattering." She smiled and tried to buffer her next words. "But it doesn't matter. Too many things have happened since we were together and I'm not the person I was a few weeks ago. And I've got too many other things to worry about," she said.

Leaning back on her heels, Madison asked gently, "Why are you always trying to make things complicated? I flew all the way up here. Doesn't that count for anything? Doesn't it tell you something?" Even as she asked the question, she felt like a huge chunk of masonry had just fallen on her head. Her behavior spoke volumes but she hadn't realized what it was telling *her*, right up until this moment. When she looked at her life, she didn't like what was reflected back.

"You're being noble?" Karlie suggested.

Madison smiled. "Why don't you give me a chance? Maybe I care about you."

A part of Karlie wanted desperately to believe the softness in Madison's eyes and the change in her tone. But she knew how vulnerable that would make her. Recognizing this fragility, she turned to the defense she trusted, pushing Madison away. "Give me a break. I know your idea of a great date is no commitment, and you've earned your reputation."

"What are you talking about?" Madison asked.

"When have you done anything to convince me I was anything but a fuck?" Tears threatened but she was determined to not let down her guard, not until Madison was gone.

"Touché." Madison knew she hadn't attempted to show Karlie she wanted more than sex from her, but that was in the past. She was here now. "I've been wrapped up in my work, with so many people and things to juggle. It's no excuse. I know that."

"Really?" Karlie glared at her. "Well, I've been a little busy myself with work and people to juggle. Oh, yeah, there's my unfaithful husband, the divorce, his death. And by the way, I'm accused of killing him."

"That's one of the reasons I'm here," Madison said.

"And I told you I'm handling it. This has nothing to do with you."

"You don't have a very good opinion of me. You're not being fair."

"Fair? That's a laugh. Who told me life isn't fair?"

Having her words continually flung back at her angered Madison. "Damn it, Karlie, I care about you. Maybe I don't show it the way you want, but I'm doing the best I can. How about giving me a break?"

"You've had your break. Now leave. Your time is up."

Running her hands through her hair, Madison said, "Okay, I'm leaving. We both need to cool off." Grabbing a piece of paper, she wrote quickly as she spoke. "Here's my hotel number and room number. You may want to call me. For your information, I have a lead on who may have killed your husband. When you get your head out of your ass, we can talk."

Throwing the scrap of paper on the coffee table, she walked away. *I ought to just pack up and fly back tonight. It's not my fault...* Her thoughts slammed into a wall of unpleasant reality. Christ, it *was* her fault that Karlie was in trouble, and Madison didn't like it. Karlie didn't deserve to suffer because she, Madison, had made some unpleasant choices. She hesitated, trying to decide how to break their impasse. She was about to make one final appeal when the door opened.

"I'm just leaving," Madison replied to her sister's unasked question and stepped back to let Dee past. Another woman followed her into the house.

The questioning look from the attractive stranger was unexpected. "Madison? Madison Barnes?"

"Yes." Who the hell was this?

Without any discussion, the woman went over to Karlie and spoke softly. "Are you okay? Sorry we weren't here."

Madison stood mesmerized. *She better get her hands off Karlie or I'll...or what?* She stared at the two women and wondered just what kind of friends they were.

"Madison, this is Sandra Bailey," Karlie said. The women gave a polite nod.

Madison barely heard what she said. When the hell had this happened? Karlie was supposedly straight. *Yeah, that's why she allowed you to fuck her. Allowed, shit, you wanted her and wouldn't take no for an answer.* Madison felt her heart begin to race. She said she wanted no commitments, and Karlie had been equally clear about looking for more? Had she found it with the woman tenderly stroking her hair as they hugged? The sight made Madison's blood rush to her head. Realizing she was winding herself up and was about to say something she would regret, she left without another word.

❖

At her hotel, Madison called Carl and arranged to meet him in the bar. "Do you ever miss being on the police force?" she asked him fifteen minutes later.

"At first I wondered what the hell I was going to do," he replied. "I was too old to go active duty, and police work was all I wanted to do after I got out of the service. A chunk of my life was gone. What pissed me off the most was that I felt my choices had been stolen from me. Then this crazy lawyer offered to represent me and help me to set up my own business." He raised his glass in a toast. "Since then I've made money and live comfortably."

"Are you happy?"

Carl twirled his glass of scotch. "These days, yes. It wasn't always so. My first marriage was a victim of my job. Then I didn't have my job. There were times when I wasn't sure I wanted to live." His smile was introspective. "But I've been given a second chance with a wonderful woman and I am not going to screw it up. I can honestly say my family has become my number one priority. How about you? Any regrets?"

Regrets? Why should she have any regrets? She made a fortune. She could have anything or anyone she wanted. *Well, almost.* "I would have said none not that long ago, but I don't know. I have everything I thought I wanted. Funny, how you get what you want and then wonder if it's been worth it. Right now, I'm trying to figure out how the hell I got where I am."

Madison rambled on but no particular answers came up. Three scotches later she knew it was time to go to bed. Looking around before speaking, she said, "We need to make sure that nothing points to Karlie when the Hidalgos go down. I'm meeting with her attorney tomorrow morning, then we go hunting."

"Madison, in all the time I've known you, we've avoided personal advice. Tell me to butt out if I'm walking on mines. I don't know what this woman is to you but..." Seeing her about to protest, he stopped her. "Wait, let me finish. What we're doing is, at best, borderline legal. At worst, criminal. If we're found out, you'll lose your license. Worse, if things go sour, you could be dead."

"I'm doing this with my eyes open, Carl."

He nodded, but insisted, "I owe you. If you leave now and let me handle this, you won't be involved. If things get rough I can handle myself, but I don't want anything to happen to you." He paused. "And you may have some personal things you need to work out."

Madison looked down into her scotch hoping an answer would suddenly appear. Her world was continuing to shift and she was unsure how to proceed. The lengthening silence finally forced her to respond, "Carl, Hidalgo threatened people I care about. I won't sit back and let something I've done cause them pain or endanger them." She paused to formulate her thoughts. "I'm not going back. I am willing to let you guide me in what we do, but I am not willing to walk away until this is over. Let me talk with Karlie's attorney first and see what happens. We'll decide what to do after that. When this is over, well, we'll see where I am with the personal things, but no matter what, I will not let it interfere with what we have to do. Deal?"

Carl nodded. "No regrets."

"No regrets," Madison agreed. "Let's get some sleep."

Before crawling into bed a little later, Madison signed on to the Internet and made reservations for her annual trip to Bali. Whatever happened in the next few days, she was determined to take her vacation and this time she was going to be gone six weeks, leaving next month, right before Thanksgiving. She wouldn't be back until after New Year's Eve. Somehow she had lost her way and she needed the peace that only Bali could offer.

CHAPTER FOURTEEN

"How did the visit to the attorney go?" Carl asked as they drove.

"Stupid pricks. So fucking righteous. They thanked me for the information, suggested I go back and talk to the cops. They even tried to explain chain of evidence to me."

"Guess they weren't interested."

"Then they said 'Don't call us. We'll call you.' At that point I left before I said something I might be sorry for."

"Hmm. Doesn't sound like things went well."

"About as expected," Madison said. "I probably would have responded the same way. But I needed to try. Now I don't feel nearly as guilty."

"When have you felt guilty for anything you've done?" Carl grinned.

"Believe it or not, I do feel some responsibility. I guess it also makes it easier to justify what we're doing."

"I don't need much of an excuse," Carl said as they turned up the driveway to the home Karlie and Rob once shared. "Nice place."

They'd driven past the place twice, making sure no one was around. The third time they turned in. Fortunately the drive curved behind the house and their car wouldn't be noticed from the road.

Carl pointed. "Police tape around the house but they haven't searched the outbuildings yet."

"I can't believe it's going to be this easy," Madison said.

"The case looks open and shut. Wife threatens husband in public place and then husband shows up dead. She doesn't have an alibi. All they're looking for is evidence that she did it. So far they haven't found the weapon. That's all they need. I'm sure Hidalgo's contractor has it stored in the area. Once he committed the crime, he probably wasn't sure what he was going to do but he needed to make people happy. He would want to have it available for further use. After he talked with his boss and with the Hidalgos, he just needed to find a way to plant it in Karlie's house." He looked around as he spoke. "Unfortunately, one, she was arrested in another jurisdiction and two, by the time he realized that he had to find another way to plant it. It's got to be around here. We just have to find it before the police do and make sure the evidence leads to the slimy brothers. Come on."

After locating the security cameras and not detecting any threats, they got out of the car and carefully searched their surroundings. Carl's contact on the local police force had given him all the information needed in order to have a good sense of the layout. Still, he said he wanted to have his own feel for the building and grounds.

"Once additional information starts showing up, the forensic team will be back up here practically tearing the place apart," he said. "Especially if drugs and money laundering are involved." He led Madison toward a small shed near the back of the property. The grounds were lined with a variety of tall trees and shrubs. Privacy was guaranteed. The shed was almost invisible. "Let's start here."

He picked the lock on the door and let the two of them inside.

"Well, look at this," Madison stared at an array of electronic devices. "I wonder what this is all about."

"Looks like some very sophisticated electronic monitoring equipment for this neighborhood. Did Karlie mention cameras or surveillance equipment?"

"No, but I didn't talk about her house."

Carefully examining the recording device, Carl put his gloves on. "A little outdated. Old-fashioned videotape." As he hit the rewind button, he watched the clock count back. "It appears to be motion activated. Well, look who we have here. That was stupid."

Madison leaned in closer. On the screen was the younger Hidalgo brother standing outside the back of the house, smoking a cigarette. A time and date stamp across the bottom showed the film was taken around the time of the murder. "This is too easy."

Carl smiled. "I'll need to erase our arrival before we leave. I'll have you pull the car around front when we're ready to leave and then reset this. Let's get in the house." Turning the unit off, he followed Madison out. "Here, put these gloves on before we go in. Don't touch anything without those on. Be careful to leave everything exactly as you found it."

Their movements were slow and deliberate, each making detailed notes about the layout and setting of each room. On the second floor Madison examined the large master bedroom. Each feature, each piece of furniture, each painting reminded her of the woman who had lived here. She ran her fingers across the edge of the bed and fought a flash of Karlie thrown back against pale cushions, her hair clinging to her damp cheeks. Everywhere Karlie was in evidence. The color, the lightness. She imagined she could smell her. Her pulse became rapid and all she wanted was to hold Karlie in her arms.

A picture of Karlie and Rob on the dresser reminded her why she was here and brought her back to the present. *Guess the husband didn't make too many changes. I wonder how long ago Karlie moved out.*

"Look here," Carl called as he opened another door. "I wonder whose computer this is." He turned to the door and called, "Hey, Barnes, we may have hit the jackpot."

Madison sat down and turned the machine on. "If we're lucky, he'll be just as stupid about computers as he was about his life. Why don't you finish looking around and I'll just surf?"

Carl nodded and continued his search. "I doubt the weapon's hidden in the house, but we better make sure.

"Looks like lots of financial data," Madison said when he returned. "This guy really wasn't very bright. It's not even password protected. He used some simplistic coding to try to hide this stuff. Some of these files look like business accounts. What's interesting is that there appears to be two sets of each account. I have a feeling he's been keeping duplicate books and helping himself to other people's money. I'm going to copy these."

"Hurry and then copy those other files on to his drive. We've been in here too long."

Madison reset the internal clock, dumped the files, and then corrected the clock. It would take a rare expert to know they were even on this machine. "I'll go move the car out to the street," she said, "while you take care of the surveillance system."

They met a few minutes later, both breathing hard. The exhilaration she felt reminded Madison of sailing. "Step one done."

"I copied the tape while you were moving the car," Carl said. "I wonder what the Hidalgos will think when they find out exhibit A shows Ramon at the scene of a murder in New York." He held the tape up with a smile of satisfaction. "I bet they'll run up here to grab the weapon. We may not have to wait long for something to happen."

"I never was patient. I wish I could see their faces when they see that tape." Madison enjoyed playing with the image of the Hidalgo brothers. She tried to focus on the tasks at hand. Concentration was the order of the day.

"They'll come looking for the original. They have to. And they'll be dangerous because they know it will tie them to the crime. We need to finish putting all the pieces in place and do it quickly. The guys will let me know when the Hidalgos leave town. Those bastards. It's taken a long time, but they'll finally pay."

Taking the tape from him, Madison added, "I have a feeling this will make New York's finest want to do a little more investigation." She planned to exact her own retribution, and it would be permanent.

❖

The shower washed away the dirt from her body but not the filth infecting her spirit. The Hidalgos had subtly drawn her into their world and no amount of washing could make Madison feel clean. She stared into the mirror as she dried her body. Unexpectedly a memory of Karlie forced itself into her consciousness and she was immediately aroused. She wanted her. Karlie's taste, her smell, her touch. Karlie on the sailboat laughing. Karlie at her parents' dinner party handling the nice, and not so nice, comments. Karlie's skin against hers.

Leaning on the sink, she took deep, slow breaths until she could focus on getting dressed. The clock read five thirty. Madison was hungry but food was not what she craved. She grabbed the car keys and headed out.

❖

Two weeks until midterms, Karlie thought as she typed the exam for her senior level literature class. Two weeks and then what? The rest of the semester.

Dee had departed on a morning flight, leaving the house as empty as Karlie's heart. She'd promised to return before the holidays, or sooner, depending on how things went with the investigation. She seemed convinced that the police would soon realize their mistake and Karlie would be cleared with an apology.

While Karlie enjoyed having Dee around and treasured the friendship, she found, this time, that she was constantly reminded of the resemblance between the two sisters. Why the hell had she ever let it go this far? Maybe Dee was right. Maybe somewhere, somehow, she'd loved Madison and the feelings had come rushing back. Or maybe she'd just needed to prove something. But what? That she could seduce her? Have power over her? Or was it about the attraction that had always unsettled her, the one she'd dismissed as a crush more than evidence of her sexuality?

Hitting the Print icon, she sent the exam to the printer. Any answer was thwarted by a knock at the door.

Opening the door, Karlie wasn't sure if she had conjured the image or if the chimera was real.

"Hi." The voice was very real. "I don't know if you've eaten or were hungry but I thought I'd buy dinner for you and your friend." Madison looked around for evidence of another person's presence. "Can I come in? It's kind of chilly out here."

Her confident grin sent Karlie's pulse into a wild gallop. She stepped aside, asking, "What are you really doing here?"

"I told you. I wanted to take you and your friend to dinner. That's all."

Karlie stood behind a chair, hoping the distance would keep her safe. "That's very generous of you, but—"

"I know…but generosity is not one of my attributes." The grin expanded. Her face was incredibly handsome. "Well, I guess I'm a little selfish. I'm hungry, and I don't want to eat alone." Her voice was husky, warm. "Or maybe I'm changing."

"Oh, can't find you some other entertainment?" Karlie returned the smile. This type of banter was familiar and easy to slip into. "Come on, you have women in every port, don't you?"

Madison shifted her weight onto the chair. "You crush me." She lifted one hand and stroked the pale cheek as she spoke. "You make me out to be some ordinary sailor. I had hoped the weekend on my boat had convinced you that I'm special. It certainly convinced me that you are."

The shift in conversation shook Karlie, but she wasn't sure why. She wanted to run away and she wanted to run into the long, tanned arms. Brilliant blue eyes spoke of hunger, raw desire.

Madison left the chair to stand only inches from Karlie, whispering, "It sounds so sexy when you say my first name. There's so much about you that I adore…your nose." Her lips brushed Karlie's nose. "Your eyes, your chin, your lips."

As she kissed each body part, she heard the intake of air that betrayed Karlie's increasing arousal. By the time Madison tasted the lips, she knew that wouldn't be enough. She needed to consume this woman and be filled by her. She needed the hope and light Karlie offered. The kiss seemed to last a lifetime then Karlie suddenly pulled away.

"I can't," Karlie gasped, trembling from the raw intensity flowing from the woman next to her. "Madison, this won't work."

A finger on her lips silenced her. Madison knew she needed to win this woman or face a life without the hope and warmth. She pulled Karlie into her arms and began to kiss her again. Gentle, tender kisses. She let Karlie lead. As Karlie's kisses grew more passionate, Madison followed. Soon Madison felt herself aroused to the point that it was almost painful. She pulled back just enough to speak. "I want you. I need you. Please let me touch you."

Karlie felt her own arousal grow, yet feared her own future. "I…"

"I want you. You, Karlie." Madison reached down and took one of Karlie's hands. "I need you. Feel how wet I am," she pleaded and then moved their joined hands down her trousers and between her legs. She groaned as she pushed Karlie's hand into her wet center.

"Oh, goddess," Karlie whispered as she leaned against Madison.

"It's you," Madison responded. "See how wet you make me."

"Yes," Karlie whispered. "Oh, yes."

"Is it okay?"

Madison's hesitation touched Karlie and sent her doubts scattering. "Well, I don't know. I haven't tried since you." The surprised look on Madison's face made her laugh. "I can assure you I'm not promiscuous. What happened between us was a complete surprise."

Taking a deep breath, Madison asked, "Are you sorry?" She was unsure if she really wanted an answer.

"No, I didn't regret it then, or now."

Breathing again, Madison asked, "Then why didn't you stay or come back with me after my parents' party?"

"Something was happening between us. Things were changing. I was changing, and I didn't know what you wanted. I realized that I was just another notch. My regret is allowing myself to begin to care for you, not what we did." Karlie hesitated and considered her next words carefully, "I found my feelings for you very intense and I couldn't stand going through being rejected. You made it clear you were into sex, not anything else. You made me feel wanted, but not needed, desired but not cherished." Averting her eyes, she asked the question that had haunted her since Madison had shown up on her doorstep. "Why are you here? Why won't you leave me alone?"

Madison stared at the thin, vulnerable woman in front of her and realized there was so much to Karlie she didn't know. Encircling Karlie with her arms, she confessed, "I can't. I don't know what this is about except that there isn't a day that goes by that I don't think about you, worry about you, wonder what you are doing. You're my oxygen. Every breath is about you. You're my sunshine and there's no life without you. There's only a dark emptiness that is cold, lonely. I don't really exist without you." She rested her cheek against Karlie's head, "I don't understand this and I've never experienced anything like this. I don't like the places I go when you're not around."

"And I thought I was the writer." Karlie stared at her. "Do you love me?"

"God, Karlie, I've asked myself that. Honestly, I don't know. Except for Dee and her family, I've never really cared for anyone. I don't have a name for what I feel. Right now all I know is that this is more than just desire. I want you. Only you. I do need you."

"I think we need to stop talking." Karlie took Madison's hand and led her to the bedroom in her small house. When she reached the bed, she faced Madison, wordlessly challenging her to prove that there really was more than a physical bond between them.

Madison instinctively knew that any hesitancy on her part might cause Karlie to bolt. She kept her eyes focused on Karlie's as she undressed her. The power of the emotions rolling through her overwhelmed her. The thought of losing Karlie was frightening. She was determined to regain control. Gently and slowly, she continued to remove garments, kissing and caressing the exposed flesh.

Karlie pulled this surprisingly gentle Madison to her and spoke softly. "Please make love to me. Even if you don't love me, make me feel as if you do." Madison started to speak but Karlie placed a hand across her mouth. "No. I don't want to know. Just make love to me."

Madison quickly shed her clothes and led Karlie to the bed. For the first time in her life, she wanted to make love, not just have sex. She leaned down and kissed the waiting lips. "That will be easy. That's all I dream about."

As Madison nibbled on her breast, Karlie put her head back and lost herself in the sensations. She allowed this woman to take her body and bring it to a place only Madison could. The hand sliding between her legs quickly buried itself in the warm, wet passion that filled her.

"Oh, Madison, please love me," Karlie cried out as she felt her orgasm begin. She clasped the woman above her and allowed Madison to feel the intensity of her orgasm. Karlie had never expected to feel this again and was overcome by her emotions. She couldn't control her tears.

Madison kissed the soft cheeks and tasted the salty tears. She stroked the thin but still beautiful face. "Karlie, sweetheart, what's the matter? Are you okay? Did I hurt you? Did I do something wrong? Please, darling, speak to me."

The incredible gentleness and the terms of endearment only intensified the feelings. Karlie struggled to speak. "No, you did everything right. I truly felt as if you were making love to me."

Madison smiled and looked around, then said, "Hmm. I don't see anyone else around. I didn't think you were into a threesome."

Karlie laughed and relaxed. "You can be a real smart-ass."

"You're the one that's the smart-ass. I thought I was the pain in the ass. Or maybe just 'that bitch.'"

"Yeah, those also apply."

"I'm crushed." She began to kiss Karlie once more. "I thought I was perfect." Karlie's groan brought a warmth to her heart. "Guess I'll just have to try harder to persuade you." Madison found the waiting lips.

For the next two hours they lost themselves in each other's bodies, each giving and receiving, sharing a special kind of passion that came from the depth of feeling each held for the other. No promises were made. No acknowledgment of the emotional strings that were slowly binding them to each other. Only the present existed. Finally Karlie fell asleep and shortly after a very relaxed Madison joined her.

When Madison awoke, it was dark, but she could tell that a set of gray eyes had been watching her for some time. "How long have I been asleep?"

"About an hour."

"Mmm. And how long have you been awake?"

"About fifteen minutes."

"And what's so interesting."

"I enjoy watching you sleep. You have this little snore."

"I don't snore."

"You do. It's a cute little snore. Hasn't anyone ever told you before?"

Madison felt awkward. She never slept with anyone, much less spent the night. She adopted a more reassured air. "I do not snore. Lawyers do not snore. It's in our code of ethics."

"Now that's the first time I've heard that one. I can see the cocky Madison is back." She lifted Madison's hands and began to kiss and suck on the fingers. "Thank you."

"You're welcome, but for what?"

"For tonight and being here. I'm sorry about the way I've talked to you. I'm not always sure how to act around you or even how you'll act around me. It's almost like there are two of you."

"I think one is enough, don't you?" Madison rubbed Karlie's back and watched her lover's eyelids closing.

"Why don't we get some sleep," Karlie said. "I'll fix you a wonderful breakfast before I have to leave for school in the morning?"

A chill embraced Madison. An old unnamed fear slammed hard into her gut and she struggled with her feelings. The familiar won out. "I would love to stay, but I have a very early meeting. Can I take a rain check on the breakfast?"

"I'll make sure you get up in time. I have to be up for school. Stay."

"Karlie, I can't."

Karlie sat up and pulled the covers around her bare chest, "Can't or won't?"

"Karlie, please," Madison pleaded. She sat up next to Karlie not caring that she was baring more than her soul.

"So help me, Madison, if this is just another one of your one-night stands, I don't ever want to see or hear from you again. I am not going to allow you, or anyone, to turn me into an emotional yo-yo."

"Karlie, I swear this is not a one-night anything. That didn't quite come out the way I planned. This is all new to me. I do know that I want you for more than one night. Probably for many nights. I'm just as confused as you are and I wish I could give you a better answer."

"Okay, Madison, what do you want of me?"

"I don't know. I need some time. I probably have no right to ask, but please just give us some time. Besides, I really have some things I've got to take care of in the morning, and then maybe we can have more than one breakfast in bed."

A wall was resurrected and Karlie felt herself letting go of the woman who was both lover and enemy. "Okay. Go. I probably need to get some sleep anyway. Could you hand me my bathrobe?"

Madison disliked the chill and silently swore. How the hell did this fall apart so fast? What the fuck did Karlie expect of her? "I'll see you tomorrow," she said as she passed the robe. "I promise I'll be back, and I never break a promise."

It wasn't much, but at least Karlie had that one promise to hold on to. "Drive safely." She struggled with her decision, frightened of the risk she was taking on a woman who seemed as unreliable as rain in the desert. "Madison, I still don't completely trust you, at least not your words. So I'll wait to see what you do."

Her honesty struck home hard, touching Madison in a tender spot she didn't know was there. "I'm not going that far away. Besides, I still want that breakfast."

Karlie merely nodded. As she closed the door to her home, Karlie tried to close the door to her heart but found it difficult to stop thinking about the blue-eyed woman who filled it. Tears ran down her cheeks as she chastised herself. "Why? Oh, Madison, I can't help myself when it comes to you. Why do we keep doing this? You better keep your promise."

❖

Karlie's house sat off the Long Island Expressway. Driving back into the city was easy with fewer cars on the road. Madison drove around for an hour, knowing she needed to sleep but restless. Finally she remembered a lesbian bar she had visited a few times when she had visited the city. Thirty minutes later she found a parking space and walked into the bar.

At two thirty in the morning, the place was still packed. The crowd seemed younger than she remembered, but she reminded herself that in the past she didn't care. Finding a place at the bar, she ordered a Chivas on the rocks.

"Strong drink," a voice purred near her. "Fits you, however."

In the mirror behind the bar Madison noticed the attractive redhead sitting to her left. Sipping her drink, she answered, "Habit, I guess. It relaxes me."

"I'm sure there are better ways to relax," the redhead promised, placing her hand on Madison's thigh.

Madison smiled but did not turn to look at the woman. *Too eager*, she thought. "Maybe, but I usually have fewer regrets with a scotch."

"Obviously you haven't had a good substitute." The woman's offer was obvious. Any other time Madison would have readily accepted. Tonight she was tired and thoughts of another woman lingered, keeping her body warm and aroused.

Getting no response, the redhead tried again. "You look like you may need some help relaxing." She renewed her strokes, trailing her nails along Madison's jean-clad thigh.

Setting down her drink, Madison sighed and gently moved the wandering hand aside. "You're probably right, and that's why I need to say good night."

The redhead reached out, but too late. Madison had already started for the door. She didn't want anyone in her bed except Karlie. And she didn't want to fuck up her chances any more than she already had.

Chapter Fifteen

I found Hidalgo's hired accomplice," Carl began as he finished his first cup of coffee. "The one who was hired to kill Karlie Henderson. The name's Larry Peck. He'll do anything for money and he had a lot of money thrown at him. This way the Hidalgos can claim they didn't do it." He poured himself another cup. "The guy lives in the city and usually leaves around nine and makes the rounds picking up a variety of payoffs. He makes his deposit around one. He grabs something to eat and then heads back to his place. If we leave soon we can get to his place, plant some listening devices, and be out of there before anyone notices."

"You think the Hidalgos will contact him before he makes his next move?"

"Well, boss, they've paid big bucks, and they'll want to manage their investment. It's amazing how careless these people are. The Hidalgos think they're fucking indestructible. That's the reason cocky punks like them generally don't live to collect social security."

"This is certainly a different side of the law."

"You've been walking both sides for some time," Carl replied. "At some point you're going to have to choose. You've never been the kind of person to be indecisive. You've got a great criminal mind and could make loads of money if you went that way."

He stopped as though to gauge her reactions.

Madison was equally curious. "That's not who I am," she said with certainty. "We're in an unusual situation and I'm doing what I have to do, but it's not a career move."

"Have you talked to Karlie yet?" Seeing Madison nod, Carl went on. "Did she say anything about the surveillance equipment out at the Hamptons house?"

"All she knows is that her husband was concerned about her being out there by herself when he had to spend time in the city, so he offered to get some security set up. I don't think she's aware of the extent."

"Does she know someone wants her dead?"

Madison shook her head. She'd decided not to share that detail. Karlie had enough to cope with.

❖

"She said what?" Karlie listened as her attorneys discussed their unexpected visitor.

"I'm sorry, but we felt we should provide you with this information," Garrison said. "This woman came in with this fantastic story and seemed reluctant to talk to the police."

"I bet. It wouldn't look good for a lawyer to admit to representing these people."

Leland Roberts, the criminal attorney, seemed surprised. "Lawyer? She never told us that. She said one of her clients had threatened you and was trying to blackmail her. We assumed she was working with a crime organization in South Florida, and we sent her away. We can't afford to ally ourselves with the criminal element."

"We should have asked more questions," Garrison said. "But she looked...seedy."

Karlie pictured Madison in her faded, baggy jeans and worn leather jacket. Obviously she didn't look like a lawyer to these men. Karlie was incredulous. Her growing feelings for Madison warred with anger over the path her life had taken. "Who are these people?"

"The Hidalgo crime family," Garrison said.

"The Mafia?" Karlie could hardly take it in. "Are you trying to tell me that my husband was killed and I'm threatened because of something Madison did that pissed off the Mafia?" She thought about the name. *Hidalgo*. It seemed familiar.

"They're not the Mafia," Garrison hastily assured her. "Just small-time organized criminals."

Karlie turned to look out the window until she could concentrate and ask a question without rancor. "What can we do?"

"We told her to talk to the police," Garrison answered, "but I doubt if she will. She appeared frustrated with the meeting and probably wanted to tell us where to go."

"I'm surprised she didn't," Karlie replied.

"We have her contact information," Leland said. "We'll talk to her again and involve the police. She won't want to implicate herself in any way, but this information could exonerate you, so we need to get it on the record."

"I'll call her. I know where she is. I'll let you know when I talk to her."

Both attorneys stood as Karlie rose. Leland Roberts stopped her. "We need to arrange protection for you, either privately or through the police. I'm afraid your husband's killer may come back for you."

Her hand on the office doorknob, Karlie thought briefly and then answered, "Organize whatever you want. I need to talk to Madison."

❖

Madison grabbed the phone on the fourth ring. She had scarcely uttered a greeting when Karlie demanded, "What the hell's going on? When were you going to tell me some jerk you do business with decided to kill my husband?"

Madison ran her hand through her wet hair and grabbed a towel. She tried to dry herself as she talked. "Karlie, I've been trying to tell you. I'll have the whole thing sorted out soon. Please, just give me a chance to explain." She grabbed her clothes and dressed as they talked.

"Explain what? That my life is at risk and you didn't bother to tell me? My attorneys think I need a bodyguard."

"Stop yelling," Madison requested. "Christ, I'm doing my best to make sure nothing happens to you. Cast your mind back. You gave me fifteen minutes to explain why I came to New York. What was I supposed to do? Just tell you some street punk has a price on your head?"

"Yes!"

"Get real. You were so angry you wouldn't have believed me. I couldn't risk that."

"Really?" Karlie's voice dripped with sarcasm. "Why? Were you worried?"

"Yes, desperately." The truth both hurt and irritated her. Madison didn't want to acknowledge what she feared. Taking a deep breath, she replied, "I thought I had to convince you that I care."

Karlie was speechless. The words were spoken with gentle tenderness. She could hear concern resonating from the other end of the line, and memories of their recent night of lovemaking flooded over her.

"Karlie? You there?"

"No, I'm in Florida." Karlie needed to distance the emotion that wanted release. She needed time to sort through the conflict.

"Can you just tell me where you are?"

"I'm five minutes from your hotel, and you better have some great explanations."

"You're coming here? I'm in room—"

"I know where you are. Just be ready to give me some answers."

A knock at the door halted conversation. "Someone's at the door. Hold on."

Carlton Best was dressed in jeans and a jacket, with gloves and a pull-down cap.

"Shit!" Madison swung the door wide to let him in.

"Not a friendly greeting. Ready to go?"

"No, can you wait?" The nod was all she needed. Returning to her call, Madison tried to think of a way to not anger the woman she was trying to win. "Karlie, look, I've got to run out. I'm going to be busy for the next few days dealing with this situation. Can I call you when I get a break?"

"If you don't talk to me now, don't bother calling."

Lowering her voice, Madison pleaded, "Karlie, I've done some not so nice things in my life, but when I make a promise, I keep it. I promise I'll explain all this to you and somehow make it up. Just give me a couple of days. Believe me, I wish I could turn back the clock and make this go away. Please? Give me a few days?"

Karlie's heart felt the plea while her mind tried to dissuade her. Her heart won. "I don't know why I'm even talking to you. You better have a great explanation. And if you don't keep your promise..."

A huge smile grew on Madison's face. Sighing, she answered, "I'll answer anything you ask and then some."

The conversation quickly ended and Madison and Carlton were headed to start their vigil.

Karlie managed to turn the car around and head back home. She hoped she wasn't going to end up regretting allowing Madison Barnes back into her life.

❖

On the first full day of listening, Carl and Madison were rewarded. The New Yorker was initially pleased to hear from his generous benefactor but was quickly defending his actions. News of the tape had reached Lawrence Hidalgo, and he was not happy.

"Look, I'll fix it. I'll find that goddamned tape and get rid of it."

"What else is left around? What did you do with the gun? I told you to get rid of the bitch, not her husband. If anything happens to my brother, your life will not be worth anything. Where the hell is Damien?"

They could hear the man's breathing change as he spoke. "I assure you the bitch will pay. I'll make sure of it. I've already got things figured out. I can get in touch with Damien and we will finish this."

"How the hell do I know you two won't screw things up worse than they already are?" Hidalgo stormed back. "It's your fucking neck."

"It's under control, man. Don't worry. She's gonna drown in her swimming pool. It'll look like suicide."

Silence on the other end, then finally a threatening voice came over the phone. "Listen, you idiot. I didn't pay for mistakes. I want that tape in my hands in twenty-four hours, or I assure you there will be two bodies in that pool. Do it quickly, and no mistakes. I don't want to have to take care of this myself."

The man swore as he hung up. More noise issued from the apartment. Sounds of objects being overturned were easily heard on any of the listening devices. Anger and fear were powerful motivators.

Madison was ready to jump out of the car. "Okay, now what? I can't let him go after her."

"Hold on. I'm calling a good friend on one of the local PDs. He's actually stationed near where your friend lives. I bet he'd love to be the one to get the collar and solve this. The newspapers have made this a big-time case, even for New York City."

He finished dialing and waited for someone to pick up. "Randy, Carl Best. Yeah, I told you I'd stay in touch. Got a minute? You know the Stockard case?" He chuckled then continued, "Yeah, that's the way it looks, but I have some info that the wife is being set up."

"Tell him about the pool," Madison urged.

With a look of forbearance, Carl continued providing details. "They plan on making it look like suicide. I can't give you details of how I know, but if someone were to examine the outbuildings at the Stockard place out on the Island, they might have the same information I have. And anyone watching the wife's house might also capture someone breaking and entering."

He agreed to meet an officer at Karlie's house before hanging up.

"Well?" Madison asked.

"Randy is on his way out to the Stockard place on Long Island. We have to be very careful, especially with the IAB and the state task force. Randy knows all about it. He's making sure someone else will meet him out there so no questions can be raised about the evidence when they find the tape. There's joint jurisdiction that way. Once Randy finds the tape and sees what's on it, he'll be hot to get in on the arrest. He'll organize the stakeout and I'm betting the Hidalgos will be here before the sun goes down. We need to convince Karlie to work with us."

"Let's do it, then." Madison pulled the gun from inside her jacket, checked the safety, and replaced it.

"Hold on, I want to see where this jerk is going first. I don't think he'll do anything until tonight, but I would like to see if he's going to contact anyone."

"Carl, I can't."

"Trust me, we'll be there in plenty of time. We just need to make sure there are no loose ends."

❖

"I don't trust him," Lawrence said as he hung up the phone. He shook his head. "I've always hoped you would become my second in command, and here I am still cleaning up after you."

Ramon tried to assuage his doubts. "I'll take care of it. I'll go now."

"No, little brother, it's too late. We'll both go. I have no intention of letting that bitch lawyer get the best of me again. I want that damn tape and we will take care of her little whore. No mistakes this time. Come on, we need to get to the airport quickly. I can get a private plane to take us to New York. No one will know we've been there."

❖

"There he goes," Madison said. "He's hailing a cab." She started the car.

"Just leave at least one car between us for now." She nodded and pulled out. In a few minutes they stopped at a tenement in Brooklyn. The man they had been following jumped out of the cab and ran into the building. A few minutes later two men exited the building and got into the cab.

"That must be Damien," Carl uttered. "Matches the guy with Ramon on the tape. The guy we're following is Larry Peck. I suspect they're both part of the same gang. Didn't think we could catch both fish together."

"Should we call the police?"

"Not yet. Let's see where they're going next."

After about thirty minutes they were headed out on the Long Island Expressway toward the end of the island. "Shit," Carl spat, "we're headed back toward the Stockard place. I can't believe this. I bet he left the gun somewhere out there. Hidalgo would not be pleased to realize how stupid these guys are."

"We can't let him get it."

"I doubt if he'll have a chance. I'm going to call Randy and give him a heads-up."

As they followed the cab back toward the house, they immediately saw the police car parked out front. The cab just drove on by. "I bet that is one pissed son of a bitch," Carl smiled. "Randy's a good man...and prompt."

"What do you think they'll do now?"

"If Damien left the weapon there, he's in deep trouble because now he has to use another one to kill your friend. The link between her and the murder is gone. Even if the police do find the weapon, it won't have her prints on it. Let's get to Dr. Henderson's."

Madison turned around and headed back to the Long Island Expressway and toward the city. "What makes you think they won't try to attack her at her house instead of the mansion?"

"We don't know. The fact that they're talking about drowning makes me think they didn't know about her other house initially.

By now, they will. The address has been in the papers. I'm guessing they'll force her out to the Hamptons and then drown her in the pool."

They would be at Karlie's in about twenty minutes. Apprehension filled Madison. Fear for her own life was nothing compared to the terror she felt when she thought of the threat Karlie faced. She would not relax until she was sure Karlie was safe and this was over. Carl's words offered little consolation.

Carl put his phone away and said, "The Hidalgos just took off in a private plane. Supposed to be going to Chicago, but I doubt that's where they're headed. We need to be on our toes."

As she nodded acknowledgment, Madison desperately needed to see Karlie, to touch her, to hold her to reassure herself that she was safe. The closer she got the faster she drove. The threat level had risen.

"This is it," she said as she turned into the driveway. Karlie's car was already parked.

An angry person answered the door. "Madison! I'm so angry I could…"

"Karlie," Madison stepped aside and allowed Carl to enter, "this is Carlton Best. He's a private investigator from Miami. Carl, Dr. Karlyn Henderson."

"Pleased to meet you. Ms. Barnes told me you're the writer Karlyn Henderson. My wife has read every one of your novels. In fact, she sometimes reads to me at night."

"Thank you, but if you will forgive the lack of pleasantries, I need to talk to this woman now."

Madison was quick to answer. "The police will be arriving here soon. We need to talk before they arrive."

"Oh, great, what now?" Karlie showed her guests into the living room and sank onto the couch.

Madison rushed over and sat next to her. "What's wrong? Are you okay?"

"I guess I should ask you the same thing. I go to my attorney's office and learn that you've been there telling them you are responsible for this whole mess. How do you think I'm feeling? So why are the police coming here? Am I being arrested again and put in jail, or are they coming after you?"

"No, they're not coming for you."

"Dr. Henderson, I hate to interrupt," Carl said, "but your life may be in imminent danger. That's why the police are coming here. The people who killed your husband are after you. We think they'll make another attempt, probably tonight."

Karlie stared incredulously. When she could finally find her voice, she said, "If this is some kind of sadistic joke, I am not in the mood. I thought you were *taking care of the situation*."

"I'm afraid she's telling the truth," Carl replied. "We need to get you out of here for a couple of days." Before he could continue, someone rang the doorbell. He pulled out his gun, released the safety, and then put it back in the shoulder holster. "I'll get it. It's probably the police, but we need to be safe in case it isn't."

Karlie sat immobile, as frightened by the thought of a gun in her house as the supposed threat on her life.

The investigator carefully opened the door. "Good to see your old face." He extended his hand.

"You aren't looking that great either, old man." The new arrival shook his hand, then stepped aside and introduced another man. "This is Dave Marsh. Meet Carlton Best."

Carl led them to the living room and introduced his friend as Sergeant Randy Baskin, a plainclothes detective. Introductions over, Baskin put on his professional face.

"Carl, we need some answers. We found the shed well camouflaged on the back part of the property. All kinds of electronic surveillance equipment was inside, including videotapes showing anyone entering or exiting the house. The tapes are time and date stamped. On one of the tapes there were two men at the crime scene about the time of the murder. Who are they?"

"The short-haired guy is a local gun for hire named Damien. He hangs out with Larry Peck. We believe he runs payoffs and occasionally does some hit work. The other guy is Ramon Hidalgo, the brother of the leader of a drug operation in South Florida. The

Hidalgo brothers have been in lots of trouble but have always managed to walk. Mostly small time stuff. They're not a big operation, but the Miami-Dade police would like to put them out of business. We overheard Damien planning the fake suicide."

"I don't suppose that was a legal eavesdropping? Never mind. We've already got crime scene out there."

Carl grinned. "Let's just say we happened to be standing on a good street corner."

"Sure. Go on with your story."

"This local guy isn't too bright. He was planning on using the same gun her husband was killed with. We followed him this afternoon back out to the crime scene. Unfortunately, you were already there. He must have hid the weapon out there. When he tried to recover it today, he got a surprise. I'm betting he's panicked."

"We found the gun. What makes you think he'll still try for the hit?"

"He's under pressure." Madison jumped into the conversation. "If he doesn't deliver, he's dead and he knows it. The Hidalgo brothers are ruthless. They want results and they want it now."

Baskin mulled over her words before asking, "How do we know it will happen? Why won't he just run?"

"These guys are stupid and careless, but they are probably smart enough to know they can't run far enough. Besides, if these two piss off these guys in Miami, Hidalgo will make sure no one in New York hires them. Hidalgo has money and will want hits out on anyone associated with this so that there are no witnesses. No place to go."

Madison was becoming impatient. "Now can we get down to what we're going to do about this?"

"Randy," Carl said, "believe me, this guy's coming. To top it off, we think the Hidalgos are on their way. They left Miami in a private plane about twenty minutes ago, supposedly heading for Chicago."

"Look, I'm out on a limb here. I trust you. I found the tape and a gun. Now I have to explain the additional search at the scene to my captain. You want me to believe another murder is going to be committed, I need more than your word. We're crossing jurisdictions."

Carl didn't blink. "I placed listening devices in Peck's apartment and we heard him tell the Hidalgos this morning what he was planning to do."

Baskin let out a sigh. "You know that's inadmissible. How am I supposed to go after this guy?"

"You won't have to," Carl answered before lowering his voice. "He's coming here. We're in your jurisdiction now. Randy, we know about the IAB investigation of the other district." Carl gave his friend a condensed version of the information he had obtained.

"Hell, Carl, you always end up in these messy plots. We've heard rumors of something going on in that precinct. We had a guy transfer to our precinct because he didn't like what some of his coworkers were doing. If IAB is involved, I've got to talk to my chief."

"He's got to try tonight. Hidalgo won't wait another day, especially if he and his brother are on their way here." She exchanged a look with Karlie, whose pale face and speechless shock told her all she needed to know. "We move Karlie to someplace safe and wait. Damien and Peck will be impatient, and they don't know they're about to have visitors. They don't want the Hidalgos up their ass."

"Help me here," Randy Baskin said. "What do I tell my chief? I'm supposed to do what? Stake out this place for who knows how many days based on illegally obtained evidence? How am I going to sell that? He's not going to want an investigation if IAB is involved."

"I don't care how the fuck you sell it." Madison was furious. "If you're not going to do anything, then get the hell out of here. We'll take care of this ourselves."

"Look, miss." Baskin was determined to exert his authority. "You are not the law around here. You do anything and I find out, I will personally arrest you. This is *my* neighborhood." Warning flashed from his brown eyes.

Carl stepped between them, trying to lesson the antagonism. He cared about both of these people, but he knew they were both single-minded. "Randy, we'll get Dr. Henderson out of here. If you'll just trust us for a little longer. If he's not here tonight, we'll go away. Can you do me this favor? Just tonight?"

Baskin looked between the two and nodded. "Until tonight. Let me get some help, and you two get the lady out of here."

They shook hands and moved their discussion outside.

Madison sat down on the couch next to Karlie. "Is there someplace you could stay tonight?"

"With you." Karlie laughed thinly.

"I wish." Madison kissed her tenderly. "But this isn't a game. I'd love to have you with me but I need you someplace where most people wouldn't think of looking for you."

Adopting a more somber tone, Karlie answered, "Sandy's, I guess."

"Sandy?" *That* woman?

"Yeah, we work together at the university. We're good friends but only a few people at the university realize how close we are. She's not that far. What's going on?"

"Get some clothes and let's go." Madison didn't want to think about Karlie with her colleague. Even if it was innocent. She didn't want to share her with anyone. "I'll wait for you outside."

As Karlie walked into her bedroom, pieces of the puzzle began to fall into place. Some idiot wanted to kill her because this Hidalgo person was mad at Madison. It made no sense. Why her? Why not Madison's family? She slammed clothes and personal items into an overnight bag.

"I need to have my head examined," she told Madison as they left the house. "I can't believe I am going along with this crazy plot."

❖

Karlie looked at the kitchen clock. It was barely seven o'clock and already it had been a long day. She stared down at the coffee cup and wondered when the pieces of her life would be in one place, much less put back together. Sandy and Marge had made her welcome. Seeing the love and commitment of the two women made her wonder what it would be like being in a real relationship with Madison. She couldn't imagine it, perhaps because the idea was pure fantasy. Madison wasn't the type who settled down.

"Do you want to talk?" Sandy cautiously asked.

Karlie's voice broke. She let the tears out. "I'm sorry I'm such an emotional wreck."

Sliding into the chair next to her, Sandy said, "Don't. You know there is never a need to apologize." She reached across to the tissue box on the counter, moving it to the table. "Is there anything I can do?"

Marge brought tea from the kitchen. This kindness made Karlie's tears flow even more freely.

Karlie tried to control her breathing as she spoke. "I see the two of you and realize how alone I am. How alone I've been for some time. Confusing, isn't it."

There were too many emotions and too many memories. When calmness finally began to descend upon her, she was slapped with the memory of Madison's parting words as they'd walked to Sandy's door: *We're going back to wait for the guy who killed Rob. If we're lucky, the idiots from Miami will also show up. Whatever happens tonight, I'm so sorry and I want you to know I love you.*

Karlie almost keeled over. Grabbing Sandy's arm, she croaked out, "Oh, God. She thinks she's going to die."

CHAPTER SIXTEEN

Madison and Carl were back at the house within an hour. "How long do you think we'll need to wait?" Madison asked.

"Tonight. Peck's life expectancy is based on how quickly he completes his job. So he's fucking scared. Damien has got to be in a panic now that he knows he is on tape and the Hidalgos are after him. I'm guessing the only way these two think they can redeem themselves is to take Karlie out quickly and get the tape."

"Having the police out at the Hamptons must have put a crimp in their plans," Madison said.

"You bet. These guys will do whatever is necessary to keep the Hidalgos in Miami." Carl looked around as they drove. "This isn't their usual neighborhood. Probably don't want to be around here when it starts to get light. Too much of a risk of being seen and remembered. It's got to be anywhere from around ten tonight to five in the morning."

"I hope those slimeballs are scared shitless."

"They are and that's what will cause them to be careless. These are locals, and they've already shown they're not very smart."

"We're almost there," Madison said. "I don't think we're being followed." She'd been carefully watching her rear and side view mirrors as she took a circuitous route. "God, Carl, this is a fuckup."

"The Hidalgos are fuckups. The idiots they hired are worse. We're just the cleanup crew."

Trying to feel some of his confidence, Madison said, "Thanks for all you're doing and have done. I just better make sure you get home to your wife or else I better not turn up at all."

She pulled into one of the many nondescript alleys that marked the older neighborhood. They found a place to hide the car close to the house and set off on foot, remaining in the shadows for several minutes to make sure no one was watching. The shadows provided cover, and the poor lighting created enough dark places to hide if necessary.

"The sounds around you," Carl whispered, "are just as important as anything you see." Less than a hundred feet from the house they crouched for several minutes in the dark, and he continued in a voice barely loud enough for Madison to hear, "Close your eyes and listen to the sounds around you. If anything sounds out of place or unusual, be alert and don't move."

Madison slowed her breathing and listened. Somewhere a dog was barking, not a threatening or attacking bark. More the sound of a dog playing in a yard. A metallic sound nearby signaled someone putting the trash out. The lid went back down. She waited and heard a door open and close. The smell of fish cooking reached her. *Damn, amazing the things you can smell and hear when you pay attention.*

Quiet settled and they inched toward the back door, their footsteps muffled by the night sounds. A few feet from the house they squatted near some bushes, their dark clothes absorbing and melting into the darkness. *A window must be open! I can hear the radio. I forgot it was on earlier.* Again they waited. When Carl nodded, they moved to the back door. Carefully inserting the key Karlie had given her, Madison slowly turned the knob and pushed the door open, allowing Carl to slip in first. Not sensing any danger, she too slipped in and gently closed the door. A soundless entry.

The kitchen was still and there was enough light they could easily see. Carl motioned her to stay there while he completed the search. A few minutes later, he returned with the all clear. "Well, I guess we can turn on the lights and wait. Might as well grab something to eat. It could be a long night."

Earlier they'd agreed on their plan. Madison would hide in the shadows in the living room providing guard for the front door. The most likely entry for the New Yorkers would be through the back of the house. Carl would wait in the hallway between the bedrooms and kitchen, where he could see and hear anyone trying to come in. At the same time he could easily cover Madison's back. Officers Baskin and Marsh would patrol the neighborhood at the top of the hour. If the front light was out they would come in. If Madison or Carl called, they could be there in ten minutes or less depending on their location. Their chief wasn't wild about the plan, but he didn't want another murder if he could stop it. Reluctantly he had given Baskin and Marsh the go-ahead for one night of surveillance.

"If, for any reason, things get out of control, I want you to get out of here and make sure you call Baskin," Carl ordered.

"Damn it, Carl, I'm not leaving you here."

"Madison, I'm not asking you to leave," he said. "Just call in the reinforcements. No hotdogging. We're in my court now. Understand?"

"I've learned a lot from you in the last few days, but I'm no idiot. I want to live." She took a deep breath before continuing. "That said, I think I can take care of myself, but I promise not to do anything stupid. Carl, if something happens…"

He stopped her. "In our outfit we had one commandment: *Thou shalt only think good things.* Just in case something happened, we all wrote last letters anytime we were sent out, regardless of the mission. We just thought it bad luck to think anything bad would happen. Whenever we headed out on a special op, we always promised we'd see each other later. Whoever got back last bought drinks." Smiling at her, he added, "In this case, I think we'll both be buying a round."

"Done." Still, there was a part of Madison that worried. Twice she sat down to write a letter but couldn't think of anything to say. Finally she just wrote, *Karlie, I love you.* She put it in an envelope and wrote Karlie's name across it. She tucked it into one of her pockets, sure someone would find it in the event…

The evening seemed to pass slowly. They sat and continued to talk. Quietly they covered a variety of topics except one: what was going to happen tonight. Each got up periodically and walked around so that anyone looking in would notice a solitary figure walking through the house. The windows were closed and locked and the curtains were drawn, but still a shadow could be seen.

Around ten, Carl suggested they turn off the inside lights and thus they began the hardest part of their vigil, silent waiting. He crouched in an L-shaped corner at the junction of the large kitchen and the hallway to the bedrooms. He had clear view of the hallway but a slightly obstructed view of the kitchen. He could not see Madison at all, but needed only to take a couple of steps to have complete line of sight of the front part of the house. Darkness hid him well.

For Madison, waiting was what others did. This seemed the longest night of her life, and only thirty minutes had passed. She kept shifting around and trying to find some position where her legs didn't go to sleep. *How in the hell do I sit still?* Pulling the couch away from the wall just enough to stretch her legs when she needed, she carefully positioned herself so that the couch obscured her yet enabled her to easily see anyone at the front door. She also had a clear view of the windows in this portion of the house. She removed her gun, released the safety, and sighted. She had a clear shot at the front door. Assured she was settled, she carefully placed the gun on her knee and waited. *Breathe,* she reminded herself.

Fatigue threatened but she fought back by remembering why she was doing this: Karlie. The last hours had driven home the intensity of her feelings. She knew she would have to deal with these when…if this was over, and she made it out alive. *What an asshole I've been. Please forgive me, Karlie. I should have written that in the letter. No, you're going to tell her in person. Remember that.*

A few minutes after midnight the sounds of the night changed. Slow-moving footsteps carelessly scuffing gravel and leaves could be heard approaching the house. Madison was immediately alert. She controlled her breathing as she heard the steps approach the back door. The door handle rattled. She was sure it was their much-awaited visitors. As she listened she thought she heard only one set of footsteps. *Where is the other guy?*

Next came the sound of a clumsy and ineffective attempt to pick the lock. More and more she appreciated what she was learning from Carl. Although he was coming in the back of the house, she remained where she was. Gently she released the safety on the gun and remained still. There were no sounds anywhere but at the back door and it continued to sound like one person—whoever it was. She would not move unless necessary or when it was safe. She carefully lifted her gun and prepared to fire, but only when she was sure of her target.

The sound of breaking glass confirmed the point of entry.

Patience. One step at a time.

❖

"What do we do now?" Ramon asked as he parked the rental car. "We've been following this idiot for thirty-five minutes. Why do you suppose he dropped Damien off?"

"What do we do? We make sure it's done right. We kill Peck and the whore. Then we go after Damien. These are a bunch of losers. How the hell did you find them? This prick has not even noticed us following him. Right now he is probably going in the back door. We will wait a few minutes and then go in after him. You will take the back and I will take the front." Lawrence Hidalgo got out of the car and waited for his brother to come along side. "Ramon, no mistakes tonight. Don't hesitate. Just kill the blond whore. We kill him with another gun, put it in her hand, then we get out of there. If anyone hears the shots, the police will be called. We don't want to be around."

"Okay, I got it."

"No, Ramon you don't get it, and that's the problem. No more mistakes. Now we will go back around to the alley until we get to the house. No talking unless absolutely necessary."

The two brothers moved swiftly into the shadows between two

houses. Fortune smiled on them. They were not noticed. As they slipped into the darkness, they moved cautiously while approaching their target.

Lawrence pulled his brother close to him and whispered, "We will wait a little and then go in." He looked down at his watch and they both moved into protected shadows.

❖

The steps were close. A shadowy form walked through the kitchen; Carl slowed his breathing, gently eased to a standing position, and counted the footsteps. He knew exactly where the intruder was. In another five steps Carl would be able to take him down. *I hope you stay put. Four. Come on. Three. You're almost there. Two.* Carl lifted his gun up and flattened further against the wall. He had the element of surprise, always a big advantage. The footsteps had stopped so close he could smell the man and hear his breathing. *Come on. One more and you're mine.* The intruder moved forward and an arm came into view, a gun held in the extended hand.

Carl grabbed the arm, stepped in front and threw the man on the floor. The man's gun went flying. "Don't move." His voice was ominous, "Don't even think about moving. Put your hands out in front of you."

Seeing a hand searching for the gun, he stomped quickly on the outstretched fingers, hearing bones break. Quickly he turned on the kitchen light and pointed the gun at the man's temple. "Next move and I start shooting." When the man hesitated, Carl grabbed his uninjured hand and twisted it behind him. "Okay, Barnes, call Randy."

❖

"Wait, something's wrong." Lawrence grabbed his younger brother and pulled deeper into the shadows.

"What's the matter?" Ramon asked.

"The light is on."

"So?"

"God Almighty. You don't turn on the lights when you break into a house."

"Maybe he's got her and is looking for something to tie her up with."

Lawrence looked at his brother and began to believe he would never fit into the family business. "Then he is more stupid than you, little brother. We need to wait a little longer."

❖

Madison called Randy Baskin and alerted him. "They're only a couple of blocks away," she informed Carl. "They just started to cruise the neighborhood." She decided to wait in the living room for the two police officers, stretching to ease the tingling from sitting still for so long.

"Who the hell are you?" Larry Peck asked.

"No questions," Carl warned. "Just answers. Like who are you working for?"

"I'm not saying nothin'."

Carl shot Peck's foot. "Forgot the gun was loaded. I just hate when that happens." The silencer had muffled the shot but not the scream of pain from the injured man.

"You can't do that." Peck's angry howl echoed through the kitchen. "You're crazy."

"I can do anything I want." Carl laughed and raised his gun, "until the police get here."

Any further questions were halted by the arrival of Sgt. Randy Baskin. Madison opened the front door for the officers. "We have one of them."

❖

"Damn that bitch," Lawrence Hidalgo swore. How the hell did the little whore do it? He was determined that the job would be finished this night. The police car arriving infuriated him. "We can't let them take him in. He'll testify."

"How do you know he hasn't talked already?" Ramon asked.

"It doesn't matter. Don't you understand that? Sooner or later he will give them our names. That's why we have to get rid of all of them. They can't leave here alive."

"They're cops. If we take out cops in New York, we will never hear the end of it. Even the local people won't work with us."

Lawrence stared, amazed. "I don't give a flying fuck who will or won't work with us, you stupid idiot. None of this would have happened if you had not gotten into trouble. Now shut up and make sure your gun is ready. Do you even know how to use it?"

Ramon nodded. "They cannot come out, do you understand? Too many possible witnesses. We have to take care of them while they are inside. They are in the front of the house." Lawrence had watched the living room lights go on when the police arrived. "You take the back and make sure no one comes out. I will go in the front and take out the cops."

"We're outnumbered," Ramon protested.

"They probably just have handguns. With this," he clutched his semiautomatic weapon, "I can take them out before they realize they are dead." Grabbing his brother by the shirt front, he added, "No one comes out alive. Do you understand?"

Ramon nodded, too terrified to object again.

"You will make sure the blonde is dead? You fucked this up and you need to get rid of her. Understand?" Lawrence pushed him toward the back of the house. "I'll go in and take care of the cops then we'll get the blonde."

Rage blinded him to anything except seeing Barnes suffer. When he got back to Miami, he would personally provide her with details of her girlfriend's death. He wished he had a camera or that he could bring the whore's head back with him.

❖

Randy Baskin pulled the suspect up off the floor and into a chair. "You want to talk to us now, or maybe we have to go out to the car and call the station for a few minutes."

"Look, don't leave me here with this crazy man. He'll kill me."

"I guess you better say something fast, because I think I need to call this in."

Larry Peck needed no further prodding. He gave detailed information, enough to put the Hidalgos away for a long time in the New York state penal system. Damien's location was also freely given. Randy and his partner quickly took notes just to make sure they had enough information to put a solid case together. With IAB around, they didn't want any problems coming their way. This had to be squeaky clean.

"Get up. We're taking you in," Baskin said.

The sound of someone outside the back of the house raised an alarm. "Wait!" Carl warned, turning off the kitchen lights. "Douse the lights," he urged in a harsh whisper.

Madison hesitated momentarily, then blindly obeyed. Baskin reached over and turned off the other lamp lighting up the front of the house. Unsure what was happening, Madison leaned back against the wall, trying to melt into the shadows. She remembered her lesson: listen. Officer Marsh, however, had already opened the door only to find an armed gunman filling the entrance. Baskin reached for the younger officer's arm and tried to pull him back. Hidalgo began shooting. The young officer went down. Baskin barely removed his gun when he was hit. He landed on the floor and rolled out of the line of fire.

"You stupid prick!" Madison yelled. She'd been sure the Hidalgos would show up sooner or later. She was not prepared, however, for this confrontation.

The sound of her voice sent Lawrence Hidalgo into a frenzy. All previous sense of caution was abandoned. "Where are you, you bitch?"

Lawrence was a man now incapable of reason. He sprayed

the room with rapid fire. At the first shots, Madison retreated to the safety of the kitchen, aware he couldn't see her. She couldn't leave the two officers unprotected, so she fired blindly trying to give them time to get to safety.

Peck was astonished by his good fortune and tried to stand to thank his rescuer. As he got up, he shouted, "You saved me."

Turning to the sound of the male voice, Hidalgo continued firing, "Yes, I'll save you from yourself. You'll make no more mistakes," he said as he killed the unarmed man. "Come on, Ramon, where the hell are you?"

As soon as the door opened, Carl had dropped to the floor in the hall and pulled himself out of the line of fire. He wouldn't have a shot until Hidalgo paused. Someone was coming into the back of the house. Ramon Hidalgo had crept through the open back door. There was no way Madison would notice him.

Carl shouted, "Madison, behind you." At the same time, he tucked and rolled into the kitchen.

Ramon saw only the dark-haired woman. He had to redeem himself, and this would be the way to do it. He raised his gun and fired, hitting her in her left arm. He smiled as he watched her spin around. Like so many things in his life, he underestimated his opponent and overestimated his own skills. Too late, he noticed the gun in the woman's right hand. Her reflexes were quick, accurate, and fatal. Ramon was dead before he hit the ground.

"Good shooting," Carl whispered, "but we still have the other brother."

The house was ominously quiet. Baskin had managed to pull himself and his seriously wounded partner behind some cover, but they couldn't wait forever. Officer Marsh had lost a lot of blood. His radio had fallen somewhere near, but Baskin wouldn't be able to retrieve it without moving into the open. Any movement would reveal his position.

Madison signaled to Carl that she was okay. The bullet had grazed her arm. It burned like hell but she was still able to shoot. The adrenaline had kicked in with the breaking glass. The wound felt more like a bad paper cut. Only later would she feel the sting. They slowly leaned around their corners to search, but Lawrence Hidalgo had cleverly used the dark and the furniture to hide his presence.

From the living room they heard, "I will never leave you alone."

"Then I guess I have to kill you like I did your shithead brother."

Distant sirens did not register with Lawrence. Instead the words of the hated woman further enraged him. "You are stupid if you think you can get me to come out by telling me such a ridiculous story."

"Someone called the cops," Carl whispered. "How're you doing?"

"Okay."

"Try to keep him talking and I'll try to figure out where the hell he is."

"Got it," she quietly answered. "Hey, Lawrence," she shouted into the darkened living room, "come on in, then, and get this lifeless hunk of shit. He's never looked so good." She watched Carl maneuver so that he could see clearly into the living room and find Hidalgo. "What are you waiting for?"

Carl slid around the corner and squeezed in behind a chair. He saw Marsh on the floor bleeding. Nearby, Baskin was sitting in a corner wounded. He feared Lawrence Hidalgo would somehow slip away. Feet scurrying behind him worried him, but the only person it could be was Madison. What the hell was she up to? If he called out, he would mark his position and he could be vulnerable. He had to trust she knew what she was doing. It was only when he saw movement at the front door he realized what she had done. She was setting herself up as a target to get Hidalgo out in the open.

"Hey, shitface. You want me? Come out and get me." She ducked and moved out onto the lawn.

From his concealed position near the door, Lawrence leapt up and darted out after her. When Madison turned the corner to go around the house, he opened fire. The bullet entering her left shoulder took her down to the ground but not out of the fight. Adrenaline coursing through her body kept her moving. Ignoring the pain, she rolled to her right and lifted her gun. Her vision blurred. She struggled but managed to aim. Before she could pull the trigger, she saw Lawrence go down.

She lowered her gun and allowed her body to relax. Her reserve was gone and now a bone-deep weariness engulfed her. He was down. It was over. *Everything will be okay. I just need to rest. Karlie's safe. I'll just rest for a while.* She put her head down on the ground. *It's getting cold. Where's my coat? Maybe if I sleep.*

❖

Madison lay on the grass with a fire burning in her back. She tried to sit up, but Carl pushed her back. "What about the Hidalgos?" she was barely able to speak.

"They're not going anywhere," Carl assured her. "Lawrence is dead. With that shot of yours, the brother is, too. You're a damned good shot. Even I'm impressed."

The bleeding had stopped, but Madison had become cold and clammy and her breathing was uneven. She knew she was going into shock. Carl pulled off his jacket and covered as much of her as he could. He kept talking trying to keep her awake. More flashing lights filled the night sky and she could hear voices coming up behind them.

"Just hang in there," Carl repeated over and over. "The ambulance is here."

CHAPTER SEVENTEEN

Carl walked into Madison's hospital room. She was sitting up staring out the window. "You're looking better. Ready for a beer?"

"I'm ready to get out of here and leave this city behind me."

"What about your friend?"

"She's safe. I need to get away from her. I need to get away from this fuckup."

"You ought to talk to her before you run out. I know. It's none of my business, but running never solves anything, Madison. It is decision by indecision. Remember when you told me that?"

"Shut up and stop being so smug." She managed a smile, even though it was very brief.

"The best thing you said to me was to not hide. It saved my life." Carl hesitated briefly. "She deserves an explanation."

"Goddammit, Carl, she deserves to live a decent life and not have to worry about crazy people coming after her for something someone else did." The burst of anger drained her. "When we started this I wondered if I would be able to shoot a gun at a human being. I had no doubts about my ability, but I did about my willingness."

When she looked up at the man who had walked with her through this personal hell, she wondered how many people he'd killed. She had now killed one.

"You acted in self-defense," Carl said. "You didn't invite these men to commit crimes of violence."

"Didn't I?" Madison thought about the times she'd made sure men like Hidalgo walked away from criminal convictions. "I never thought about whether or not I would shoot when I heard your warning. I wanted the shot to have maximum effect. I wanted him dead. I didn't even know he had hit me until I got to the hospital and looked at the blood on my arm." She looked down at her right hand and again felt the pull of the trigger. Not looking up, she asked, "Do you ever forget?"

In a muted voice, Carl answered, "Never."

Madison took a few minutes to tread through the mud of her chaotic emotions, knowing he'd been there. The silence was punctuated only by the ticking of the second hand on the wall clock.

"Are you going to try to talk to her?" Carl finally asked.

She picked at the sheet and wondered how to answer. Her reply was the only answer she had come up with. "What the hell can I say? I don't understand how this whole thing got so out of control. Both my sister and brother-in-law recently accused me of not thinking or caring how my actions affected other people. I thought they were crazy because I always prided myself on my thoroughness. They were right. When I lose my temper, I don't care what I say or do. How the hell am I supposed to explain it to her? I don't know if there is anything I can say or do that will ever help her understand. Her husband was killed."

"Why don't you start by explaining what's going on with you?"

The physical wounds were not life threatening, but the emotional ones were. Madison glared at the man standing by her hospital bed. "There is nothing going on with me. Now, just give it a rest."

She turned away not wanting to be reminded of the last few days. She needed to learn to control her temper and her actions. What was it Karlie said? Something about judging her on what she *did*?

"What are you going to do, then?"

"Go home. Sleep. After that, I don't know. I've got my annual vacation planned. I'll get the hell out of town where I won't have to worry about anyone or anything. Just sit in the sun, drink a few beers, and try to find myself." She laughed, but it was more a bitter, denigrating snicker. "God, I sound like some college kid who goes into senior year not knowing what to major in."

"No, you just sound like someone who needs a vacation. Remember I've been there, done that."

She remained silent, wondering if life would ever be normal. "Mind if I catch a ride back to Florida with you? I think I'd like to drive back and get lost in some scenery."

"Not at all, boss. I'll have us packed and ready to leave when I pick you up."

The phone in her room rang a few times but Madison ignored it. Finally she just unplugged the cord from the handset. "Whoever you are, just go away."

Her heart hoped it was a certain very attractive woman, one whom she had made a promise to. Her mind was busy fighting the images of the last twenty-four hours. Sleep that night was haunted by blood and the sound of guns. Her targets had always been inanimate objects, the goal the highest score. *How many points do I get for a human body?* She tried to rationalize the events of the previous evening but she couldn't hide the image of Ramon Hidalgo's surprise when he saw the gun. He froze. He fucking froze. *Yeah, but he had already taken a shot at you. If Carl hadn't shouted, you would be the one dead.* He was never going to turn thirty. Or have kids. Or finish his college classes. He was dead. *He's a piece of shit!*

And what are you?

❖

"Thank you both," Karlie said as she stood between her attorneys. Four weeks after the shootings, she had been cleared of all charges and suspicions. The last of the legal documents placing all former joint property into her name alone had been signed. Now she only had to wait. Wait for the filing of the documents with a variety of sources, wait for their processing, and finally wait for final documents. *And wait for the nightmares to stop.* "How long should all this take?"

"Normally," Garrison Snyder began, "anywhere from a couple of days up to six weeks. Having gotten Rob's death certificate, and now that you have been cleared of any involvement in his death, there should not be any unusual delays. We will get the deeds for the two properties delivered to the courthouse today."

"I can't believe this nightmare is almost over."

"This is not an easy experience," Leland Roberts reminded her. "As an attorney, I can guide you through the legal process, but I realize there is more to this than what happens in the court."

When Karlie was sure she could control her voice, she said, "Most days it was all I could do to get through the day." She looked at the two men who had handled her legal affairs. "Again, thank you both."

"You are more than welcome," Leland Roberts answered. "The real gratitude, however, should go to your friends. That good-looking attorney from Miami and the guy she was with. Apparently it was their evidence that was convincing to the police. By the way, how is she?"

By the time Karlie had learned the details about the events at her house, Madison had already been discharged from the hospital. At first all Karlie knew was that several people were dead and others were taken to the hospital. No one had names. A frantic call to her attorney had gotten the information that Madison had been admitted to City Hospital. Karlie tried calling but never got an answer. When Karlie tried the nursing desk, she was told that they were only allowed to give information to family members. Fearing the worst, she headed into the city only to arrive thirty minutes after Madison had left.

Dee flew into town not long after, but Madison wasn't returning her calls either.

"Fine," Karlie answered her attorney. "I guess. She got on a plane and left as soon as she could. Apparently her wounds were not serious."

❖

Walking into Sandra Bailey's house, Karlie smiled and enjoyed the smells emanating from the kitchen. "What are you cooking?" she asked. She was actually hungry.

"We thought we would fix something special to celebrate," Sandy answered as Karlie entered the kitchen. Turning to face her, Sandy and Marge both pulled her into a hug.

"What's that about? What are we celebrating?"

"You! Your legal problems are behind you. The future is bright and you can begin to live again."

Karlie smiled but it was halfhearted. There were still holes in her life and she knew it. "I'll go change and be right back."

As she climbed the stairs to the room she had been occupying, Karlie's thoughts kept circling. *Why didn't she at least say good-bye? Why did she leave so quickly? Damn her, she promised to come back to me!* Changing into jeans, she forced the unanswerable thoughts as far away as she could. By the time she entered the kitchen, lunch was on the table. "Wow, this looks wonderful. Thank you."

Sandy smiled her delight. "Have a seat. I even have some wine."

"In the middle of the day? This is a celebration."

Marge put the food on the table and motioned for Karlie to sit. "Besides, red wine is good for the heart and I believe we need to be healthy. I prescribe it to many of my patients."

Karlie laughed and joined the two women in enjoying conversation and food. Eventually talk returned to the recently completed pre-registration for classes for next term, in particular a problem student who was in one of Sandy's classes. "I can't imagine him signing up for your class again." Karlie laughed.

"I got the registrar's list today or else I would have accused someone of playing a bad joke. I hope he has gotten serious about learning, because I am not going to tolerate his usual excuses and flippant remarks."

"Good for you." Karlie emphasized her point by hitting her spoon on the table. The others looked at the loud implement and laughed. "Sorry. Guess I got too excited."

"Well, your class schedule is in there, too. You may have more to exclaim about after you look at it."

Some of the shine on the day began to fade. "Sandy, I don't know what I am going to do. So much has happened in the last few days, months. I don't know what I want to do or where I want to be."

Seeing the light fading from her eyes, Sandy made a decision. Taking Karlie's hand, she began, "Karlie, you don't have to make any decisions right away, but have you thought about talking with Madison? It has to mean something for her to go out on the limb she did for you."

"She left and didn't even try to call me. What am I supposed to think? She promised she would be back but disappeared." Karlie paused while fighting the tears. Putting her hands back on the table, she continued, "I thought I knew Rob. I thought we were in love, then he wants a divorce and I find out he has been cheating with other women and has nearly financially destroyed me." Her voice quivered. "I don't know what to believe about anything…or anyone…anymore. To be honest, I'm having trouble with trusting… me as well as anyone else."

She took a deep breath and wiped the tears away. "Right now, my life is a mess and I guess I need to find me first. If Madison didn't call, then I have to believe that she had a reason and I need to try and put my life back together. Without her."

Marge looked at her partner and then walked out of the room. "Did I say something?" Karlie asked.

Sandy sighed and shook her head. A few minutes later Marge walked back in with a small package. "The police dropped this off today. They said it was taken at your house but is not needed as evidence. They said that since it was kind of personal, they thought it might be better to give it to you."

Karlie took the package to her room and carefully opened it.

Inside was the well-worn leather jacket she had often seen Madison wear. Her breath caught when she saw the blood. "Oh, Madison." As she finished pulling the jacket out, an envelope fell to the floor. Her name was written across it in a bold hand. She slowly opened the envelope, pulling out the single piece of paper.

Moments later, Karlie found herself picking up the phone and trying to call Madison. The answering machine beeped and she left a hopeful message.

She tried again many times over the days that followed. When a week passed and no call was received, she left another message. "Please call," she whispered into the phone. "I got your note."

Seeing her moping around, Sandy finally put aside her reservations and interfered. "You know, Karlie, I'm sure the university would understand if you wanted to take a break until the next semester. I can cover your classes and you can take time off."

"Sandy, what would I do with time off? Classes, right now, are my sanity."

"How about go down to Miami? How about spend some time with Dee? How about tracking down that untrustworthy hoyden and give her a piece of your mind?"

A lump in Karlie's throat threatened to keep her from speaking. She swallowed and finally found enough courage to speak. "I've tried calling, but she's not returning my calls. I've been a fool."

"Maybe she's afraid to talk to you because she's feeling guilty. Maybe she's in the hospital with an infection. Maybe she's…"

"Okay, I get the picture, but what would I say?"

"Karlie, I can't help you with that, but it took some courage for her to finally admit she loved you. I have no doubts about your feelings for her."

❖

Over a glass of juice, Karlie finally broached the subject that had never been more than moments away during the flight to Miami and the drive to Dee's house. "How's Madison?"

Dee looked tense. "When she got back, she was exceptionally quiet, especially for her. Her wounds were healing nicely."

"Wounds? More than one?" Karlie couldn't hide her surprise.

"I thought you knew. She had a deep cut on her arm where a bullet had grazed her. Then there was the bad one in her back, in her shoulder. I'm amazed they let her out of hospital so fast."

Karlie wasn't. "She can be very...persuasive."

And she was running away as fast as she could.

Dee looked closely at her before continuing, "Sorry, I can't believe you didn't know. The way she was talking, I thought... Never mind. She called yesterday and said she's fine." Seeing the pale look of her dearest friend, she added, "There's something I don't understand. She goes up to New York because she is worried about you, and then she leaves and you don't know what is going on?"

Fragments of conversations cascaded into a waterfall of confused thoughts. Karlie felt the weight of friendship bearing down. Half-truths and deceptions, she feared, would rend the fabric of her relationship with Dee, the only constant in her adult life. "Dee, I need to talk about Madison."

"Before you start, I want you to know that I am no longer going to allow either of you to say anything bad about the other. She's my sister and you're my best friend, and I think you both, at heart, genuinely care for each other."

"Yes, we do. That's why I'm here." Karlie took Madison's note from the small velvet pouch she kept tucked in her bra, over her heart. She spread it out on the table in front of Dee and said, "I need to find her."

Dee stared at it for so long, Karlie had to prod her. Finally Dee asked, "Are you involved? As in romantically involved?"

"Sexually involved would be a more accurate description. I guess I'm still trying to figure out the rest. I mean it was definitely sexual. It was never like that with Rob."

"Stop. Too much information. I'm sorry, but as far as I know I have only one sister. The bitch. Garbage mouth. That despicable pain in various parts of your anatomy. And on your more literate days, the cruel, callous curmudgeon who prefers rigidity to rectitude, salaciousness to celibacy, and denigration to decency."

Karlie winced as she was reminded of just a few of the many names she had used to describe a certain woman. "Goddess, how the hell did you remember that?"

"I had to look up a couple of the words to make sure I understood what you said. Now, is this the person we are talking about? My Madison?" Dee shook her head in astonishment. "How did this happen? How come I'm just finding out? You know, there were times I've suspected something was going on but I just couldn't believe it. I guess I refused to believe it was possible."

How many times have I asked myself the same question? Karlie tried to put her thoughts into words she had not yet found. "I don't know how. I'm sorry. I've wanted to tell you since that weekend in August but was afraid you would think less of me or that I would lose your respect."

"Oh, Karlie, you have my unconditional love. Don't you know that by now?"

"Yes, but we are talking about your only sister. I'm so sorry I didn't say something sooner."

"When did this start? Was that the first time?"

"To be honest, I think it started the first time I saw her."

"In college? I've always thought you were straight. I mean... Not that... It isn't that I... Oh, shit! I'm beginning to sound like the narrow-minded bigots my parents entertain at dinners."

Karlie laughed. "If I'm honest with myself, I've probably had crushes on girls growing up. But Madison is much more than that. So...where is she?"

Dee's face went pink, then pale. "Bali."

The sound she heard was more of a squeak than an answer. "Bali?"

Dee nodded. "So, now what?"

"Damn. I guess I was hoping she'd be around so I could talk to her. I need to have some kind of closure. What happened between us was too intense. I will always ask what if, yet I don't want to spend my life chasing after some illusion. Especially one that is unavailable. I know this is getting old, but I really don't know."

"Karlie, I just wish I could wave a magic wand and make things better. I'm at a loss to know what to do or say."

"I don't know either."

"I love Madison. As much as I love her, she does and says things that…hurt other people. Her morals, well, the best I can say is that they leave a lot to be desired. As a partner I wouldn't recommend her to my enemies, much less my best friend. The funny thing is that, at the same time, I wouldn't want to see anyone hurt her." Dee paused. "Do you love her?"

"I alternate between loving her and wanting to wring her neck. She can be incredibly tender and then incredibly thoughtless." Karlie took another sip of her juice. "The bottom line is I need to know how she feels. I need to know why she wrote me that note." She stared at her glass as if some answer could be read in the amber liquid. "All this may be moot, Dee. We have such different lives. She lives for work. She's driven by money and success. She…I don't know. At this point in my life I want stability, love. A relationship of equals who share the big and little moments in life. I want to wake up in the morning and feel loved."

"Hmmm, doesn't that sound wonderful and ideal?"

"Ah, there's the rub. Passion versus peace. Choppy seas versus a calm, smooth lake. I'm not sure how well I could handle another disaster right now."

Dee jumped up from her chair. "That's not going to happen." She grabbed Karlie's hand and dragged her up. Come on."

"Where are we going?"

Dee regarded her as though she'd asked a very silly question. "We're going to pack your clothes and get your passport. I'm putting you on a plane to Bali."

CHAPTER EIGHTEEN

Fatigue and doubt her uncompromising companions, Karlie wearily walked out of the airport and looked for a taxi. She had spent most of the two flights dozing and arguing with herself. *Did I make the right choice? What if I've screwed up? Suppose this doesn't work. Suppose she doesn't want a relationship.*

Finding a taxi, Karlie climbed in and gave the address. The anticipation was almost over. The only thing she was sure of was that today would either be the beginning of a new life or just another disaster added to a year already filled with enough adversity for a life time. She sighed. *No, I've made the right decision.* She gazed out the window. The scenery was exquisite, unlike anything she'd ever experienced. She could not have imagined a more entrancing place. Warm, gentle breezes caressed her skin when she stepped out of the taxi at the Bali Hyatt. A slightly salty scent wafted up from the sea. Colorful tropical flowers grew in abundance in the manicured gardens. Her breathing slowed, and she felt the smile growing across her face. No matter what happened, she was going to enjoy the next few days.

Walking into the hotel, she was immediately struck with the elegance and grace of her surroundings. Open, panoramic vistas. Casual ambience. She had moved into a slower, gentler world. No wonder Madison loved this place so much. It had been four weeks since they'd seen each other and now that Madison was physically close, Karlie was again unsure of if she was making the right decision.

She had carefully rehearsed opening lines and conversations from Miami to Los Angeles. From LA to Hong Kong she'd tried to sleep and ignore the reason for her trip. It was too late to turn back.

"I'm meeting a friend here," she told the registration clerk after she'd completed signing forms. "Madison Barnes."

Looking at her watch, the clerk answered, "She is usually out on the beach in the afternoon. Just take the path down past the Regency Lounge. It's an outdoor bar area." She smiled. "I hope you enjoy your time with us. Do you have any special plans?"

"I'm working on a book, so I'll be doing some research," Karlie said.

"What's your book about?"

"It's a romance."

"Does it have a happy ending?"

"Don't know yet. I hope so."

"Good luck. Let us know if we can be of service." The clerk called for someone to carry the luggage to Karlie's room.

Thanking her, Karlie headed for the elevators. An hour later, she had showered and changed into white cotton shorts and a sleeveless green V-neck top. She looked into the mirror, and for the first time in months, she recognized the ravages of stress. Her blond hair had been cut before she left New York, and it was curlier. While she'd regained some weight, the shorts she wore hung at her waist. She was almost as white as the pants. *I look like a horrific apparition. Definitely need to put more weight on.* She crawled on top of the bed and let the pain of the past weeks cascade out. A*m I making the right decision? Hopefully we will have the rest of our lives to decide.*

Tears flowed easily and ended only when sleep captured her.

❖

Madison put down the book she was reading and watched the petite blond woman walking in the surf. The woman had arrived three days ago and spent most of every afternoon walking along the beach. Sometimes alone, sometimes with another woman. The first day she'd shown up had sent Madison reeling. Too many troubled nights had been filled with dreams of a certain blonde. Seeing the new visitor walking so casually at the water's edge had shaken her out of her self-imposed torpor.

Getting up from her chair, she grabbed her book, towel, and other belongings. "Why the hell did she have to stay at this hotel? I hope she's leaving soon." Rushing through the lobby, she headed to her room. She had to get hold of herself. Either she had to forget her or call and beg her forgiveness, bare her heart and soul, and plead with her.

As if she would even believe me.

Sliding her sunglasses on, Karlie walked out into the blazing sun. Awe filled her as she walked out of her ground level room into a tropical setting. Running her hand through her thick locks, she said, "I think I'm going to like this. Well, just remember that if this doesn't work."

Karlie walked around the outdoor bar and down the sandy beach. Nowhere could she find the one person she had traveled so far to see. Disappointment threatened to cloud the sky, but she struggled to remain positive. "I know she's here. She's got to be here."

Taking off her sandals, she continued down to the water's edge and walked along the beach, her eyes ever watchful for a certain tall, dark-haired woman.

"Damn, there's another one!" Madison swore as she looked out the window and realized there were two blondes walking along the beach. "I'm having dinner someplace else."

She stormed around the room, struggling with the growing discontent. "I may have to change fucking hotels." Sure, that would keep her from seeing Karlie in nearly every woman around. Damn it, sooner or later she was going to have do something.

❖

The nap had helped, but after walking for an hour Karlie was again tired. The sun had warmed her skin and was turning it a bright pink. By the time she arrived at her room, she had gathered enough courage to call Madison's room. Three attempts proved futile. After ordering dinner in her room, Karlie crawled into her bed determined to try again the next day. *I can't believe I have come this far and still I'm not any closer to resolving this. Where are you?* With no ready answer, she gradually allowed sleep to again claim her.

CHAPTER NINETEEN

The morning sun streamed into Madison's room. Sitting up, she felt the weight of a sleepless night. Memories of Karlie were intermingled with gunfire and darkness. She had already made arrangements to move to another hotel the next day. Two blondes at this hotel stirred too many thoughts and feelings that remained unresolved. A late breakfast, lunch on the veranda, and then sitting on the beach in the afternoon. Afterward she would pack and prepare for her move the following day. She preferred the more organized life, one without dreams or nightmares.

Walking through the hotel lobby, Karlie didn't see anyone familiar. Again heading outside, she remained hopeful. *If we don't make contact today, then I will have to let go. It wasn't meant to be.*

Stopping to get oriented, she found the sound of tropical music coming from her left. Heading in that direction, she saw the large, shaded lounge area and a tall familiar figure standing at the bar. Even from the back, she recognized the woman who had dominated so much of her adult life. The woman she had traveled thousands of miles to see. *Madison!* Karlie hesitated. She walked over to a palm tree and moved into the shade where she hoped she wouldn't be noticed. She needed to gather her courage.

Madison looked thinner…and browner. A bright blue swimsuit was visible from the waist up while a blue print sarong wrapped her from the waist down.

Feeling her breath catch, Karlie knew her feelings for Madison were strong and they weren't going to easily fade away. Deep inside was the awareness that it was more than lust. It was the feelings that were first lit in the naïve, adoring, eighteen-year-old freshman and, in spite of years of bickering, had simmered over all the years of adulthood, and finally exploded into an inextinguishable fire last summer.

My God, I really love her! Why had she never realized it? She knew the answer. She hadn't wanted to know.

As Madison shifted her weight from one foot to the other, Karlie watched fascinated as an attractive much younger female bartender flirted with her. The bartender was obviously infatuated. Karlie wondered what they were talking about. Maybe that was her newest conquest or her next one. Her insecurities found a friendly home and invaded the more pleasant thoughts. She'd traveled across the world and here she was hiding just a few feet away. As she argued, she noticed the object of her ruminations straighten, turn, and look in her direction. Karlie pulled herself farther into the shadows and waited. A few moments later she gathered enough nerve to peek around the edge of the large tree base. Madison was gone and the bartender was serving another customer.

Gathering up the remnants of her courage, she headed toward the beach. She had to know. Before she could do anything else, she had to know. *You've owned my heart for so long, Madison. I have to know.* What a jolt to the ego. The person she'd detested for so long she was in love with. Standing at the edge of the lounge area, she looked out over the beach. Madison was easy to spot. The blue swimsuit she wore was even brighter in the sun and highlighted her every move.

Karlie watched her settle into a rattan chair, take a sip of the drink in her hand, and pick up a book. *A book? She reads? Stop! Remember why you are here before you blow it.*

Her determination firmly in place, Karlie gathered every ounce of courage she possessed, reminded herself of the love in her heart, and walked out onto the hot sand. If she did not risk, she might lose the chance for happiness. *She can still say no,* she reminded herself. "Yes, but I can, too."

Her thoughts flew around in so many directions, she was immobilized with hope and fear at the same time. The writer was at a loss for words. Her heart hammering in time to her racing pulse, she searched for some clever opening line. As she stopped a couple of feet behind Madison, she noticed the book she was reading was a Karlyn Henderson romance. She smiled.

Nervous but feeling more confident, she struggled with what to do next. Madison stretched out. As she did, the fabric covering her lower body slipped back and revealed long, tan legs. Karlie took a deep breath and closed the distance between them. Walking up behind Madison, she cast a short shadow across the pages.

"I know the writer," she said, shaking. "I've been told she doesn't know jack shit about romance."

Madison tensed in disbelief, tugging at the scar on her back. Hope snatched her breath and sent her blood roaring in her ears. She waited, desperate not to wake up and find she was only dreaming.

"Of course, she's written quite a few rather successful romance novels, so there must be a lot of people who believe her. What do you think, Madison?" Karlie held her breath. Madison's lack of a reply was disconcerting.

Either I'm certifiable or I've been given a gift. Removing her sunglasses, Madison found the empty place inside herself beginning to fill. "I'm not an expert when it comes to love, but I think she could teach me a lot." Madison slowly stood and turned around. "If she was willing to."

The lump in Karlie's throat began to dissolve. She took a step forward until she was close enough to feel the warmth emanating from the tanned body. She reached up and stroked the sensuous lips. She felt the intake of breath against her fingers. "Madison," she whispered. "Why are you smiling?"

"Because I'm in Bali. Because it's a sunny day." She gazed into eyes as tranquil as the ocean. "Because you called me Madison. Most of all, because you're here."

Karlie's smile was more dazzling than the tropical sun.

She ran her fingers across the angry red scar on Madison's arm. "Why did you leave New York without talking to me or even seeing me? You made me a promise. Remember?"

"I'm sorry." She looked around. A few people had walked by and stared at them. Madison was aware of how close they were standing and of the fact that she wanted to kiss this very real woman. "Will you come to my room and we can talk? I'm staying here."

"I am, too."

"Really?" Madison's smile became hungry. "Your room or mine?"

"Well, it's good to know some things haven't changed. Actually, our rooms are near each other." Seeing the grin growing, Karlie quickly added, "Your sister arranged it."

"Remind me to do something really nice for her and Bonehead."

Karlie paused, she needed to talk and she needed to do it someplace safe. Recognizing the nascent pressure building in her body, she was sure there would not be much talking if she were alone with this beautiful woman. "Mind if I pull a chair up next to yours for right now and just enjoy the sun before we go up?"

Madison nodded. "Absolutely. Anything you want." She quickly moved them to a pair of chairs nearby. Every fiber of her being wanted to hold and kiss Karlie, but she knew it was no longer possession she craved. *I want you to love me, Karlie, if only half as much as I do you. I will wait for you.* "Can I get you something to eat or drink? The food is not elaborate out here, but it is good."

"I'm starving. I'll eat anything." Karlie blushed, distracted by the thought of what she wanted most to taste.

Madison headed back to the veranda and ordered. Five minutes later she placed the food on a small table between them and sat down. "I can't tell you how many times I've dreamed about you being here," she began. "In fact...never mind."

"Never mind what?"

"There's been a blonde walking up and down the beach for the last few days. She's from England. She doesn't look anything like you except for having blond hair, but every time I see her I think of you. In fact, yesterday, there were two of you, the English woman and another blonde." As laughter bubbled in her companion, Madison asked, "What's so funny? My going crazy or seeing two of you?"

"Neither. Yesterday I was out here on the beach looking for you. I didn't find you. Where were you? Why didn't I see you?"

"It was *you*? I was inside my room. I had decided to change hotels tomorrow so that I wouldn't be haunted by two blondes. Oh, God, Karlie, to think I might have missed you." She grabbed her hand.

Karlie couldn't answer. Too many feelings were sparring. Her stomach rumbling reminded her that hunger and thirst were now the more prominent sensations. The tropical drink was wonderful and Karlie cautioned herself to slow down or she would be asleep fast. She reached for a sandwich and knew she had plenty of time.

After a couple of bites, she felt secure enough to again ask, "Why did you leave without even saying good-bye? That was the last thing I expected. I thought you cared. You promised."

Too many times she had asked herself the same question and always the answer had been the same: Karlie deserved to be happy. Now this woman was asking her to explain. Suddenly her excuse sounded as weak and shallow as it was. "I'm sorry. There was no good reason. I tried to convince myself that you couldn't love me and that I had nearly gotten you killed. After that it was easier to say you deserved to be happy and I didn't."

Her heart as filled with warmth and beauty as the Bali landscape, Karlie touched Madison's trembling hand. "That's the stupidest thing I have ever heard you say."

"Do I get a second chance, then?"

Karlie plunged ahead. "You've told me you were not interested in a relationship with me. You said you wanted to see more of me and yet didn't make an effort to contact me. Finally you promised me you were not walking out on me, and then you disappeared." The teasing was back but there was something warm and comforting in it. "Hmm, one more chance? Okay, and you better make it good."

"I have always taken for granted that I got whatever I wanted. Seeing you with your professor friend, realizing you were in trouble because of something I did, not you…" Madison let go of Karlie's hand as she stumbled on her own honesty. "I didn't want you hurt anymore than you already were. I wasn't sure I was capable of loving you the way you should be loved. Besides, if your friend could make you happy, I didn't want to interfere. I didn't have the right. Finally, I was afraid. I didn't know what you wanted and, as I just said, I didn't know if I could make you happy."

Stunned by the admission, Karlie struggled to swallow the last bite of her sandwich. "Madison, I adore you."

Madison fidgeted. She wanted to stand, pace, walk away, but she knew she was given a second chance with this incredible woman sitting near her and she wasn't going to mess it up. "Karlie, if I could do it over, I would crawl to where you were and beg you to forgive me and give me another chance. I would plead, cajole, do whatever it took to convince you. I'm so sorry."

"Begging is good. So is crawling." Seeing Madison get off her chair and kneel in the sand, Karlie continued, "Oh, Madison, you never have to beg." She reached over and stroked Madison's arm. "Please get up. I just wanted to know that you cared for me as much as I do you."

Madison's heart was full. Karlie's words had given her hope. She stared at the beautiful face and smiled. One thought caused her to hesitate. "What about your…what about Sandra Bailey?"

"What about her?" Karlie asked, well aware of the intent of the question.

"Is she…what does she think about you coming here?"

Karlie was enjoying this moment. "Well, as I said, we're friends. I think she and her partner are hoping you'll sweep me off my feet."

"Her partner?"

"Yes. Marge. They've been together for sixteen years."

"Her partner?"

"Madison, I'm concerned about you. I'm having to repeat things. Her partner. They are the ones who talked me into coming to Florida to find you."

"Her partner!" Madison smiled. "Well, I guess I will have do something for them, too."

For the next hour, they sat side by side and chatted while watching the waves gracefully dance along the white beaches.

"I can't believe how lovely this place is," Karlie said as they watched some swimmers romping in the surf. *I haven't felt this relaxed since the weekend we spent on the boat. This could be addictive.*

"Why don't we get cleaned up and I will take you for a short tour," Madison said.

"Promise I get some real food and I'm all yours." She put her hand on Madison's arm as they walked back toward the hotel.

"Why do you think I'm here?" Karlie asked as they walked across the outside lounge area toward sliding glass doors in one of the hotel's suites.

"To eat real food?" Madison slid the door open and allowed her to enter first.

"Are you humoring me?" Karlie asked.

Closing the door, Madison pulled her into an embrace before answering, "God, yes. And I just wanted to make sure I could give a proper answer. I think you're here because you couldn't stay away. You think I am wonderful, sexy, and incredible as a lover."

Lover! Karlie is my lover. Madison played with all the words she had heard others call each other. *Partner, best friend, significant other.* This was new to her and she was enjoying it.

"Really, you haven't changed."

"There is one thing that hasn't changed. Dearest love, I just want to hold you. You feel so good." Madison basked in the feel of Karlie against her body. She was becoming whole.

"Madison," Karlie whispered. Before she could say anything

else, Madison captured her lips and let all her emotion flow into that kiss. When she could finally breathe, Karlie said, "I love you, Madison. And that's why I am here."

"Good, because I'm madly in love with you and I don't want to waste any more time." She began to pull Karlie toward the bed.

"You what?" Karlie stopped.

Looking into the eyes of the woman who had long ago crept into her heart and captured it, Madison spoke slowly and precisely, "I love you, Karlyn. I don't know how and when it happened." Her eyes became distant. "When I was at your house waiting for the Hidalgos to show up, all I could think about was protecting you. I realized I would do anything to make sure nothing ever happened to you. When the shooting started, I didn't think. As soon as I was on the ground in firing position, I didn't hesitate. I lifted my gun and aimed."

Her eyes refocusing, she looked at Karlie, ran her fingers through the blond, short curls, and continued, "Never mind. That story can wait."

"Hush, Madison, don't. You don't have to tell me."

"Karlie, that day at your house…I have never been so frightened in my life. Not for me, but for you. The thought of losing you was more than I could stand. I didn't think. I did things I never thought I would do but I knew I would do again to protect you." Madison pulled Karlie closer. "When it was all over and I heard the ambulance coming, I found myself praying that I would live. I didn't want to die, Karlie. I wanted to live. There was so much I wanted to say to you. Even to just see you." She continued to run her hand through the golden strands. "I kind of like your short hair."

Tears fell easily as Karlie rested her head on Madison's chest. "Why did you leave, then? I tried calling you at the hospital and then decided to see you but you were gone. No message, no call, no visit. At first I was angry and then I was hurt. I don't understand."

"I'm truly sorry, and I don't understand either. I've never felt this way before. Guess that's another example of my not thinking about anyone but me." She kissed Karlie before continuing, "I am sorry for being such a selfish pig."

Karlie looked up in astonishment. This woman had said *I love you*, called herself a selfish pig, and said *I'm sorry* in the same day.

Madison grinned. "I know. I know. Humility is finally coming. Believe me, I've not only learned to say I'm sorry but to also say thank you."

"Madison, you continue to amaze me, but why did you disappear?"

"You can be so single-minded, but I love you anyway. Okay. Carl rode with me to the hospital and I remember him saying hang on. At that time all I could think about was seeing you. They only kept me in the hospital overnight, but I lay there and began to think about all the reasons it wouldn't work." Recalling that night, Madison reluctantly admitted, "Karlie, I've never been able to make a commitment before, and I'm not sure I know how. I tried hard to convince myself that somehow I could make it work, but I guess I had less confidence in me than you do." She ran a thumb down the side of Karlie's cheek before again putting her hands in her lap. "If I didn't trust me, why should you? By the time the sun came up, I couldn't figure out what a gentle, loving woman like you would want with me. I guess I was afraid."

"I can't believe what I'm hearing. What happened to the cocky, self-assured, conceited Madison?"

Again kissing her, Madison answered, "I'm still here."

"And now?" Karlie allowed herself to fit snugly into the arms of her lover.

"I'm still afraid," she said as she kissed the golden head beneath her chin. "I also know that I don't want to spend another day without you in my life. I am empty without you. Yesterday I had stopped to get a drink. I felt as if you were watching me. I turned around and you weren't there. I can't tell you how many times I've done that. Looking for you. Then there was one, then two, of you on the beach. I even miss your smart-ass comments. My life, Karlie, is incomplete without you. I still can't figure why you would want me."

Karlie put her arms around Madison's neck and pulled her down into an inviting kiss. As they pulled apart, Karlie spoke, "You still drive me crazy, but I love you."

"Enough to put up with me every day?"

"Are you asking me to marry you?"

"Well, I'm taking the first step and asking you to live with me. I've got to find out if you can put up with me for more than a weekend."

"And if I can't?" Karlie teased.

"Then my heart and my life will be empty and I will do everything in my power to convince you to give me still another chance."

"How many chances do you think I should give you?"

"As many as I can talk you into."

"And suppose I do stay for more than a weekend?"

"Then I will try to persuade you to stay for a week, then a month, then a year, then…"

"I get the picture."

"You complete my life. Living with you will be paradise every day. You've become my dream, even more than Bali."

"Wow, I don't know what to say."

"Am I convincing? Live with me, Karlie. We can live anywhere. I don't care."

Karlie continued to be amazed. "You'd give up your practice and leave Miami?"

Madison continued caressing Karlie, enjoying the feeling of being alive. "I would live in a tree house and paint posters for liberal Democrats as long as you were with me. I have enough money. I don't need to work."

Karlie pulled back and reached up to touch her lover's forehead. "Now I am hallucinating."

"Answer me. Will you live with me?" Madison's voice had become serious.

"Are you sure you want to do this? We could date and vacation together, spend time getting to know each other."

"I've wasted too many years not taking advantage of getting to know you. I don't want to lose one minute, not even one second. Will you live with me?"

"Yes, I will live with you, but I've got to tell you I am old fashioned. I believe in marriage, commitment. All those things. You know…commitment?"

"God, you are one insistent woman. Well, then, I'll buy you a ring as soon as I can find one."

"And a dog?" Karlie teased.

Madison laughed, "Karlyn Henderson, I love you. Anything, even a dog." She pulled her lover close and kissed her. "I can't believe I just said that." She leaned down and kissed her again. "Mmm, I can't believe how much I want you." Madison's voice had become low and breathy. "How about another lesson in seduction? I've suddenly discovered I'm a slow learner."

Karlie laughed and removed Madison's sarong. "Good thing I'm a patient teacher. I warn you, however, that I expect a tour of this island. I've flown I don't know how many thousands of miles and I want to see something other than this bed."

Madison laughed again and realized this was the best dream of all. The beauty of the paradise outside was nothing compared to that inside her heart.

About the Author

C. J. Harte was born in New York but lived in many places while growing up. After her family finally settled in the South, she attended college in the Deep South where she obtained her degrees as well as a significant Southern accent and a unrelenting sense of humor.

During her residence in the South, C. J. was a political activist while maintaining a full-time job in health care. She edited a women's newspaper, wrote political editorials and satire, and was a speech writer for political candidates. She eventually climbed down the corporate ladder and moved out west, where she works in health care and continues to write from her Cheyenne home. She and her partner have homes on two continents since they live on opposite sides of the ocean much of the year.

When not working or writing, C.J. Harte is either commuting between continents or spending time with her four-footed friends in her beloved Wyoming, looking out at the mountains and blue sky.

Books Available From Bold Strokes Books

Green Eyed Monster by Gill McKnight. Mickey Rapowski believes her former boss has cheated her out of a small fortune, so she kidnaps the girlfriend and demands compensation—just a straightforward abduction that goes so wrong when Mickey falls for her captive. (978-1-60282-042-5)

Blind Faith by Diane and Jacob Anderson-Minshall. When private investigator Yoshi Yakamota and the Blind Eye Detective Agency are hired to find a woman's missing sister, the assignment seems fairly mundane—but in the detective business, the ordinary can quickly become deadly. (978-1-60282-041-8)

A Pirate's Heart by Catherine Friend. When rare book librarian Emma Boyd searches for a long-lost treasure map, she learns the hard way that pirates still exist in today's world—some modern pirates steal maps, others steal hearts. (978-1-60282-040-1)

Trails Merge by Rachel Spangler. Parker Riley escapes the high-powered world of politics to Campbell Carson's ski resort—and their mutual attraction produces anything but smooth running. (978-1-60282-039-5)

Dreams of Bali by C. J. Harte. Madison Barnes worships work, power, and success, and she's never allowed anyone to interfere—that is, until she runs into Karlie Henderson Stockard. Eclipse EBook (978-1-60282-070-8)

The Limits of Justice by John Morgan Wilson. Benjamin Justice and reporter Alexandra Templeton search for a killer in a mysterious compound in the remote California desert. (978-1-60282-060-9)

Designed for Love by Erin Dutton. Jillian Sealy and Wil Johnson don't much like each other, but they do have to work together—and what they desire most is not what either of them had planned. (978-1-60282-038-8)

Calling the Dead by Ali Vali. Six months after Hurricane Katrina, NOLA Detective Sept Savoie is a cop who thinks making a relationship work is harder than catching a serial killer—but her current case may prove her wrong. (978-1-60282-037-1)

Dark Garden by Jennifer Fulton. Vienna Blake and Mason Cavender are sworn enemies—who can't resist each other. Something has to give. (978-1-60282-036-4)

Shots Fired by MJ Williamz. Kyla and Echo seem to have the perfect relationship and the perfect life until someone shoots at Kyla—and Echo is the most likely suspect. (978-1-60282-035-7)

truelesbianlove.com by Carsen Taite. Mackenzie Lewis and Dr. Jordan Wagner have very different ideas about love, but they discover that truelesbianlove is closer than a click away. Eclipse EBook (978-1-60282-069-2)

Justice at Risk by John Morgan Wilson. Benjamin Justice's blind date leads to a rare opportunity for legitimate work, but a reckless risk changes his life forever. (978-1-60282-059-3)

Run to Me by Lisa Girolami. Burned by the four-letter word called love, the only thing Beth Standish wants to do is run for—or maybe from—her life. (978-1-60282-034-0)

Split the Aces by Jove Belle. In the neon glare of Sin City, two women ride a wave of passion that threatens to consume them in a world of fast money and fast times. (978-1-60282-033-3)

Uncharted Passage by Julie Cannon. Two women on a vacation that turns deadly face down one of nature's most ruthless killers—and find themselves falling in love. (978-1-60282-032-6)

Night Call by Radclyffe. All medevac helicopter pilot Jett McNally wants to do is fly and forget about the horror and heartbreak she left behind in the Middle East, but anesthesiologist Tristan Holmes has other plans. (978-1-60282-031-9)

I Dare You by Larkin Rose. Stripper by night, corporate raider by day, Kelsey's only looking for sex and power, until she meets a woman who stirs her heart and her body. (978-1-60282-030-2)

Lake Effect Snow by C.P. Rowlands. News correspondent Annie T. Booker and FBI Agent Sarah Moore struggle to stay one step ahead of disaster as Annie's life becomes the war zone she once reported on. Eclipse EBook (978-1-60282-068-5)

Revision of Justice by John Morgan Wilson. Murder shifts into high gear, propelling Benjamin Justice into a raging fire that consumes the Hollywood Hills, burning steadily toward the famous Hollywood Sign—and the identity of a cold-blooded killer. (978-1-60282-058-6)

Truth Behind the Mask by Lesley Davis. Erith Baylor is drawn to Sentinel Pagan Osborne's quiet strength, but the secrets between them strain duty and family ties. (978-1-60282-029-6)

Cooper's Deale by KI Thompson. Two would-be lovers and a decidedly inopportune murder spell trouble for Addy Cooper, no matter which way the cards fall. (978-1-60282-028-9)

Romantic Interludes 1: Discovery ed. by Radclyffe and Stacia Seaman. An anthology of sensual, erotic contemporary love stories from the best-selling Bold Strokes authors. (978-1-60282-027-2)

A Guarded Heart by Jennifer Fulton. The last place FBI Special Agent Pat Roussel expects to find herself is assigned to an illicit private security gig baby-sitting a celebrity. (Ebook) (978-1-60282-067-8)

Saving Grace by Jennifer Fulton. Champion swimmer Dawn Beaumont, injured in a car crash she caused, flees to Moon Island, where scientist Grace Ramsay welcomes her. (Ebook) (978-1-60282-066-1)

The Sacred Shore by Jennifer Fulton. Successful tech industry survivor Merris Randall does not believe in love at first sight until she meets Olivia Pearce. (Ebook) (978-1-60282-065-4)

Passion Bay by Jennifer Fulton. Two women from different ends of the earth meet in paradise. Author's expanded edition. (Ebook) (978-1-60282-064-7)

Never Wake by Gabrielle Goldsby. After a brutal attack, Emma Webster becomes a self-sentenced prisoner inside her condo—until the world outside her window goes silent. (Ebook) (978-1-60282-063-0)

The Caretaker's Daughter by Gabrielle Goldsby. Against the backdrop of a nineteenth-century English country estate, two women struggle to find love. (Ebook) (978-1-60282-062-3)

Simple Justice by John Morgan Wilson. When a pretty-boy cokehead is murdered, former LA reporter Benjamin Justice and his reluctant new partner, Alexandra Templeton, must unveil the real killer. (978-1-60282-057-9)

Remember Tomorrow by Gabrielle Goldsby. Cees Bannigan and Arieanna Simon find that a successful relationship rests in remembering the mistakes of the past. (978-1-60282-026-5)

Put Away Wet by Susan Smith. Jocelyn "Joey" Fellows has just been savagely dumped—when she posts an online personal ad, she discovers more than just the great sex she expected. (978-1-60282-025-8)

Homecoming by Nell Stark. Sarah Storm loses everything that matters—family, future dreams, and love—will her new "straight" roommate cause Sarah to take a chance at happiness? (978-1-60282-024-1)

The Three by Meghan O'Brien. A daring, provocative exploration of love and sexuality. Two lovers, Elin and Kael, struggle to survive in a postapocalyptic world. (Ebook) (978-1-60282-056-2)

Falling Star by Gill McKnight. Solley Rayner hopes a few weeks with her family will help heal her shattered dreams, but she hasn't counted on meeting a woman who stirs her heart. (978-1-60282-023-4)

Lethal Affairs by Kim Baldwin and Xenia Alexiou. Elite operative Domino is no stranger to peril, but her investigation of journalist Hayley Ward will test more than her skills. (978-1-60282-022-7)

A Place to Rest by Erin Dutton. Sawyer Drake doesn't know what she wants from life until she meets Jori Diamantina—only trouble is, Jori doesn't seem to share her desire. (978-1-60282-021-0)

Warrior's Valor by Gun Brooke. Dwyn Izsontro and Emeron D'Artansis must put aside personal animosity and unwelcome attraction to defeat an enemy of the Protector of the Realm. (978-1-60282-020-3)

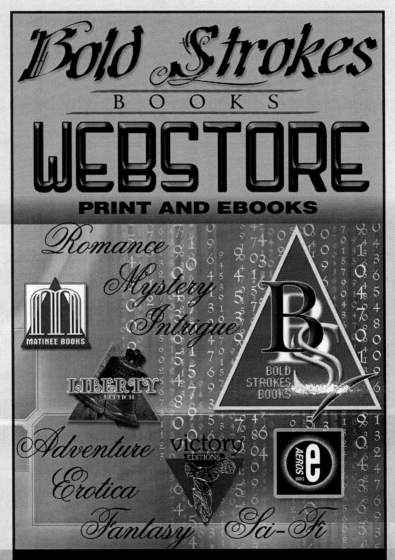